both sides now

**peyton
thomas**

DIAL BOOKS

DIAL BOOKS
An imprint of Penguin Random House LLC, New York

First published in the United States of America by Dial Books,
an imprint of Penguin Random House LLC, 2021
Copyright © 2021 by Peyton Thomas

Visit us online at penguinrandomhouse.com.

Library of Congress Cataloging-in-Publication Data
Names: Thomas, Peyton, author.
Title: Both sides now / Peyton Thomas.
Description: New York : Dial Books, 2021. | Audience: Ages 14+ | Audience:
Grades 10–12 | Summary: "A transgender teen grapples with his dreams for
the future and a crush on his debate partner, all while preparing to to
debate trans rights at Nationals"—Provided by publisher.
Identifiers: LCCN 2021021360 | ISBN 9780593322819 (hardcover) |
ISBN 9780593322833 (epub)
Subjects: CYAC: Transgender people—Fiction. | Debates and
debating—Fiction. | Love—Fiction. | LCGFT: Novels.
Classification: LCC PZ7.1.T46546 Bo 2021 | DDC [Fic]—dc23
LC record available at https://lccn.loc.gov/2021021360

Printed in the United States of America
ISBN 9780593322819
1 3 5 7 9 10 8 6 4 2
SKY

Design by Jennifer Kelly
Text set in Minister Std Light

For Lena,
my best reader, my truest friend

●

This novel was written on the ancestral and
contemporary territories of the Mississaugas of the
Anishinaabe, the Haudenosaunee Confederacy,
the Huron-Wendat, and the Dakhóta.

The cover of this book draws from the transgender
pride flag designed in 1999 by Monica Helms,
a tireless advocate for the rights of trans people,
especially trans veterans and servicemembers.

chapter one

"Sorry—*we're* the Soviets? You and me?"

"Come on, Finch: When have I ever steered you wrong?"

He's got a point. In all our years of debating together, Jonah Cabrera has only steered me right. In my bedroom, back home, there's a bookshelf that groans and sighs and threatens to split under four years of blue ribbons and gold medals. It's an inanimate testament, that shelf: Listen to Jonah, and you, Finch Kelly, will go far.

Still, I'm skeptical. "You want us to role-play as Stalin's cronies?"

"Oh, no. Not his cronies." Jonah swivels to the blackboard, scrawling his points in white chalk. "It's 1955. Stalin is six feet under. The Cold War's getting colder. Eisenhower just rolled out the New Look."

I watch him, hunched over my desk and chewing hard on a yellow No. 2. "Remind me what the New Look was?"

"More nukes, more cove-ops," he says, standing tall, sounding sure of himself, "and way more American propaganda getting piped past the Iron Curtain."

"Got it." I pull the pencil—now a beaverish twig—out of

my mouth and take some notes. I won't lie: He's selling me. "Keep talking."

In ten minutes, the two of us will stride out of this classroom and onto the Annable School's Broadway-sized stage. We will stand before hundreds of spectators, and we will argue, in speeches lasting not more than eight minutes, that every nation on Earth—no matter how rich, poor, or prone to the incubation of terror cells—deserves endless nuclear weaponry.

Do we actually believe this? God, no. Least of all Jonah, the clipboard-toting, signature-gathering student-activist bane of our local power station's nuclear existence. Among the many buttons presently dotting his backpack, I can see a little one, the color of sunshine, reading: *NUCLEAR POWER? NO THANKS!* But still, he stands before the chalkboard, doing his utmost to build the case for Armageddon.

"Both teams—the U.S., the U.S.S.R.—they're fully ready to plant mushrooms all over the map," says Jonah, with a grand sweep of his arm across the chalkboard. "And the only reason they're not raining burning hell all over the planet . . ."

". . . is mutually assured destruction." I glance at my stopwatch: eight minutes left, scrolling faster than I'd like. "This idea that the only defense against nuclear weapons . . ."

". . . is more nuclear weapons," Jonah says. "Because why hit the Russkies when you know they'll hit you right back?"

As he says this to me, Jonah scribbles a series of suggestive illustrations on the blackboard: smoke, flames, innocent civilians disintegrating into radioactive ash.

If the whole Greenpeace thing falls through, he might have a future as an artist.

Of course, if either of us wants any kind of future at all, we'll have to go to college first. And if we best the Annable School in the final round of this tournament, the North American Debate Association of Washington State will award us an enormous, gleaming trophy—one that would look *great* on college applications and, more urgently, on scholarship applications. Jonah's mom is a registered nurse. My dad's on his sixth month of unemployment and his seventh step of Alcoholics Anonymous. Neither of us can afford to shake sticks at this particular hunk of golden plastic.

"Okay, but, Jonah, Annable knows *exactly* how to refute that case."

"Not if we run the case in the 1950s," Jonah pleads. He's literally a blue-ribbon pleader; he is *very* convincing. "Come on, Finch. Time travel? Ari is *never* going to see this coming."

He's talking about Ariadne Schechter: the Annable School's prodigy of a debate captain, my worst enemy, my arch-nemesis, the freshwater to my salt. I despise her. I truly do. For so many reasons. Her noxious lavender vape fumes. Her unironic love for one milk-snatching Maggie Thatcher. And, not least of all, her early admission to Georgetown's School of Foreign Service. I settled for a purgatorial deferral letter. I'm still upset about it.

I think I'd be less upset, mind you, if Ari's dad hadn't donated forty million dollars to erect the Schechter School of Sustainable Entrepreneurship on a high cliff at the edge of campus.

But I can't fall into that swirling vortex of a grudge just now. Not unless I want to lose this round, and this state title, and fall even further out of Georgetown's good graces.

"This 'pretend to be commies' angle is definitely . . . creative." I'll give him that. It may be the *only* thing I give him. "I'm just worried it's too creative. Rule-breakingly creative. The kind of creative that'll send Ari whining to the judges."

"Okay, point one: You're never not worried," Jonah says, perching now on the teacher's broad war-chest of a desk. He gets like this when he's antsy—pacing, snapping his fingers, sitting on anything but, God forbid, a chair. "And point B: You know we need to spice it up this round. End of the day. End of the weekend. Everyone's five seconds from falling asleep."

"You included, apparently," I say. "You just said 'point one' and 'point B.'"

"Did I? Damn." He flashes me a sheepish grin, and then a yawn, his arms flying high above his head. "Guess we need to get creative, then. Wake ourselves up"

"By arguing the whole round in Russian accents?"

"Who said anything about accents?" he says, all innocent.

"I saw you in *The Seagull* last semester, Jonah. I know you're *dying* to flex your dialect work."

"But . . ."

"Not the time," I tell him. "Not the place."

"Fine. No accents. Serious business only." Jonah, still fidgeting, drums his knuckles against the top of the teacher's desk: sturdy antique oak, the furthest possible cry from the particleboard and plastic of our own Johnson Tech, ninety minutes away on the outskirts of Olympia. "If we go with the standard case here—like, define 'this House' as NATO, or whatever—we basically have to argue that more nukes are a good thing."

"Right. Hard case for anyone to make. Especially you, tree-hugger."

"But if we set the debate in the Cold War? Cast ourselves as the Soviets? Make Annable argue for the U.S. of A.?" Rocking to and fro on the desk, he disrupts a decorative apple—*World's Best Teacher*, etched in the glass. It teeters. I hold my breath. "We don't have to hash out all the boring, entry-level arguments," he says. "We don't have to touch M.A.D. We can run a more historical case. Talk about communism."

The apple steadies itself. I exhale.

"And capitalism," I say, and sit up straight, and snap my fingers. "And the Truman Doctrine, and HST, and . . . oh, oh! If we can link that last one to de-Stalinization, we could even . . ."

His hand finds my wrist, halting my Ticonderoga.

"Knew I'd get you on board." He winks. "Comrade."

I've never met a president, but when I step out onto that stage, I can imagine, just for a moment, how it feels to be one. I am five feet and five unremarkable inches tall, with a thatch of disobedient red hair that falls somewhere between Chuckie Finster and just plain Chucky. I don't get to feel like a president all that much.

But here, beneath the tremendous light-rig of the Annable

auditorium, staring into the ocean of the audience and soaking in their applause, I feel like I could do . . . I don't know, anything. Deliver the best speech of my life. Cinch the state title. Win a spot at the school of my dreams. Maybe, one day, I could become the first trans person in Congress. None of it—*nothing*—seems impossible.

I take my seat next to Jonah at the desk reserved for the people arguing *yes, nukes, more of them*. To our left, at a desk of her own, Ari Schechter is squinting through the bangs of her Hillary Rodham haircut, scribbling a final few words onto her cue cards. She's paying zero attention to Annable's principal—apologies, *headmaster*—who's standing at the podium, delivering his opening remarks in a throaty *Masterpiece Theatre* accent. He's saying things like "free inquiry," and "open dialogue," and "the dissemination of diverse perspectives," and I'm wondering how "diverse," exactly, the "perspectives" can be, at a prep school that costs $25,000 a year.

"Representing the proposition, from the Johnson Technical High School," says the headmaster—and it's very funny, that snooty extraneous "the"; it makes us sound like we belong in a very different tax bracket: "Jonah Cabrera and Kelly Finch."

I cup a hand around my mouth. "*Finch* Kelly!"

I'm very proud of my name. I gave it to myself, after all. It's a good one. But it never fails to trip people up. "Like Atticus," I always tell them. "From *To Kill a Mockingbird*," and then, usually, they get it, and they nod. "Atticus" was my first choice, for what it's worth, but my parents vetoed it. They were mostly fine with their daughter becoming their son. Less fine with their son strolling around under the bizarre appellation of a second-century Greek philosopher.

"Ah, yes." The headmaster pushes his glasses up his nose, peers once more at the paper on the podium. "Finch Kelly. My apologies."

Light applause. A lone, shrill whistle. That's Adwoa, most likely—our coach, rooting for us from the cheap seats.

"And, of course, representing the opposition: Annable's very own Ariadne Schechter and Nasir Shah!"

From the crowd: thunder. It's like we're at Bumbershoot on opening night, a wave of sound rolling off the audience. This theater is stacked with Annable kids who volunteered this weekend: timekeepers, moderators, tabulators. They are loud. They are many. But they are not the people we need to convince.

I lower my eyes to the judges, that sentry row right up front. They're stone-faced, not clapping. How do we reach them? Make them love us?

Or, at least, love the bomb?

"And now, to open the final round of the N.A.D.A. Washington State Championship, arguing in favor of the resolution—'This House would allow all states to possess nuclear weapons'—please welcome Jonah Cabrera!"

Jonah stands. There's more of that polite, disinterested, away-game applause. But then he steps forward, and he shifts loose the tallest button on his dad's Sunday-best blazer. And you can feel it: the audience falling, suddenly, just a little bit in love with him.

Understand: Jonah Cabrera is *hot*. I mean, objectively. He's campaign-trail handsome, all square jaw and sharp cheeks and warm brown skin that goes almost gold when he gets some sun. Like a Kennedy from Calabarzon instead of Camelot. You look at him, and you want to keep looking. No, no, not just look; you want to *listen*.

"Good afternoon, Mr. Speaker, honorable opponents, guests," Jonah says, and then pauses. "Or, should I say: Good afternoon, *comrades*."

He tilts his head to the right. This is a private grin, just for me. I smile right back at him. A delicious, dangerous feeling blooms in my gut.

Like we're breaking the rules.

Like we're going to get away with it.

"The resolution before us today is, 'This House would allow all states to possess nuclear weapons.'" Jonah clears his throat. Across the stage, the polite calm is beginning to slough from Ari's face. "Today, we've decided to define 'this House' as the Security Council of the United Nations, circa 1955, and we've defined 'nuclear weapons' as . . ."

Ari Schechter leaps to her feet, arm flying out like a bayonet. *"Point of order!"*

Jonah could stop talking. He could take Ari's question.

He doesn't.

"My comrade and I," he says, "will be arguing on behalf of the Central Committee of the Communist Party of the Soviet Union, in the wake of the death of our great leader, Joseph Stalin."

Ari brings her Gucci loafer down on the stage once, twice, three times: "*Point! Of! Order!*"

Annable's headmaster, seated front and center, surrounded by judges, lowers his glasses. He lifts his hand.

"Yes, Ms. Schechter? You called for a point of order?"

"Mr. Speaker," she says, her teeth a gritted cage, "my opponent has defined the resolution in such a way as to . . . to render this debate . . ." She stops, scowls, shakes her head, and tries again: "The definitions brought forth by our opposing team are not, I believe, in the spirit of the resolution."

The judges tilt together for some debating of their own: Is Ari right? Have we broken the rules? Or is Ari coming across like a petulant preschooler throwing a temper tantrum in the Hatchimals aisle at Toys "R" Us?

In a world where Toys "R" Us wasn't eaten alive by venture capitalists like her dad, I mean.

"Our judges have reached a verdict." The headmaster, lifting his head from that huddle of judges, sounds—I think? I hope?—sad. A good sign for us. "So long as the definition doesn't unfairly limit the terms of the debate—and the judges don't believe that Mr. Cabrera has done so—the team from Johnson Technical is fully within their rights to define the debate in a historical context."

"But . . . but . . ." Is that a wobble I hear in Ari's voice? Is she about to start crying? "Mr. Speaker, if you remove the resolution from the post-9/11 epoch, you effectively strip it of—"

"*Thank* you, Ms. Schechter." This is one of the judges, a woman with sleek black hair, raising her voice to speak over

Ari. "You may continue," she says, and smiles at Jonah, "Comrade Cabrera."

The audience—*this* audience, so full of Annable students, so firmly with Ari and Nasir, so utterly against us—they actually laugh! Out loud! Ari crashes into her seat with murder in her eyes. Jonah turns to me, another tiny, private grin on his lips.

This one says, *I told you I'd steer us right.*

After the round, which was honestly less of a bloodbath than I would've liked, the four of us are ushered into a tiny white-brick chamber behind the stage. It's what you'd call a greenroom, I guess, outfitted sparsely: a coffee table, a single threadbare couch. I'm keyed up after our near-hour of arguing, eager to sit down and relax. But Nasir is a step ahead of me. He dives vindictively for that single couch and sprawls out across all three cushions.

"Do you mind?" I ask him, tapping a tired foot. "I might like to take a seat."

He doesn't answer. He shuts his eyes, stretches his legs even longer, and points both middle fingers skyward.

Jonah laughs. "And the award for Miss Congeniality goes to . . ."

"Congeniality? *Congeniality?*" Ari sounds huskier than usual, pulling generous rips from a Juul the color of Pepto-Bismol as she paces the room. "You guys totally twisted the resolution in your favor, and *you* . . ." She stops, points her vape squarely at Jonah: "You referred to a genocidal dictator with a body count in the millions as a *great leader.*"

"Hey, remember when you asked the judges if we were breaking the rules?" Jonah leans against the white brick, giving her one of those broad, easy smiles. "And remember when they confirmed that we weren't?"

"Exactly." I'm still in the mood to argue. "You're just mad you didn't think of the Cold War angle."

"You're right. It never occurred to me to cheat." She coughs, thick with phlegm. "Whatever. The top two teams at State automatically move on to Nationals. What more do you want?"

Says the girl who wants for nothing—including a spot at my dream school. The one she cheated to get.

"Remind me, Ari: How many buildings at Georgetown are named after you?"

"God, Finch. Get over it." Even through the vapor, I can see her eyes roll. "It's not my fault early admission kicked your ass. There were nine thousand kids competing for nine hundred spots."

"Yo, keep it down." Nasir pops out an earbud. "I'm trying to bid on this Twitch streamer's bathwater."

I ignore him. We all do.

"And you don't think you had a leg up on the competition, Ari?" I step toward her, into her fog. "Sitting on your ass while your dad wrote check after check after . . ."

Her eyes are still rolling. "He wrote *one* check, Finch."

I yelp so hard my voice cracks: "For forty *million* dollars!"

"Really?" She exhales purply. "I thought it was fifty."

I sort of lunge at her—to do *what*, exactly, I don't know. I've never been in a fight, and I'd definitely lose. Ari's twice my size—taller *and* stockier. I'm a twig next to her. Lucky for me,

Jonah's cooler head prevails. He puts his hands on my shoulders. He pulls me back.

"Settle down, guys." He says this to me and her both. "Not the time for a fistfight."

"No, of course not," Ari says, shaking her head. "You'd probably find a way to cheat at that, too."

At my sides, against Jonah's advice, my hands curl into angry fists. "We did *not* cheat."

Just then, the room's one and only door begins to open: the winged tip of the headmaster's shoe steps in. Ari fumbles to stash her Juul, Nasir pushes his phone into his pocket, and I shake my fists back into hands. By the time the door's all the way open, the four of us are standing at attention, model students. If the headmaster notices the violet mist circling Ari, he doesn't let on.

"Ms. Schechter? Mr. Shah?" He turns to me and Jonah, thinks hard—no paper to read from, not this time. ". . . Others?"

"Mr. Kelly," I offer, and Jonah supplies, "Mr. Cabrera." The headmaster smiles falsely, sweeping his arms to the open door.

"Wonderful," he says. "We're ready for you."

"What a spirited, rigorous final round to conclude this tournament."

The headmaster glances over his shoulder, and grins at Ari—who's struggling, with ballooning cheeks, to contain a vapory cough—and Nasir. No smile for us, though. Fine. Let him count us out. It'll be that much sweeter when he rips open that envelope and reads our names.

"Without further ado," he says, "it is my pleasure to announce the winners of this year's Washington State Senior Debate Championship."

His fingers click lightly against the wood of the podium—the one percent's version of a drumroll, I guess. He takes the envelope in hand. He tears it open.

And just as I'm readying myself to rise to my feet, he says, "Congratulations . . . to Ariadne Schechter and Nasir Shah!"

I don't rise. I don't breathe. I can only watch as Ari and Nasir stumble to the front of the stage, stupefied, to accept a trophy the size of my body. I look to my left, to Jonah, only to find that he's already looking at me, bewildered.

"Second place," he says, tentative. "Second place still goes to Nationals. Second place is . . . fine. Right?"

Wrong, I want to tell him. Second place is *not* good enough. Not for me, not for us, and definitely not for Georgetown.

But I don't answer him. I can't. For the first time all day, the power of speech has deserted me.

chapter two

"How'd it go, champ? Didya kick some Annable ass?"

Dad's blurry in the lens of the living room desktop, scratching at the midlife crisis on his chin. He calls me "sport" and "champ" a lot—all in the name of, like, masculine affirmation. I don't mind it, usually, but I lost the right to call myself a champ today. Lost the right publicly, mortifyingly, in front of hundreds. I wince, remembering; Dad catches it.

"What's the matter? Why are you making that face?" He's leaning forward, brow folding, a storm gathering. "Did one of those spoiled brats say something about your clothes again?"

"Is that Finch?" Behind Dad, I see a flurry of flannel: It's Mom, pulling up a chair, peering at the webcam. "What's wrong, honey? You don't look happy."

When the spotty discount-hotel Wi-Fi allows for it, I usually video-call my folks after tournaments. But I've never briefed them on a catastrophe before. I'm not sure how to do it. And I'm not sure I want to, either—deliver bad news to people who don't need another ounce of it.

Just then, while I'm searching for words, my little sister arrives in the frame. She rakes back her hair—once as red as mine, recently box-dyed black.

"Wait. Did you guys *lose*?" she asks, disbelieving. I nod grimly. She lets out an emphatic: "*Fuck*."

Dad calls out—"Ruby! Language!"—but his heart, I know, isn't really in the scold. To judge by the dark cloud gathering on his brow, he's ready to curse out Annable himself.

"Well?" Mom, an arts reporter for the *Mountain*, knows her way around a tough interview. "Can you tell us what happened?"

Should I lie? Coat the whole thing in sugar, at least? No, no; Mom would interrogate the truth out of me. Better be honest about this, about who I am now: a loser. A person who loses.

"Annable beat us in the final round, yeah." I scratch at a dehydrated zit on the side of my nose. "Not sure how badly. We won't know until we get our ballots back."

"Oh, Finch, sweetie," Mom coos. "I'm so sorry. You must—"

"What about your college apps?" Dad interrupts. "You were gonna send those D.C. schools your results from State, weren't you? Try to drum up some extra scholarship dollars?"

Good to know I can always depend on Dad to speak my deepest anxieties aloud.

"Well, we did come in second," I begin, slowly, trying to smile. "So we're still advancing to Nationals. That's something, at least."

Jonah said this to me earlier, on the stage, when the loss was still fresh. But it's only now, repeating it out loud, that I realize: Second place *is* something. Nationals is something, too. Don't I deserve to be proud of these somethings? At least a little?

"But you can't go to school in D.C. without a full ride," Dad says. "We don't have it like that, kid. We've talked about this."

We have. We have talked and talked and talked. Apparently not enough, though; Dad never misses a chance to shake salt on this particular wound. He and Mom are lobbying me to look in-state, but I've got my heart set on the other Washington, the one where progress happens, where good people fight the good fight, where history breathes in every brick. Georgetown is my dream school, but I've applied to American, too, and George Washington. I just want to *be there*, you know? I want everything the city has to offer.

And, of course, I want to huck a carton of cage-free eggs at Mitch McConnell's brownstone. No school in the Seattle area will give me that.

"Dad. Please. I know." I've got a bad habit of going single-syllable when he grills me like this. "I do my best. I work hard. This was just a bad day."

"Everything counts right now," he says, not listening. "Every grade. Every test. Every tournament."

I catch his glare. I swallow. I no longer have even a single syllable in me. So I go mute. I lift a hand, find a peeling hangnail. I chew.

"Jesus Christ, Mitch, would you ease off him?"

"What? What'd I do?"

"He just lost his big round. Maybe save the lecture for another day."

"Well, if he's got his heart set on these Ivy League schools all the way across the fucking country, he's gonna have to work for . . ."

"*Ughghghghghghghghghghghghghgh.*" Roo moves close to the camera, peers at me through fingers curled into claws. "They've been like this all weekend, Finch. Come home. Rescue me. Please. I'm fucking dying."

"Okay!" Mom calls out. "That's it!" She and Dad can fight all they want—all day, all night, apocalyptically—but God forbid Roo drop an f-bomb. "Go to your room, Ruby."

"Seriously?" Her eyes, made up in clumsy, raccoonish circles, roll and roll. You're the ones going World War Three in front of Finch."

"Go. To. Your. Room."

"Fine. Whatever." Roo lifts her hands, half hidden in the long sleeves of her hoodie, and rises. "Sorry you lost the round, Finch. Tell that girl from Annable to go suck a—"

"*Ruby!*"

With that, Roo's gone, off-camera, before I can blink. There's a faint echo in my headphones as she stalks heavily into her room.

Mom says, "Sorry about her," and I tell her, "It's fine, really," because if there's one thing I can't stand, it's my parents confiding in me about how *difficult* Roo can be.

"Well, hey," Dad says—spilling salt into my wounds, still, "if you win Nationals, those D.C. schools will open their pockets for sure."

"I hope so." Even though I'm bruised from this tournament, I've already started plotting for the next one. "There'll be some stiff competition from those boarding schools out in New England, but . . ."

"Hey, Finch! Shower's all yours!"

I was so caught up in my call that I missed the bathroom door clicking open. But it's impossible to miss Jonah emerging—ringed in a cloud of pale steam, towel riding dangerously low. I slap a palm over my webcam. I do *not* want Mom and Dad to see what I'm seeing.

"Finch?" Mom calls out, disoriented. "You still there?"

"Yep!" I chirp. "Sorry. Just having an issue with the camera." Jonah bends over a suitcase, his towel slipping even lower. I will not be moving my hand anytime soon. "Can I call you later? After the banquet?"

"Sure thing, sport." I've never played a sport in my life. Dad knows this. "Hang in there."

"Thanks," I tell him, and forcefully *end call*.

The danger is past. Jonah is pulling his pants on.

"Congrats," I say. "My parents officially know you've been working out."

Jonah laughs and whips his towel at me. I dodge it, but just barely. It meets the mattress with a lewd, wet smack.

"I'm actually super out of shape right now," he says, which, of course, is a lie, because I *saw* his biceps flex when he whipped that towel. They are *right there*, shimmering with little drops of water from the shower. It's honestly obscene. "No musical this year means no boyfriend busting my ass in dance rehearsals. I'm getting sloppy."

"Seriously, Jonah?" I lift a hand, gesture at his . . . everything. "In what world is *that* sloppy?"

It comes out more bitter than I mean it. I just can't help feeling jealous, looking at Jonah, all lanky, all sun-kissed. Someday, Blue Cross willing, I'll sculpt my body into something I don't despise. But all the surgery in the world won't make me taller. Or smooth my frizzy hair. Or keep my paper-white Irish skin from igniting at the mere suggestion of sunlight.

Jonah's boyfriend, Bailey Lundquist, the star of Johnson Tech's drama department—he's pale, too. Paler, even, than me. There's something delicate, elfin, about his features. It can be off-putting sometimes, a little alien, but he looks good next to Jonah. Among their Halloween costumes in recent years: a medieval knight and a fairy prince; a swashbuckling pirate and a deep-sea merman; Jon Snow and Daenerys Targaryen, with Jonah's beloved mutt, Toto, tagging along in papier-mâché dragon wings.

"Well, hey, look on the bright side," Jonah says—maybe hearing that bitter note in my voice, maybe trying to cheer me up. "We lost the final round, but we won something *way* more important."

"Really?" I perk up. "What did we win?"

"Two tickets to the *gun show*, baby!" he says, and lifts his arms, curling them like a bodybuilder.

"I hate you." I toss a pillow at him: right in the abs, *bull's-eye*. "Put a shirt on."

"I was thinking blue for the banquet," he says, tossing the pillow aside, bending over his suitcase. "And maybe my *Hamilton* hoodie for Nasir's after-party. The one that's like, 'Talk less, smile more.'"

I laugh. "Good advice for Nasir."

"You know what?" Jonah lifts his head, points. "You should come with."

"Come with? You? To Nasir's party?"

"Yes to all three."

". . . *Why?*"

I've never been to one of Nasir's blow-out bashes. You may have already guessed, given that nobody in the history of parties has ever referred to one as "a blow-out bash." But I've heard stories of the carnage: bones broken, babies conceived, tiled floors turned oil-slick with beer and bodily fluid. Not exactly my scene.

"A party might cheer you up," he says. "Take your mind off the final."

"Even though the party's host destroyed us in said final?"

He doesn't answer; I've won. And so I smirk, and make for the shower. "Hope you didn't use up all the hot water."

"Please," he says. "You *know* I only do staggered showers."

I do know this, actually, from all our past stays at Super 8's and Quality Inns. I still like to tease him about it. "Sounds miserable, Greta."

"You know what? Just for that, I'm timing you while you're in there." He taps his wrist, an invisible watch. "Tell you exactly how much water you're wasting."

I scowl at him—so I like long showers; sue me!—and step into the bathroom. There's only a little steam in the air after Jonah's brief round of room-temperature water torture, but I still have to lift my hand to clear the mirror. When I get a look at myself, I'm surprised: There's a strawberry-blond shadow sprouting on my chin. It shocks me every time, still. I wonder how I'd look if I let it grow into a beard. Scraggly? Pubertal? Deeply unconvincing?

I sigh. I reach for the razor.

After eighteen months of testosterone and a year of puberty-delaying Lupron, I'm finally able to pass . . . as a thirteen-year-old boy. I get a lot of kids' menus. A lot of well-meaning strangers being like, "Are you excited to start high school, young man?" I don't love the "young," but I'll take the "man." It's all I've ever wanted. People look at me, and they think "he." They think "him." They *don't* think about it.

I do, though. I think about it. Especially when I'm alone like this. I meet my own eyes in the mirror and I pick myself to pieces. Are my cheeks too round? Is my jaw square enough? Should I cover my acne, or would strangers catch the makeup and think "girl"?

The best way to banish all these questions is to step into the shower, tilt the dial all the way up, and let the jets sear me. This is how I prefer to unwind. Not partying. I've never been to one of Nasir's ragers, but given the sure-to-be-copious amounts of alcohol, and given Dad's history with the stuff, shouldn't I steer clear?

I don't know. Maybe it's the hot water pouring over me, calming me down, but I'm beginning to think Jonah's onto something. Wouldn't some music and movement put me in a better mood? I could avoid beer, couldn't I? Drink Sprite. Dance, even, if my back stops killing me.

That reminds me: I'd have to bind all night, wouldn't I? I do *not* want to put my binder back on. For the first time all day, I can actually breathe: all the way in, all the way out. Nothing is pushing down on my chest, my ribs, my little lungs. The price of this relief, though, is being reminded. Of them. And how obvious they are. And how obviously wrong for me. I've got my surgery scheduled for this summer. It can't come fast enough. In the meantime, though, I bend beneath the showerhead and let the heat strike the sorest spot, right between my shoulders, where the binder's been pressing all day.

I'm reminded, bending, looking at the long streams of water racing down my legs to my ankles, that I haven't cried today. Not once. I should be crying. Shouldn't I? Debate is the one and only place where I'm invincible, where I can talk circles around anyone, about anything. And I lost! I lost the state final! One of those rounds that truly matter. A round that would've meant something to the admissions committees of Georgetown and American and George Washington. I'd like to cry about it. Really, I would. I wish I could squeeze my eyes shut and wring everything out: the anger, of course, but the fear, too, and the embarrassment.

This is the thing about taking testosterone, though, the thing nobody ever tells you: Some guys, through some bizarre confluence of biology and chemistry and endocrinology, lose the ability to cry. You still get sad, of course. You still get that hot, familiar ache behind your eyes, and that same old tightness in your throat. But you can't actually make your sorrow real. The water never shows.

Speaking of water, I've used *way* too much of it. If I don't exit the shower soon, Jonah will give me one of his . . . well, no, *lecture* isn't the word. *Guilt trip*, more like. Whatever it's called when your debate partner pulls out his phone and takes you through the greatest hits: turtle with plastic straw jammed bloodily into nose, seahorse curling perfect tail around Q-tip, skeletal polar bear shambling pathetically over tundra of trash.

Manipulative as hell? Yes. *Unbelievably* effective? Also yes.

I step out of the shower. Before I can grab a towel, I catch a blurry glimpse of myself in the mirror. The twin peaks of my chest rising and falling. I turn away. I wish—not for the first time—that I lived in a different body.

In the hall, at the mirror, Jonah's trying—well, *failing*—to do up his tie. It's kind of funny: Jonah, who's been a bona fide boy all his life, can't pull off a basic knot to save said life. But me, the guy raised in ruffles and bows? I've got it *down*.

Jonah looks jealous as I pull up next to him, tugging my tie effortlessly into place. "*How* are you so good at this?"

"I practiced the Windsor knot 'til my fingers bled," I tell him. "Trying to hide the fact that I don't have an Adam's apple." He laughs. I beckon him closer. "Come here. Let me work my transmasc magic."

He turns to me. The ends of his tie hang long and loose. "Do your worst," he says as I take one end—stripes, blue and red—and the other—white, studded with a golden starburst—in my hands.

"What's this pattern?" I ask. "I want to say the Stars and Stripes, but the colors aren't quite . . ."

"Yeah, no, it's the flag of the Philippines," he says. "My dad gave it to me for this tournament. I wanted to pull it out tonight as, like, a very subtle middle finger to the judges who look at me and think, 'No way this kid speaks English.'"

I know exactly what he's talking about. It happened more when we were younger—ninth graders, newbies. But even now, with our shelves of trophies, we encounter the occasional judge who frowns when Jonah enters the room, before he's even begun to speak. Or a moderator, maybe, who reads the rules just a little too slowly. Sometimes we'll even get an opponent who compliments Jonah, during the courteous round-concluding handshakes, on his lack of an accent.

"You're better than all of them." My hands go still on his tie. "You know that, right?"

I look up, waiting for a smile. A nod. Something to let me know he understands me. Instead, he says, "I'm sorry."

I frown. "Sorry for what?"

"The Soviet thing," he says. "That's what sank us. And it's my fault. A hundred percent. I take full responsibility."

I look down: my hands, his tie. I can't meet his eyes. How, *how* does he think the loss is his fault? *It's mine*, I think, *my fault*, instead of paying attention; I miss a crucial step in the knot, botch the whole thing. The thin tail's dangling loose, all the way down to his belt.

"Don't apologize." I pull the knot apart, smooth down the red and blue and gold. "We lost because I wasn't ready for Ari's proxy war argument."

"No, no. You covered all your bases." Jonah sighs. "She didn't have a comeback when you brought up imperial overstretch. Your whole Paul Kennedy spiel was great."

"Didn't slow Nasir down," I mumble, in no mood for compliments. "Remember when he was all, 'The same Paul Kennedy who made his way onto Osama bin Laden's bookshelf?'"

"God, that was such a dick move," Jonah says, and shakes his head. "You know what else they found on bin Laden's hard drive? Like, fifty episodes of *Naruto*. Does that make Sasuke a terrorist? Wait. No. Bad example."

"Hold still," I tell him, because he gets excited when he talks about anime, waving his arms around. "Don't move your shoulders." I tighten the knot at his neck. "And don't blame yourself, either."

He lets his hands fall to his sides. "I just . . . I know how much this meant to you. Because of Georgetown. And D.C. And . . . everything."

"Well," I breathe out, and tug his blue collar. "We can still take Nationals."

"Damn right, dude."

We smack our palms together—a high five that feels like a promise.

"Well?" he says. "Ready to go? We don't want to be late for the banquet. *Or* the after-party."

"Oh, I can't *wait*," I deadpan, following Jonah out the door. "Tonight's the night I *finally* find out what a party looks like."

But my pan must have been *too* dead, because Jonah looks back at me, over his shoulder, with wide eyes.

"Wait," he begins, slow, trying to figure me out. "Are you

serious? You, Finch Kelly, the calmest nerd alive—you want to come with me? To a Nasir Shah rager?"

Am I serious? I don't know. I was in the shower a long time, talking myself into this party and right back out of it. I could stand here even longer, going back and forth with Jonah, picking over the pros, the cons.

But I've been debating all day. I'm tired of talking. And so I shrug, and I give Jonah a single, simple syllable: "Sure."

"Yes!" Jonah pumps his fist. "You and Ari can *finally* do something about all that sexual tension."

I shove him, hard, through the open door. He laughs and shoves me right back. We stumble out into the hall, throwing punches too soft to really land.

We arrive at the party a little less than an hour late. Blame Seattle's buses. The sky is blacker than black above the sleek steel-gray mansion Nasir calls home, and the festivities are in full, grisly swing. I take a balletic little leap over a puddle of oatmeal-y vomit to get at the doorbell. There's a terrible sound like a swarm of buzzing horseflies before Nasir throws the door open: turquoise shutter-shades, no shirt. "'Bout *time*," he shouts. "Ready to get fucked up, my [hair-raising racial slur Nasir's got no business deploying]s?"

Before I can ask where he's taking us, or complain about the hair-raising slur, Nasir's ushering us through a gleaming white foyer into an even more gleaming and white kitchen the size of an airline hangar. He sweeps his arms across a countertop cluttered with glassy alcoholic bottles—and a single dented carton of Tropicana.

"That's for me," I say, and pour myself a tall orange glass.

"Yo, what the hell?" Nasir grimaces at my juice. "You're drinking straight mixer? Who *does* that, man?"

"Don't worry, Nasir," says Jonah, hand around the neck of a green-bottled beer. "I'll drink enough for the both of us."

"Won't you get all red in the face, though?" Nasir asks, sincerely. "Since you're Asian? Or is that just chicks?"

Jonah takes a deep breath—a long one, almost exactly to the count of five. "Nice chatting, Nasir." And then, before I can protest, or beg him to stay, he's gone.

He hasn't left me alone with Nasir. Not quite. There are maybe fifty people packed into this kitchen—debaters I recognize, volunteers I don't. The girls are in the same slinky stuff they wore to the banquet, and the boys have pulled their ties loose, rolled their sleeves to their elbows. They're pouring beverages, belting off-key to pop songs I can't place, carrying on drunk versions of the arguments we've been having all day. They look at home here. Comfortable. Like the leap from podium to party is the most natural thing in the world. Where does that confidence come from? And where can I find some?

Nasir nudges my side. Lucky me. In this whole, wide room, I'm his only conversational target.

"So, what's with the O.J.?" he says. "Why don't you drink?"

I hit Alateen meetings with Roo every week. I know exactly how to handle this question. "Well, not many people know this, but alcohol causes cancer," I tell him. "The World Health Organization actually classes it as—"

"But you're Irish, right?" He ruffles my red hair. "I thought you guys loved this shit."

Seeing as we're at a house party in the twenty-first century and not, like, Ellis Island, the abject Hibernophobia catches me off guard. Alateen didn't prepare me for this one. I have no idea how to answer him. And before I can figure it out, I hear a familiar voice: "Fuck's sake, Nas. Leave the ginger alone."

I turn to see Ari Schechter at the tap, filling a glass slowly to the brim with water. Unlike every other girl in the room, she didn't dress for a party. She didn't even change out of her uniform. She moves through the crowd to us, plaid skirt swaying. Does she know how strange she looks? How out-of-place? Does she care?

"Rodham!" Nasir crows, thumping her broad back. "Thought you weren't coming out!"

"I never pass up a victory lap." Ari grins at me, smug. "How you feeling, Finch? Didn't see that verdict coming, huh?"

Remind me: *Why* did I think this party would cheer me up?

"And we're gonna hit you *again* at Nats!" Nasir lifts his bottle, lets out a jubilant shout: "Bé salamati!"

I don't join his toast. Neither does Ari.

"Teams from the same state don't debate each other in regular competition at Nationals," she says, all matter-of-fact, "which you'd know if you ever opened my emails."

"Ugh! Don't kill my buzz!" Nasir shuffles back, spilling beer. "This is a party! I gotta find me some Pootie Tang!"

I look at Ari, baffled, as he caroms out of the kitchen. "What's he talking about?" I ask her. "Pootie Tang?"

"He means *poontang*," she says, and sighs. "Derogatory slang for the vagina. From the French *putain*, or *prostitute*."

"Oh," I say. "I see."

We both go quiet. Ari sips her water. I sip my juice. There's a feeling, as the party flows around us, like we're stuck at the kids' table during a family gathering. Everyone else is having abundantly more fun than we are. Just like that, we're not arch-nemeses anymore—only the two most boring people at this party.

"So, hey," she says, leaning into me a little. "About that thing in the greenroom earlier."

I give her a sidelong look. "When you accused us of cheating, you mean?"

"I was out of line," she says. "I mean, sure, I didn't love you guys setting the debate in the Soviet Union. But also, like . . ." She sighs, shrugs. "Fair play?"

"Wow." It's almost an apology. I'm impressed. "Are we having a Camp David moment?"

"Oh, no." She laughs, falls away from me, shaking her head. "Not at all. We fully deserved to win. I concede only that my hissy fit was a bad look. Unsportsmanlike." She pauses, tapping the rim of her glass against mine—a tentative, non-alcoholic toast. "So: No hard feelings?"

"Oh, no." I pull my glass away. "My feelings are *very* hard."

Her dark eyes go wide, and she says, "Um," which makes me realize what I've said, which makes me open my mouth and go, "Not . . . not like . . . I didn't mean . . . I wasn't trying to, uh . . . to like, *seduce* you, or . . . or anything like . . . like . . ."

"No, yeah," Ari giggles. "That was *very* clear from your complete and utter lack of game."

"I have game!" I step forward, spilling a sip of orange juice on the floor. "I definitely have game!"

"Totally," she says. "Spilling orange juice? Tried-and-true seduction tactic."

"That was an accident."

"Well, I'm still waiting for the receipts." She sips coolly from her tap water, lifts a suggestive brow. "Some proof of this alleged game."

I start to speak—"What are you . . ." but before I can even land on *talking about*, I realize: Ari might be hitting on me.

I mean, I *think* she is. Was Jonah right? Is there . . . *tension* between Ari and me?

I turn away from her. I look at the tiled floor. The clean white walls. The bottles cluttering the countertop. Anywhere but Ari. If I'm right, if she *is* flirting with me . . . well, that's awfully suspicious, isn't it? Not only am I her worst enemy, I'm . . . well, I'm *me*. Not exactly what you'd call a catch.

In the entire course of my life, I've only ever had one girl-friend: Lucy Newsome, a lesbian who laid me off the second I came out as a boy. (The breakup was amicable; she's now my best friend.) Nobody's ever flirted with me. Let alone at a party. A party at a bona fide mansion with plenty of bedrooms upstairs.

What would even happen if I ever found myself in a bed-room with a girl? Would she want to kiss me? Touch me?

Peel off my clothes? Her hands would find the binder. She'd scream. Reel away from me. Tell all her friends that I . . . that I'm . . .

I need air. I need help. Where the hell did Jonah go, anyway?

"Can I . . . I just . . . I need to go find Jonah. Just touch base."

"Sure. No worries." Ari's got her phone out. I look at her; she looks at the screen. "See you later, I guess?"

I guess? What does *that* mean? Does she *want* to see me later? And why am I agonizing like this over *Ariadne Schechter* of all people?

I don't know. I can't say. I need to find Jonah. He'll know what to do. About Ari. About all of this. Even though he's gay, even though he's never been with a girl—he'll know. He's confident in all the ways that matter. All the ways I'm not. He knows me. He'll know how to calm me down.

And so I go looking for Jonah. It takes longer than I'd like. I peer into devastated bathrooms, climb beer-sticky stairs, interrupt no less than half a dozen drunk debates. Real intellectual variety here: A big group over by the pool table wonders where you put all the rapists if you abolish prisons; some guys in line for the bathroom argue about which YouTube starlet is operating the most worthwhile OnlyFans.

I finally find Jonah out on the balcony, facing south against the skyline. The view here's worth millions: Space Needle, skyscrapers, snowcapped mountains rising through the clouds. He's a tiny black silhouette against all this splendor.

I'm just about to step through the screen door when I see he's got his hand to his ear. There's a glint: a phone. I pause behind the mesh. Should I leave, I wonder? I don't want to eavesdrop.

Until I hear my name.

"No, no, Finch was flawless. The whole thing was my fault." There's a pause. He listens; he laughs. "God, Bee, how do you always know the *exact* right thing to say?" Another pause— longer, this time—as he listens to his boyfriend's voice. "Right. Exactly. Not a total wash. We're going on to Nationals. We still got silver medals." A puff of breath, visible in the cool March air. "Enough about me, though. How are you? How was your rehearsal? Did you run through your duet with . . . Oh, awesome. I can't wait to see it. I can't wait to see *you*." He sighs; the hand with the phone falls from his ear.

I'm just about to step forward, join him on the balcony, when I hear a crackle of static. Jonah's holding his phone aloft, dangling it daringly over the railing. "Can you see it?" he says, and it's then, only then, that I realize what he's doing: filming the skyline for Bailey. "Mount Rainier, right there, behind that cloud?" I can't hear what Bailey says in reply, not from where I'm standing, but Jonah seems touched by it. "I'm so glad you picked up," he says. "I get so lonely at these things."

Jonah sounds a little strange, different than he does when we talk. I've never heard his voice this low, this loving. It's so big, this thing he's got with Bailey. So much brighter than anything I've ever felt for anyone.

"I miss you," Jonah says. He waits a moment; he says, "I love you, too."

None of this is a mystery to him. He's figured it out. All of it. He's in love.

And here I am, a total infant, too afraid to even hook up with a girl at a party.

I retreat, fast, before Jonah can see me. I don't return to the party. I don't wish Ari a good night. I shuffle, instead, out a side door, and down a long driveway. And then, alone, on a vacant side street, I climb onto an empty city bus and head to the Holiday Inn.

chapter three

"So, what, Ari said you had no game? And you took that as her begging to bone you?"

"Well, when you put it like that, I sound like an idiot."

We're on the bus to school, Lucy and me, her fluffy pink head lolling against the window as she pops a bite of tempeh into her mouth. This is the bacon in the vegan bacon-egg-'n'-cheeses her mom made for us this morning. Lucy's mom is a renowned restaurateur in these parts, the proprietor of Viva Vegan. I'm no health nut, but I've never been one to turn down free food.

"All due respect, Finch, you can be kind of an idiot when it comes to, like, knowing yourself." Lucy takes another bite of tempeh. "I mean, you thought you were a girl. For, like, a decade and change."

"No, no. That's not true." I sit up straight, wag a finger in her face. "I always knew—I *always* knew—something wasn't right. I just didn't know exactly what 'til I joined the GSA."

That's where I first met Lucy, on the first day of seventh grade in a math classroom decked out in rainbow crepe. She was a pink-haired punk even then, her skin studded with temporary tattoos that she's since replaced with a small army of self-administered stick-and-pokes. I was, and remain, her diametric opposite: small, freckled, and shrinking into myself. I'd been dispatched to the GSA after seeing a school counselor for what I thought, at the time, were standard pubertal issues: feeling my body sprouting; wanting to die about it. Lucy was kind to me, that first meeting, as we nibbled on vegan renditions of the Genderbread Person. When it was just about time to go home, she asked me on a date. Her idea of romance? A die-in on the floor of Jim McDermott's constituency office. It was love at first act of civil disobedience.

"So, okay, scale of one to ten," Lucy presses. "How hot is Ari Schechter?"

"I . . . I can't . . . I don't know!" I splutter. "I don't want to say something misogynistic!"

"What the hell is that supposed to mean?" says Lucy, looking at me the way she does when I say something misogynistic.

"It means I don't want to rate her appearance on a scale of one to ten!" I yelp. "Can't I just tell you how she looks?"

"Sure," says Lucy, blowing a strand of pink hair out of her face. "I just wanna know if she's my type."

"Well, she has brown eyes. Brown hair. Short. Her hair, I mean. She's not short. She's tall. Not abnormally tall, though. Normal height."

"Wow," says Lucy. "It's like I'm there."

"I'm sorry!" I throw up my hands, defensive and baffled, equal parts. "I have no idea how to talk about girls! You're still the only one I've ever . . . you know."

"Ever *what*?" She chews on a mouthful of chickpeas, grinning slyly. "Held hands with?"

"Dated."

She snorts. "Finch, we were, like, twelve."

She's not wrong. Our relationship ended about a month into the summer before eighth grade. In her bedroom, the door locked tight, I told her that I couldn't be her girlfriend. She took the news well. She told me she loved me. She hugged me so hard I thought my bones might break. And then she told me that I couldn't be her boyfriend.

"Well, I still feel like I'm twelve sometimes," I tell her. "Especially when I listen to Jonah on the phone with Bailey. That conversation was just so . . . I don't know, *grown-up*."

"Okay. Radical idea here." Lucy takes a careful bite of tempeh, and speaks slowly through it, crumbs falling from her mouth: "Given that this story involves you experiencing so much anxiety you can't even speak to a girl, and ends with you getting so emotional about a guy talking to his boyfriend that you had to flee the premises, have you considered that you might be . . ."

"*Lucy*," I groan. "Just because you're gay, that doesn't mean everyone else . . ."

"I'm just saying!" She throws up a hand, half a shrug. "Something to think about!"

I do wonder, just for a moment, if it *is* something I should think about. This isn't the first time I've had this talk with Lucy. She's fond of asserting—much like her hero, Kurt Cobain, once did—that everyone is gay. She tells a story about the time she told her mom she liked girls. The very first time. When she was five. She made her announcement, and her mom was like, "What about boys?" and Lucy thought it over, then answered, "No. Just girls." Lucy's mom, recently divorced and wary of men, threw a hand over her heart. "Oh, sweet pea," she said. "What a *relief.*"

Me, though? I've never been that sure about who I love. The more important question, I think, is this: Will anyone ever love me?

Before I can fall too deep into a spiral of self-loathing, the bus driver calls out, "Next stop, Johnson Tech!"

Lucy rises. "This is us," she says, helpfully.

"I don't know. I might stay on for a few more stops." I sigh, and slump even further into my seat. Not even eight o'clock in the morning, and already my binder is murdering my back. Surgery *cannot* come soon enough. "I'll skip first period. And second. And third. Just ride the bus east into the rising sun."

"Uh-oh." Lucy hoists her canvas backpack onto her shoulders. "Behind on homework again?"

Every tournament, I tell myself: This one will be different. I'll manage my time. I'll balance my priorities. I'll devise a color-coded Urgent/Important scale, à la Eisenhower, and follow it to the letter.

And every time, without fail, I fully ignore all my homework for the entire week leading up to the debate.

Well, no. Not "without fail." There has definitely been some failure. Mostly in calculus.

"I really need to get it together," I tell her as I stand and step into the bus's narrow corridor. "If my grades tank this semester, there's no way I'm getting into Georgetown. Or any of these D.C. schools."

Lucy follows me to the door of the bus. "You know, you don't have to go to D.C. to make an impact," she says. "You could stay here. Work for a state senator."

"But there's no *action* here," I say. (Okay, whine.) "I want to go to D.C. Where all the world-historical political fights are."

"Why not go to Evergreen?" She's talking about the granola-crunchy state college here in Olympia. "You know how many world-historical political fighters went to Evergreen?"

I shoot her a doubtful glance. "Name one."

"Uh, Rachel goddamn Corrie?"

Okay. She's got me there.

I spent most of my life being hopelessly confused about the whole Israel-Palestine thing. Then, last spring, the topic for Regionals rolled out: This House believes that the United States should impose sanctions on Israel. I went grumbling to Google to get started on research, and I found those photos of Rachel Corrie. The ones where she's lying in the tracks of a bulldozer, blood streaming from her nose.

And suddenly, I wasn't confused anymore.

"That is *not* fair," I complain. "I'm nowhere near as brave as Rachel Corrie. I could never stand between a bulldozer and somebody's home."

"Well, could you stand in front of a home here in Olympia?" Lucy asks me, as the doors of the bus accordion open.

"What are you getting at?" I ask her, as we step onto the sidewalk.

"Denny Heck's leaving Congress this year." Lucy pulls the straps of her backpack tight over her shoulders. "My mom says there's this really cool trans lady running to replace him. Alice Something. She came by Viva the other day with some brochures." She shoots me a sideways smile as we reach the crosswalk. "If you stayed here in Olympia, you could knock on some doors for her campaign."

I shouldn't feel disappointed. But I do. "*I* want to be the first trans person in Congress."

"Dude, you're like, five years old," says Lucy, rolling her eyes. "You don't want *anyone* to get there before you?"

"Staying in Olympia to *volunteer* for a campaign," I say, stubborn, "is *not* the same thing as going to college in D.C. so I can learn to *run* a campaign."

"No. Not the same. Better, probably."

"You *would* say that," I huff, as the walk signal flickers and we cross. "You're not even going to college."

We have this argument every day. Lucy thinks college is a scam—a *bourgeois* scam, even, if she's especially riled. I, on the other hand, think my life won't start 'til I get to George-town. Neither of us ever budges an inch.

"I don't need a degree," Lucy says, confident. "I know how to edit videos. I know how to write scripts. I know how to turn on a camera. All I need is a Patreon, and I'm in business."

She's explained it to me before, this political-activist You-Tuber thing. They call it "BreadTube," I think, in reference to some obscure Russian philosopher who, I guess, wanted to give people bread? I don't understand YouTube. I definitely don't understand how Lucy plans to make a living through YouTube. I want to grab her by the shoulders sometimes, shake her, tell her, "You *have* to go to college."

But I'm a good friend, and good friends don't get into knock-down-drag-out brawls with one another. Not first thing in the morning, at least, with a long day of school ahead. So when I take her by the shoulders on the brick steps of Johnson Tech, all I do is squeeze, gently. I tell her, "I'm rooting for you."

"I'm rooting for you, too, Finchie," she tells me. "All the time. Always."

And then she kisses me on the forehead. Nobody else gets to do that. Only her.

"There he is! Our very own loser!"

On my way into debate club after school, Adwoa doesn't just meet me at the door. She full-on tackles me—whipping her arms around me, rocking me back and forth.

"Get in here!" she bellows, even though my ear's not even an inch away, as she hauls me into the cluttered history classroom that houses our club. "I made cake!"

She sure did. There, on the teacher's broad desk, is a sheet cake almost the size of that desk. It's coated in elaborate, every-color-of-the-rainbow icing. *CONGRATS TO OUR LOSERS*, it reads, the letters piped by an impressively even hand. How late was she up, baking this thing, frosting it? And how did she know that it was exactly the consolation prize my heart needed?

Well, not just my heart. My stomach, too.

"Drop out of law school," I beg her. "Open a bakery."

"I'd love to," she says, giving me a spirited whack between the shoulders. "But litigation pays better."

When Adwoa's not coaching us, she's wrapping up her last year of law school up in Seattle. Every Monday, after a long day of classes, she hops on a bus and rides down to Olympia to argue with us. She talks about moving on to a high-powered job at some big tech firm, like Microsoft, or maybe Amazon. She works hard, dreams big, takes no shit. She's everything I want to be when I grow up—but trade Silicon Valley for Capitol Hill, and subtract the knife-point acrylics.

"Jonah? Finch?" She gestures with said acrylics, bedazzled today in silver. "You guys gonna cut this cake, or what?"

With one glittering hand, she passes me a butter knife; with the other, she beckons Jonah forward. The freshmen and the sophs part for him in neat, clean lines. When his hand closes around mine on the handle of the knife, his palm feels warm on my skin. Not sweaty; warm. Are my hands cold? Is that it? People tell me all the time I've got cold hands.

Before I can think too much more about the respective temperatures of our hands, Jonah brings them both down, and we slice through LOSERS, and the club cheers like we've never lost a round in our lives.

It's nice, being admired like this, looked up to. Not literally, of course. I'm shorter than most of the club.

"Here's to kicking butt at Nationals!" Jonah lifts our hands, still joined, and tries to get a chant going: "First place! First place! First place!"

"Attaboy!" Adwoa claps his shoulder. "Keep that energy going! The resolution for Nats is out tomorrow morning."

"Wait. The resolution is coming out *tomorrow?*" Isn't that awfully soon? We've only *just* finished worrying about State. Adwoa is too busy to answer me, mobbed by cake-hungry students.

"Is it chocolate or vanilla?" says Tyler, one of the juniors, squinting at the cake through his funny frameless glasses. "I can't have any if it's chocolate. I'm allergic."

"You're allergic? To *chocolate?*" says Ava, a freshman who doesn't quite clear five feet. "How do you even *live?*"

"I got you, Ty. Pure Madagascar vanilla." Adwoa passes Tyler a slice of lily-white cake. "Y'all know there was an 'allergies' line on that permission slip back in September, right? I'm not about to serve up shellfish cake with peanut-butter frosting."

"Damn," says Jonah, with a full mouth. A vanilla crumb falls to his chest; I reach out, brush it away. "That's, like, ninety percent of Pinoy food off the table."

This is very true. I'm no expert in the culinary arts—my skills run the gamut from Frosted Flakes to instant mac—but I'm over at Jonah's place enough to know the Cabrera family practically runs on peanuts, fried up with salt and garlic. His mom serves them every time we prep for a tournament at his cluttered kitchen table. I love them. I may even *need* them.

"This cake is *it*, Adwoa," says my favorite soph, Jasmyne, moaning through her last bite. "I'm with Finch. Open up that bakery."

She reaches out to me, bumps her fist against mine. I've never told her, not in so many words, but I think she's the best debater in the club. She's only fifteen, but someday, no doubt, she'll eclipse me, eclipse Jonah, outshine us both. I have a feeling I'll turn on the TV in forty years and see her perching at a podium, running for president.

"Aww, Jas, that's so sweet." Adwoa claps her hands over her heart—and then, suddenly, her gooey smile turns mischievous. "I'm still not letting you out of today's practice round."

Jasmyne pouts, but I know she's only pretending. She sees Adwoa as a kind of big sister, I think—an older Black girl killing the game. She's constantly trying to impress her. And she loves nothing more than a good off-the-cuff argument. The instant Adwoa turns to the whiteboard, Jasmyne's pout dissolves. She shoves her empty plate aside, reaches for her pen and notebook. She is *on*.

"Let's see . . . today's resolution is . . ." Adwoa rises, on tiptoe, to render the words in big, black, bubbly letters: *This House would enact a carbon tax.* "Jas, you're on opposition, along with . . ."

"Adwoa!" Jasmyne drops her notepad, crosses her arms over her chest. "You *always* make me argue for the evil side!"

"Mmhmm," Adwoa hums, capping her marker. "N.A.D.A.'s not gonna let you skip a round if you disagree. Neither can I."

Jasmyne swings her feet, kicking at the legs of her desk.

"But you never let me talk about the stuff I *do* agree with."

"'Cause you're smart enough to play devil's advocate, honey." Adwoa points her marker into the crowd. "Now, on prop, I want to see . . ."

"I mean, if you only ever defended things you agreed with, debate would be completely pointless." Tyler's voice is a little more patronizing, a little more *duh*, than I'd like—especially since we, as a club, have some version of The Devil's Advocacy Argument, like, once a week. "You're *supposed* to put your personal feelings aside."

"That's not how it works in real life, though," Ava offers, her mouth full of cake. No one else is eating right now; she's either gone back for illicit seconds or started poaching half-eaten slices abandoned around the room. "Like, in the presidential debates, you don't see the Democrats talking about why the Republicans are so great."

And then, suddenly, *everyone* is talking, one voice piling over another. It's impossibly loud, a cacophony—but, hey, at least we're all debating.

Adwoa hooks two fingers into her mouth. She blows out a high whistle. "Pipe *down*," she commands, and we do, because if Adwoa's learned one thing in law school, it's how to drop a convincing *order in the court*. As we settle, she swings herself onto the teacher's empty desk.

"Let me ask you something, Miss Jasmyne," she says, and tucks a couple of braids behind her ear. "Is there anyone you admire who's done something you don't agree with?"

"I mean, sure. Yeah. We've all got a 'problematic fave'"—

Jasmyne's fingers curl into quotation marks—"or whatever, but I'm talking about people who are, like, straight-up *evil*."

"Like who?" Adwoa asks. She holds out her hands, sweeps her gaze across the classroom. "Who is so straight-up evil that we shouldn't even waste our time asking how they justify straight-up evil?"

"Donald Trump," Jasmyne answers, instantly. Bravely, too, given that there are more than a few conservatives in our club. I see Tyler raise his hand to offer up some apologia; I see Adwoa silence him with a steely look.

"And how do you know that Donald Trump is straight-up evil?" Adwoa says. "Can anyone give me an example of an especially evil thing that he—"

"When he separated all those immigrant children from their parents," I cut in, before Tyler can. "Literally tore babies out of their mothers' arms."

"Exactly," says Jasmyne, bringing her palm down on a desktop. "There's no *why* there. No excuse. Trump's just evil. Period."

Adwoa's being awfully quiet. I wonder, for a second, if Jasmyne's got her beat. If she's about to cede the whole argument. But then she crosses her arms, lifts her head, and levels her eyes at us.

"You know," she says, "Obama locked immigrant kids in cages, too."

We're silent. All of us. No words going her way. Only wide, stunned stares—and a smug look from Tyler.

Jonah's the first, finally, to speak. "No, he didn't," he says—

and then, a second later, less confident: "Did he? Actually?"

"Yup. Obama locked all the same brown kids in all the same cages," Adwoa says, nodding. "Forced them to sleep on the exact same concrete." She laughs, joyless. "One of his speechwriters tweeted out those photos—you know, with the tin-foil blankets, the chain-link fences? And he was all, 'This is terrible. Trump's a monster.' He didn't even realize that the photos were from 2014. When *he* was writing Obama's speeches."

I wonder, with a sick, sinking feeling in my stomach, how any of this can be possible. How could this man, who literally put words in Obama's mouth, not know what those words were propping up? And then I wonder how it's possible that *I* didn't know. I pay attention, don't I? I read the news. Is that enough?

I look to Jasmyne. She looks like she doesn't feel very well. Adwoa must see the illness on her face. She gives a kind of sad half-smile.

"Just ask yourselves this," she says, her voice soft now, consolatory. "If someone like Barack Obama, who's so much smarter than me, who's done so much more for the world than I'm ever gonna do—if *he* could miss something so obvious, what am *I* missing?"

She pauses. Her fingers drum along the desk.

"Good people get talked into evil all the time," she says. "I'm just teaching you to recognize evil when it talks—then talk right back at it."

She stops speaking, but her words linger, heavy, in the air. I feel that sinking sickness, still, but I feel something more, too. Like I don't have to drown in that feeling. Like I can lift my arms, steel myself, and swim forward. Good or evil, right or wrong—whatever I am, I'm not helpless.

"And on *that* happy note," says Adwoa, with another flick of her braids over her shoulder, "it's oil tankers versus tree-huggers in fifteen."

When debate club lets out, the sky is the color of coal dust. A few of my least favorite things about living in Olympia: the prevalence of white people with dreadlocks, the constant threat of seismic catastrophe, and the descent of night, in wintertime, at only four o'clock in the afternoon.

When it's dark out, I take the bus home, for safety, with a small group. Adwoa's got the farthest to go, so she claims the window seat, and I settle for the aisle. Behind us, Jonah tosses an arm around Bailey.

"You guys had *cake?*" Bailey nestles under Jonah's wing. "And you didn't even save me a slice?"

He pouts, just a little; Jonah kisses him calm.

"You'd better get that boy some cake," Adwoa says, giving them a fond look. "Treat him right."

"Oh, trust me," Jonah says. "I give him *plenty* of cake."

Adwoa laughs, shocked. Jonah and Bailey giggle, too. But I've tuned out, eyes on my phone. *The Economist*'s daily newsletter rolls into my inbox around this time every afternoon, and I don't want to miss it. Not with the resolution for Nationals landing tomorrow morning. There might be a hint in this e-mail, some newsworthy item we'll wind up debating. This is what I need to focus on—not romance, not cake. There will be plenty of time for dating *after* I've secured my place at Georgetown. 'Til then: Focus, Finch.

Adwoa pokes me. "Hey," she says. "You heard back from any schools yet?"

"Still deferred at Georgetown. No word from the others yet." I can't help it; I sigh. "I thought the state championship might give me a leg up, but—"

"I know *exactly* how you're feeling," Bailey interrupts, with a sigh of his own. "My final Juilliard callback is this weekend."

"Fingers and toes crossed," Jonah says, and he really does lift a hand, cross his fingers. As for his toes, I can really only guess.

"So I'll be flying out to New York for that," Bailey goes on, "and then I'm flying out again in June for the Jimmy Awards."

"The Jimmy Awards?" Adwoa lifts a brow. "I'm not familiar."

"The National High School Musical Theater Awards," Bailey recites. You can hear the hope in his voice. "I've been before, but this is my last chance. I really want to make it count."

"He's being modest," says Jonah, clearly loving this opportunity to brag. "Bailey's been nominated for Best Actor *twice*. Last year, he was a semifinalist. Top four in the whole country."

Bailey is so pale that I can actually see the blush spreading under his skin. "I don't want to jinx it," he says. "I've never won anything."

"Not yet, you haven't," Jonah says, and taps Bailey on the tip of his elfin nose. Then he turns to us. "He's switching it up this year. Taking on a bigger role."

"Wait—didn't you play Sweeney Todd last year?" I'm confused. I've never been a theater kid, but I know that Bailey's roles are big ones. Starring ones. "And Jean Valjean the year before that?"

"Yeah! I came to see *Les Mis* when you guys were sophs. And, Jonah, you played . . ." Adwoa pauses, aiming a thumb at Jonah. "Wait. Don't tell me. I wanna say . . . M-something?"

"Marius Pontmercy." Jonah gives Bailey a look so loving I feel embarrassed just witnessing it, like I've walked in on the two of them making out. "That's how I first met Bee. He saved my life. Carried my wounded body through the sewers."

Bailey drops his head onto Jonah's shoulder. "We always say 'Bring Him Home' is our song."

"Guys, *stop*," Adwoa squeals, throwing her palm over her heart. "I'm getting cavities over here."

"So what musical are you doing this year, then?" I still have questions. "What 'bigger role'?"

"Well, this year, I actually got to *choose* the show." I can see the corners of Bailey's mouth tilting up as he speaks. "And I picked *Thoroughly Modern Millie*. It's about this flapper who moves to New York in the Roaring Twenties, meets a rich man, falls in love . . ."

"So you're playing the rich man?"

"No, no. I'm playing *Millie*." Bailey's smile cracks all the way open, a wide moonbeam, on this last word. "We renamed it: *Thoroughly Modern Billie*. She's a boy now. It's a gay love story."

"For real?" Adwoa gasps a little, then lifts an arm over the seat-backs, shakes Jonah by the shoulder. "Jonah! Why didn't you try out? You could've played the rich man! I mean, don't get me wrong, I'm glad that I've got you all to myself for tournament season, but . . ."

She's asking an innocent enough question—so why is Bailey's grin getting dimmer by the second?

"Oh, well, you know," Jonah mumbles, "I was already juggling debate with college apps and family stuff, and I just . . ."

Jonah's saved by the banner at the front of the bus. It lights up: his stop. After a quick kiss goodbye for Bailey, and even quicker nods to me and Adwoa, he's hurrying down the corridor, slipping through the doors and out onto the rain-slick sidewalk.

I turn, head over my shoulder, to watch him walk away. Bailey's doing the same. There's something deeply unhappy in the cast of his moon-white face. It makes me think—suddenly, weirdly—of that ludicrous thing Lucy said this morning. That I'm, you know, gay. Secretly. And jealous of Jonah and Bailey. If that were true, I'd turn away, wouldn't I? I'd let Bailey's sadness fester. I definitely wouldn't offer my help.

And so, to prove Lucy wrong, I take a deep breath and ask, "Hey, Bailey?"

He meets my eyes. "Yeah?"

I lower my voice. "I know it's none of my business, but are you guys . . . I mean, are you okay?"

"Oh, yeah," Bailey says, though his tone seems more *oh, no,* at least to my ears. "It's really nothing." It is, absolutely, something. "We're just figuring out college and stuff."

"You two gonna try long distance?" Adwoa asks. "Or is Jonah following you to Manhattan?"

"Yeah, he applied to NYU," Bailey says, sighing. "And obviously, that would be ideal. But . . . you know. Money."

We nod. We know. I've been agonizing over scholarships for months, and law school's left Adwoa with a pile of debt the size of a house. She likes to bring it up every time someone in debate club is naive enough to voice an interest in law school—a hard, cold reality check.

"We'll figure it out, though," Bailey says, voice bright. "Our two-year anniversary's coming up soon."

"Two years?" Adwoa whistles. "That's a long time."

Bailey laughs, but he's pulling away from us, retreating into the blue world of his phone. This is, I guess, a sensitive subject. I may have to keep prodding. But not today. Not now. Adwoa's turning to me, lowering her voice.

"So," she says, "we never really talked about your college plans, huh?"

She's right. Bailey really ran away with the conversation just now, huh?

"I just wish Georgetown would give me a real answer," I tell her. "I can't stand this deferral thing. I want a yes. Or a no."

"You do *not* want a no. Trust." She laughs—and, fine, I laugh, too. I could use it. "I've been interviewing for a few jobs lately, and . . ."

"That's exciting!" I lean close to her. "Have you heard back yet? Do you know where you're going?"

"Well, I may or may not be flying down to Alabama next Saturday," she says, lifting her hands, inspecting her silver nails, "for a lil' final-round interview."

"Wait. Alabama? What's in Alabama?" As long as I've known Adwoa, she's dreamed of Silicon Valley. What happened to Big Tech? And, besides, if she gets this job . . . if she moves to Alabama . . . "You're not coaching debate club next year?"

She chews on her lip. "Remains to be seen," she says. "I've got a few leads up here, around Seattle, but this Alabama job, man . . . I'd literally be freeing innocent folks from jail. Every day, I'd be helping people get out on parole, go back to school, start brand-new lives." Her voice is soft, tender. She's talking about this job the way a kid might talk about Disneyland. And then the spell breaks, and she laughs: "It'd be a massive pay cut, though. These people do *not* have Amazon money. I wouldn't be able to pay off my loans. Not in this lifetime."

"But who's going to take over for you?" I'm being rude, but I can't help myself. "Here in Olympia, I mean. As coach."

She curls her fingers into her palm, frowns: a tiny piece of polish is chipping away.

"Honestly," she says, "if you weren't heading off to D.C. . . ."

I fall away from her. "Don't jinx it."

"I'm just saying," she says. "You'd better coach a team of your own someday. You'd be great. Those kids? They love you."

"Thanks, Adwoa. That means, um . . . it means a lot to . . ."

That banner at the front of the bus flickers on. We veer to

the curb, come to a halt. I reach for my backpack, wishing I'd found better words, something beyond the obvious *thanks*. I want Adwoa to know how much it means, her faith in me.

"Get a move on, Finch," Adwoa says, hugging me tight. "I'll text you the resolution for Nats first thing."

And then, after giving Bailey a brief nod, and getting a friendly wave in return, I step unsteadily off the bus, into the rat-gray rain.

Have I mentioned that I hate the rain here? Hate it. Just hate it. Can't escape it. There are entire months in Olympia where my socks feel like they'll never be dry.

As I walk up the path to my front door, this is how I console myself: *Just a little more rain, Finch. A few more months of rain, and you're free. You can fly away to the other Washington, the one with seasons. Then your life will begin. Your real life.*

I climb onto the porch, fishing my keys out of my pocket. My parents are audible through the door, lurching into something that sounds like another fight. I'll have to be quiet when I turn the handle. Quieter when I slink down the hallway that always smells like wet dog, although we don't even keep plants, let alone pets. Quietest of all when I close the door to my own room, to keep my parents—and their fights—at bay.

At a quarter after midnight, the time blinking bright through the black from the clock on my nightstand, there's a knock at my door. I lift my head from the pillow. A beam of weak light floats into my room: Roo, stepping carefully inside.

She moves on tiptoe, slowly, although she really doesn't have to. Our parents are in the kitchen, screaming so loud I'd be stunned if they can hear a single thing we do. She's got a video game in hand, deployed as a flashlight, and blankets, too. A whole mess of them. If Mom and Dad insist on waging war all night, we're better off huddling in a blanket fort than struggling to sleep in our own separate rooms.

I lift a blanket, flicking my wrists as it flows out into the air, a long wave. Through the walls, Mom's yelling something about "fifty thousand dollars a year, Mitch! What's your plan? I sure as hell can't send him to school on my dog-shit salary." I wince. This is my least favorite flavor of familial fight: one where I'm the offstage star.

"Because he couldn't just go to a fucking state school!" Dad's shouting, too—just as loud, twice as venomous. "No, he has to go all the way across the country and pay out the ass to get something he can get for free right here!"

Roo, pinning a blanket to my desk beneath a heavy trophy, gives me a tortured grimace. I see her mouth form *yikes*, but I don't hear her, because Mom is yelling: "He's a fucking genius! He deserves a good school!"

I've seen enough of my parents' fights to understand: This is no compliment. It's bait. If my dad takes it? If he goes, *No, he's not a fucking genius*, or *No, he doesn't deserve it*, the fight will no longer be about money. It'll be about me. Whether my parents love me. Who loves me more.

And so, for the sake of my own sanity, I think I'm better off tuning out tonight.

What a profound relief to curl up with Roo under all these draping layers of cotton and wool. I turn my pages. Roo's thumbs tap her screen. I munch on my late dinner, a cereal bar. We make a rhythm, the two of us, with these little movements. I choose to focus on these sounds, instead of the argument pushing faintly through the walls we've built. I feel lulled. Safe. I lose track of time, and I'm surprised when Roo lifts her head.

"Hey, Finch?"

I look up, blinking at her in the dim light. "Yeah, Roo? Everything okay?"

"Does it ever bother you?" She gnaws on her lip, not meeting my eyes. "When they talk about you like this?"

The answer, of course, is *Yes, it does bother me, very much*. But I know that these fights aren't really about me. Not all the time, anyway. They're bigger than I am, usually. They're about the biggest thing of all: money.

"Well, Mom and Dad, they've been under a lot of stress for a long time," I begin. "Dad being unemployed, Mom's newsroom getting whittled down, I mean . . . none of that has anything to do with me. Or them. Or any of us. It's not their fault that the government won't . . ."

"Finch, seriously? Can you please be a human being? For one second?" Even in our low light, I can see the frustration on her face. "Instead of going off about politics?"

"The personal *is* political."

She groans. A curtain of black hair falls over her eyes. "Man," she mutters, behind this veil, "I'm really going to miss your nerd ass next year."

"*My* nerd ass?" I can't help it; I laugh. "Sorry—how many hours have you logged playing Mineshaft?"

"It's called *Minecraft*, and I think you know that."

"Sorry, sorry. I meant Fortwatch."

"*Finch.*"

I'm still laughing: "Overnite?"

"Okay. That's *enough*."

She throws her game aside, comes at me on all fours. I lift my book up, a makeshift shield against the tackle I'm sure is coming. It never does. Roo, with a small, scared sniffle, is collapsing into my arms, going limp in my lap. I'm so startled that it takes me a second to lift my hands, pull her to my unbound chest. Roo, usually, isn't down for physical touch, let alone a full-body cuddle.

"I wish you weren't going away for college." Her voice is quiet, almost vanishing in the folds of my pajamas. "D.C.'s too far away. You should stay here. Live at home."

I rock her, gently. "But where would I go to school?"

"Evergreen," she says. "Lucy's always talking about it."

My turn to roll my eyes. "She's roped you into her conspiracy, huh?"

"You could get an apartment with her and I could come and live with you guys," she says. "I wouldn't have to listen to them yelling at each other every single stupid night."

"Oh, Roo." She's heavy in my arms. "I have to go away to D.C. I just have to. But it has nothing to do with you. Promise."

"It *does* have something to do with me," she insists. "What happens if you leave? I won't have anybody."

She's right. I know she is. Who does she have without me? The pixels on her screen?

"Well, listen: Three years from now, you'll be in college, too, and—"

"Oh, I'm definitely not going to college." She snorts. "My grades are crap. And, plus, you don't need a degree to be a game dev."

"Okay. Fine. No college. In three years, you can move out, and start making your own games, and . . ."

"Right. Great. Three more years of trying to sleep through all this screaming. I wish they'd just give up and get a divorce."

"Ruby!" Her real name rushes out of me. "You don't mean that. You don't actually want—"

"Maybe I do!" Roo's like me—she hardly ever cries—but I can see she's on the verge now. "It's been, what, a year? And he's not even looking for a job anymore! He just sits on the couch and he . . . he . . ."

"He's almost sixty," I interrupt, gently; I can feel her running out of steam. "It's hard to find a new job when you're that old."

"So what does he do, then? What do *we* do? Seriously, Finch: When's it gonna get easier?"

I have nothing to say. Nothing. At least I can tell myself that I'll be out of here in a few months. But what about her? How is she supposed to endure this? All I can summon are little niceties, useless ones: *Hold on, hang in there, keep your chin up.* But I'd rather say nothing at all than give her something so empty.

"I don't know, Roo," is what I land on, finally. "Let's just go to bed. I need to get some sleep."

"Fine," she says, huffily, but she settles down as we pull the blankets around our bodies, wrap ourselves up. Even now, after an argument of our own, we both know it helps to have someone nearby. A person who loves you. Who won't leave.

And yet, when Roo rests her little head on my shoulder, it's all I can think about: leaving.

chapter four

Next morning, all morning, I feign calm as best as I can. A little more shut-eye might've helped in my battle against nervous wreckage—thanks, Mom and Dad—but nothing would've kept me from panicking about the incoming Nationals resolution. Especially after Adwoa's text comes through on the bus to school: res dropping @ 11:30 AM, b ready, followed by a helpful YouTube link: Europe—The Final Countdown (Official Video).

When the hour—well, the half hour—finally rolls around, I'm trapped in the back row of calculus with Mr. Mah. Emphasis on *trapped*. If Mr. Mah sees me using my phone, he'll take it; if I don't read the resolution at precisely 11:30:00 AM PST, I will spontaneously combust.

So I've fashioned a shield out of my textbook. Protecting my phone from his prying eyes, you know. Not that he'd be wrong to pry, since I'm openly checking texts during his class. I've gotten three silent, buzzing false alarms now: an invite from Jasmyne to play Words With Friends, a new episode of *Pod Save America*, and a missive from Lucy in exuberant, misspelled all caps: OMFGGGGGG LINSAY ELLFIS JUST DMED

ME BACK ON TWITTER! GONNA TRY TO INTERVIEW HER FRO MY CHANNEL WSISHE ME LUCK!!!!!!!!

I'm about to do exactly that—tap Lucy's message, wish her luck, and ask her who this Linsay Ellfis person is—when I feel a fourth buzz.

ADWOA DOUNA: guess who got the nats topic (it's me) (i got it)

I lift my head and flash Mr. Mah an I'm-definitely-listening smile. He smiles back. Perfect. I've just bought myself five minutes of suspicion-free screen time.

ADWOA DOUNA: lemme just copypaste the email i got from NADA

ADWOA DOUNA: Kylie Jenner Hosted a Handmaid's Tale Themed Birthday Party and It Was Everything

ADWOA DOUNA: omg sorry wrong thing

JONAH CABRERA: wait did she actually? the handmaids tale???

FINCH KELLY: Is Kylie the one who did the pepsi ad with the riot police or is that a different one

JONAH CABRERA: finch i know how much time u spend reading thinkpieces abt the kardashians being the downfall of civilization

JONAH CABRERA: there is no. way. u don't know kendall from kylie

ADWOA DOUNA: okay sorry copypaste take 2

I wait. I watch the gray bubble. Those three little dots grow darker, darker. This is it: the gun going off at the starting line. Whatever Adwoa types next, it will rule the next month of my life. I will spend every kernel of spare time I've got plugging these words into Google. I will devour every article I can read for free, and, with Roo's assistance, hack around the paywalls barring me from the ones I can't.

ADWOA DOUNA: The National Championships of the North American Debate Association will be held at the Gray School, in Washington, D.C., from March 29 to March 31.

The topic for this year's championship is:

This House would allow transgender students in public schools to use the bathroom facilities of their choice.

No. No, no, no. I'm not breathing. My vision is blurring. The breakfast I ate on the bus is leaping up into my throat. Of all the things we could argue about, all the culture wars in all the towns in all the world, they walked right into mine.

"Finch?" Mr. Mah slices through my stupor. "I'll be taking that phone now."

He reaches out a hand, beckons for the phone buzzing busily behind the lousy makeshift barricade I'd erected. I am so, so nauseous; it takes real, conscious effort to open my mouth and dispense words, not bile.

"Family emergency," I tell him, not convincingly. "I need . . . need to . . ."

He shakes his head, bifocals glinting in the halogen light. "Give it here, Finch. You can have it back after class."

I don't know how I muster the strength to drop the phone into his hand, but I do, and then I'm alone at the island of my desk. It's hard work to breathe in and out. Even harder work not to be horribly, vividly sick all over the sixtieth and sixty-first pages of *Calculus: Concepts and Contexts*. I cannot believe this is happening to me.

You're never just for or against at Nationals, is the thing. You take turns. In the first round, you're *yes*; in the second, you're *no*. Both sides. No getting around it.

If I go to this tournament, I will have to stand behind a podium and argue against my own right to take a shit.

I'll have to argue against people who've never met a trans person. Who don't know the first thing about who I am. Who believe everything J. K. Rowling posts on Twitter. I do daily backflips *not* to engage with these people. Almost no one at this school knows I'm trans, and for good goddamn reason: I wouldn't be a person anymore. I'd be a political issue.

I spend the rest of calculus in queasy rumination. What the hell am I going to do? I can't just boycott this tournament; this is *Nationals*, for Christ's sake. I have to go. If I want any chance at Georgetown, I have to *win*. Stand behind a podium, deliver a speech about why I don't deserve to pee, and win.

God knows my calculus grade isn't going to clinch Georgetown. I barely absorb the stern warning Mr. Mah gives me on my way out of the classroom, stumbling into the hall and stabbing frantically at my cell phone. I've missed upwards of a dozen texts. The most recent one—the first one I see—is:

JONAH CABRERA: well still finch u must be excited

. . . What is he *talking* about? Jonah is among the very few at Johnson who I've told I'm trans. Shouldn't he know that I'm less than thrilled about the prospect of a weekend spent hearing—no, *repeating*—the case for my own personal banning from every bathroom in the United States of America? I text him back with shaky thumbs:

FINCH KELLY: Why would I be excited haha

JONAH CABRERA: uhhhhhh maybe because washington??

JONAH CABRERA: district????

JONAH CABRERA: of columbia??????????

Wait. Pause. Is he . . . are we really . . .

I scroll up, and I see it: *The National Championships of the North American Debate Association will be held at the Gray School, in Washington, D.C.*

I am going to Washington, D.C. *I am going to Washington, D.C.*

The nauseous wave breaks over me. I don't feel dizzy. Not anymore. I feel awake, suddenly. I feel *better*. So what if every round is a transphobic dumpster fire? Who cares? We're talking about dumpsters full of world-historical trash, glowing bright and defiant against white-brick monuments.

Jonah's words are like sunlight piercing fog. I can see the resolution for what it is: a test. If I win this tournament, I'll transform my wildest dream into reality. I will go to Washington, D.C., and I will make history there. Years down the line, I'll be debating trans rights on the House floor, and I'll look back on today's little flutter of fear and I'll laugh and laugh and laugh.

I bring my thumbs to the keyboard once more. I grin.

FINCH KELLY: Bring

FINCH KELLY: It

FINCH KELLY: On

There's a corner booth at Viva Vegan that Lucy's claimed as our personal property. Woe to anyone who settles into this booth for a smoothie, sweet potato fries, or spaghetti squash lasagna while we're around. We can get—*have* gotten—physical with would-be usurpers.

Today, an after-school snack awaits us there, courtesy of Mom Newsome: pita chips, bean dip fragrant with garlic and lemon, and two darkly purple drinks, almost black, brewed with some exotic berry I couldn't even guess how to pronounce.

When Lucy and I go out to eat, especially at Viva, we observe a strict ban on cell phone usage—enforced by Lucy, inherited from her mom, and shared, apparently, with Mr. Mah. *Be present with one another*, say the placards, in a trembling font, taped up all over the dining room. *Mindful eating makes for mindful conversation*. It sounds like woo-woo to me, but there must be some truth to it. Lucy's so mindful that when I glance down at my lap for a second, a *split* second, she catches me, and pounces.

"For those of you just tuning in," she says, a finger to her ear, like she's speaking into a headset, "we're getting word that area teen Finch Kelly is sexting—yes, Tom, that's right, *sexting*, in public, in broad daylight . . ."

"I am not *sexting!*" I cry out. "That's not even a real word!"

"Though Mr. Kelly denies the accusation," Lucy goes on, "and also denies that *sexting* is a totally valid step in the natural evolution of the English language . . ."

"You mean the *degradation* of the English language."

". . . One thing remains clear," she continues, and flips me a deeply un-newscasterly middle finger. "Mr. Kelly is staring at his cell phone while sitting in the corner booth at Viva Vegan with his best friend, Lucy Newsome, in violation of a long-standing agreement to refrain from texting while eating." She pauses, and then, solemnly: "Back to you, Tom."

I take a sip of my smoothie. "Who's Tom?"

"Uh, *Brokaw?*" she says, like I just asked if the sky's green. "Who were you texting, anyway?"

"The debate club group chat." I drop my phone into my backpack, then lift my hands, displaying my empty, innocent palms. "We got the topic for Nationals this morning."

"Oh, God. What is it this time?" She reaches for her smoothie, eyes rolling. "Pouring trash into the oceans? Arming kindergarteners with assault rifles?"

Lucy is *not* a fan of debate club.

"I don't remember the exact wording." I'm lying. Of *course* I remember the wording. I've been repeating the sentence to myself all day. But I want to avoid a fight with Lucy, who remains skeptical about the ethics of arguing for, like, the U.S.S.R.'s right to unlimited nuclear bombs. "But it's something about, um . . . trans people. And bathrooms."

"Oh, Finch." The snark melts right off her face. "I knew it'd be bad, but I didn't realize it'd be, like, *personally* bad." She takes a deep breath, scans my somber face. "Shit. You're not actually going to do it, are you? Go up there and say you don't deserve rights?"

"This is Nationals," I say. I hope that's enough for her.

It's not. "So?"

"So you can't pass on a topic if it's about you."

Lucy makes that face she makes—lips pursed, nose wrinkled—when she smells something gross, or accidentally eats meat, or lays eyes on a really *Republican* Republican.

"This is why I never joined debate," she says, voice brittle and hard. "I could never get behind a podium and pretend to be Satan."

"That is *not* the point of debate." My turn to make a face at her. "It's about understanding an issue from every angle. I'm not talking about right or left. Not even right or wrong. I mean, to really dig into tough issues, get at the nuance, the really complicated—"

"No thanks," she interrupts, picks up a pita chip, and brings her teeth down: *crunch*. "Don't need to walk a mile in a Proud Boy's polo to know he sucks."

"Oh, well," I mumble, eager to end this conversation before she gets really heated and calls *me* a Proud Boy, "at least the tournament's in D.C."

"Oh my God, Finch, why are you so obsessed with D.C.?" She brings her drink down, hard; a splash of smoothie leaps out, paints the tabletop purple. "There are people *right here* who need your help."

"Like who?"

"Uh, like the homeless people camping in Sylvester Park?"

"Oh, totally. Forget D.C." I know I sound like a brat. I don't care. "I'll just stay here and end homelessness all by myself."

"Who said anything about doing it yourself?" She rises from

the table and snatches a postcard from her mom's corkboard. "Alice Brady for Congress," she says, and hands it to me, her face smug.

I take in the postcard: a young, redheaded woman, dressed in bright blue, pledging Medicare for All, Bold Climate Action, and Housing as a Human Right.

"Is this the lady you were telling me about?" I ask her. "The trans woman who's running to replace Denny Heck?"

Lucy nods. "If you want to devote your life to helping trans people, give her a call." She taps the number on the postcard. "Don't fly to D.C. and argue you shouldn't be allowed to piss."

I set the postcard on the table. Alice Brady smiles back at me, upside down, unfazed.

"You're very persuasive," I tell her, sipping my smoothie. "You would've made a great debate partner."

"Yeah, right. We both know I can't hold a candle to Jonah. He's your debate soul mate." She pauses, laughs: "Your debate mate."

"Oh, shoot." I look up, frantic, to the clock on the wall. "I have to meet Jonah in fifteen."

I'd asked him if we could prep after school—at his place, preferably, so I could gorge myself on his mom's peanuts. But he was already booked: Bailey had roped him into attending this afternoon's *Billie* rehearsal. Adwoa told Jonah that a date was not a valid reason to skimp on prep—not with Nationals only a few weeks away, no sir. I offered a compromise: We'd meet *after* Bailey's rehearsal. This way, Jonah could honor both of his commitments: to his boyfriend, and to us.

It worked. Peace reigned. Be the change you want to see in your group chat.

"Well, you'd better get going, then," says Lucy. "Gonna take ages to crowbar Jonah out of Bailey's arms." She must realize she's being a little mean; I barely have to side-eye her before she walks it back. "I don't blame him, though. I mean, have you *seen* Bailey?"

"I have seen Bailey, yes." I stand up, sling my backpack over my shoulders. "And honestly? Of the two? Jonah's way more conventionally attractive."

I say this flatly, like it's the plain, unremarkable truth— because it *is*—but Lucy leaps on it anyway, grinning like the devil. "*Is* he, now?"

"I don't mean it like *that*," I huff. "And I'm not even saying Bailey *isn't* good-looking. Just that Jonah's more . . ." I search for a way to say this, one that won't, like, *implicate* me: "He's like a man you'd see in . . . in a black-and-white movie. Or, uh . . . an ad for trench coats." My stammering isn't helping. Lucy's still grinning. "Stop looking at me like that."

"I'm not looking at you like anything." She lifts her hands, feigning innocence. "And you *definitely* don't like boys."

"You're right! I don't!" I bring a palm down on the tabletop, insisting: "I pay attention to the way boys look because I *am* a boy, and I want to look more like one."

"Whatever you say, bud." She laughs, slurping up the final dregs of her smoothie. "Text me later, okay? Tell me how 'conventionally attractive' Jonah's looking these days."

"Will do," I say, giving her the finger. "Love you."

"Love you, too," she says, her middle finger just as high in the air as mine.

Because I haven't suffered enough today, I push open the door to the auditorium just in time to hear the very last words I wanted to hear: "Okay, everyone! From the top!"

The swell of the orchestra helps to drown my groan of despair. The loud clatter of the dancers' tap-shoed feet helps, too. They move into the wings and leave Bailey alone, center stage, in a tiny pool of light. I watch for a moment—mesmerized and envious—as his Adam's apple rises and falls in the snowy expanse of his throat.

Jonah's seated center orchestra, right beneath the tech booth—best view in the house. "Hey, Jonah." I slide into the plush chair next to him. "How's the rehearsal going?"

"Great!" He sounds awfully upbeat for this late in the afternoon. "They're really getting the hang of these big dance numbers."

I eye him, suspicious. "Why don't I believe you?"

He hesitates for a second. "Honestly, this musical is kind of . . ." But then the lights are going out, and the music's starting up, and Bailey's opening his mouth.

His voice. Holy shit. No wonder Jonah's in love.

There's something impossible about Bailey's singing: innate, practiced, magical? I've heard it before, but never in a space this empty. Without so much as a microphone, his voice finds us in this cavern and holds us captive.

He's all alone up there, just him and his light. I lean close to Jonah. "Is this a one-man show?"

"No, no," Jonah whispers back. "Bailey opens it solo, but then . . ."

But then! The music explodes, the stage erupts in color, and every dancer in the drama club bursts forth and swirls around Bailey. They crowd him in careful formation. I lose sight of him, almost, his duck-fluffy blond head disappearing behind arms, elbows, fluttering hands.

"Guy? Hey, guys?" Bailey is barely audible above the storm of tap shoes. "I'm gonna need a little more space for the quick change! Tiffany, can you back up?" Tiffany, I guess, ignores him, because Bailey laughs—not happily. "Don't make me shout, okay? I can't strain my vocal cords, or—*Tiff, seriously?*"

It startles me, this little wave of attitude rippling through his voice, cresting at *seriously?* I've never seen this side of Bailey before. If I didn't know any better—didn't ride the bus with him, didn't know he treats Jonah like a prince—I might think he was a diva.

Is he? Have I missed something? I look at him now, back in his spotlight, with two whole rows of dancers swaying at his back, and I can't recall him ever once being humble. At the song's end, when he throws his hands up and bellows the highest note, he is, literally, shining. With sweat. But still.

I look to my left: Jonah is shining, too. In the places where his dark brown eyes are darkest, I can see the reflection of the stage lights. It's striking, seeing him like this: genuinely starry-eyed. But I don't get to look for long. He's on his feet in an instant, bringing his hands together, whooping, cheering: "*Bailey! Bailey! Bailey!*" It's funny, hearing an ovation this vigorous in a space this empty. Does anyone else think it's weird? The cast, the drama teacher? Whoever? It's like the rest of us aren't even here. Like nothing matters but Bailey's excellence, Jonah's admiration.

I can appreciate Bailey's talent, of course. I can even clap for it. But I'm not in love with it. Not the way Jonah clearly is. When the teacher frees the cast to go, he bounds down the stairs to the stage, two or three at a time. I trail after him, the sluggish senior dog to his hyperactive puppy. He hits the stage first and lifts his boyfriend high in the air, swinging him like a ragdoll.

I wonder, watching them, if anyone will ever hold *me* like that.

"Jojo!" Bailey shrieks. "Oh my God! Put me down, baby!"

Jonah does eventually set Bailey down, carefully as a china teacup. But his joy doesn't dim, not one lumen. He tucks a white-blond curl behind Bailey's ear and he says, "You were *stunning* today, Bee."

"I'm stunning every day," Bailey says, and swats Jonah's chest. "But you already knew that, didn't you?"

There's a brightness about Bailey, even without the spotlight. I feel dull, dingy, just standing next to him. Next to *them*, I mean. It's like I've walked into a private moment, even though there are dozens of people around, all in careless, messy, post-show dishabille. I turn away from them to face the red velvet curtains bordering the stage. Lifting my hand, I start to trace a little pattern in the fabric. Just something to do 'til Jonah finishes, and finds me, and we can go and get to work.

It's cold out after the rehearsal. Dark. The sky's shedding the first tears of a storm as we make our way across the parking lot. Jonah pauses to open his backpack, fumbling for his defiantly yellow umbrella.

"Scale of one to ten," he says to me, as the polyester canopy blooms above our heads, "how excited are you to fly to D.C.?"

"A hundred," I say, without thinking. "No, a thousand. A million."

"We should stop by Georgetown." Jonah gives me a grin. "Give you a preview of campus life before you move out there in the fall."

My stomach flips. "Don't get my hopes up."

"Why not? How's any school going to turn down a national debating champion?" he says, and before I can protest—because I meant what I said, about hopes and directions—he points to the bumper of his humble used hybrid. "Hop in. I'll turn on the butt-warmers."

A car was never even a conversation in my cash-strapped family, especially after Olympian transit went mercifully zero-fare a couple years back. Jonah was lucky enough to get this car as a birthday gift from his mom and dad last year. It came with the expectation, of course, that he'd use it to ferry his siblings to Little League and Girl Scouts while his dad visited ailing parishioners and his mom worked night shifts at Providence St. Peter. But Jonah's the type who never drives *unless* he can carpool, and so, on the days we don't bus, I find myself in his passenger seat.

Tonight, his eyes are on the road. Mine are on my lap. I've got my agenda open, along with a fistful of highlighters—all the colors of the rainbow, an old Pride gift from Lucy.

"So: Seventeen days 'til Nationals. Two debate club meetings between now and then." I find the yellow marker, drown each Monday in sunlight. "If we can get together and prep every Wednesday and Friday after school, and maybe book some lunchtime meetings at the Green Bean, that'll bring us to . . ."

Jonah lets out a laugh. A quiet one. I lift my head, curious, and look at him. His eyes have left the road. They've found me.

"What? What is it?" There's something funny about the way he's looking at me. Actually, no, not *at* me; *into* me, more like. I feel myself go stiff. "Why are you staring at me like that? Do I have something in my teeth?"

"Do you remember that first debate club meeting?" he says, just as I bare my teeth at the rearview, searching for parsley. "Freshman year. Adwoa paired us up."

"She's got good instincts," I say, running tongue over teeth, satisfied I'm not missing anything. "How many of those other random pairings are still around, four years on? How many of them went on to Nationals? We owe her a lot."

"We really do." He laughs again. "I don't know what the last four years would've looked like without you, man."

It's raining now. Hard. He's still looking at me.

"Thanks," I tell him. "Eyes on the road."

He turns his head away from me. The moment, whatever it was—it's over, I think. I lower my eyes to the agenda in my lap.

"Right. So. If we can swing a few extra meetings on the weekends, that'll give us an edge, I think, in terms of—"

"I guess I'm just trying to say I'll miss this."

I lift my head, startled. "Miss what?"

"Next year, you know," he begins—and he's sort of stumbling over his words now, like he's embarrassed. "When we're on opposite coasts, and you're drilling somebody else with your color-coded calendars."

"Opposite coasts? I thought you were following Bailey to Manhattan. Money permitting, I mean."

Jonah goes quiet a long moment, chews on his lip. When he speaks again, his voice is soft.

"I got into the University of Washington," he says. "And I'm going. I got the Doris Duke scholarship. Majoring in atmospheric science, minoring in ecological restoration."

"And Bailey doesn't know?" I'm so shocked that I don't even say it politely, don't soften it with congratulations. I just bray it out: "You didn't tell him?"

Jonah turns away from me, wincing. "Not yet," he says. "But Bailey knows I want to stay close to my family. And he knows UDub's got, like, the best environmental science programs anywhere."

". . . Makes sense," I say, though I'm reeling: Why is Jonah telling me something he hasn't told Bailey? "There's not a lot of wilderness to save in Manhattan."

"Exactly." Jonah laughs freely. "I don't like cities all that much. I need trees. Rocks. Dirt."

I understand this, of course. I know Jonah. Any weekend we're not debating, you can find him climbing Mount Eleanor, or hiking out to Sheep Lake, or swimming in the ice-gray water at Priest Point. In another life, he might've been a lumberjack, a mountain man. I can see Bailey on Broadway, but I can't exactly see Jonah in Tribeca.

"So are you guys going to do the long-distance thing?"

"I mean . . . I want to try." Jonah half laughs. "And it'd better work, or I'll spiral."

"Spiral how?"

"Oh, like, party 'til dawn, eat nothing but takeout, fail every single class." He stops; that half-laugh again. "My mom and dad are gonna get a call at Thanksgiving, like, 'Come get your son,' and they'll show up, and they'll find me buried in my dorm room under a big pile of Jollibee bags."

I can tell he's joking—trying to, at least—but he sounds more worried than I've ever heard him. More worried, even, than me on my very worst tears about college, money, the future. What's going on here? *He's* the one who cools *me* down. I only know what to say next because he's taught me how.

"I don't think you have to worry about spiraling," I tell him gently. "I know you, Jonah. I know how hard you work. I think you'll be in your element at UDub. Doing what you love."

"Doing what I love?" he asks.

"Saving the planet!" I throw my hands up. "Patching holes in the ozone! Throwing water on forest fires! Slurping plastic out of oceans!"

"Slurping?" he says, laughing—for real, this time, which makes me laugh, too. We pass beneath a billboard, and a sheet of light rolls over us. But before I can even blink, it's gone. He's quiet. We're back in the realm of dull, dish-watery gray.

"It's just a big change," he says, voice flatter—no peaks of fear, no jokey valleys. "A lot of stress. They say college is supposed to be way harder than high school."

He looks at me like he wants me to reassure him. Like I'll tell him it's not true, that college is a breeze. But I can't. I'm worried about all the same things.

I shrug; he sighs.

"Maybe I'll feel better when I'm there," he says. "You could lend me some of your confidence. That'd help a ton."

"Confident? Me?" What's he *talking* about? "My factory-default setting is punishing existential anxiety."

He throws his head back with another giddy, genuine laugh. "Still, though, you get shit *done*."

Do I? All I do, all day, is worry—about my grades, my debate scores, my odds of getting into Georgetown. Jonah's not like that. Not like me, I mean. He's better. So much better than me, objectively, in every conceivable way. He's book-smart, of course, but he stars in school musicals, too, and sits on the student council, and serves dinner to homeless people at his dad's Filipino American Fellowship every Sunday night. He was homecoming king last fall, for God's sake. Why would he need to borrow confidence—borrow *anything*—from me?

We pull into his gravel driveway. He pauses, hand on the gearshift.

"Hey," he says. "You mind keeping all this between us?"

"Of course," I say, and I feel a weird, dark thrill. I've always been on his team, in his corner; now, I get to keep his secrets, too. "You want to tell Bailey on your own time. I understand."

"Thank you," he says, and breathes out. "So much."

He opens his door, and I open mine, and I follow him up the driveway. There's a basket of soft sandals in his home's small, cluttered entryway, right next to the umbrella rack. Jonah's little blond dog, Toto, yips at my heels as I shuck my shoes and pick out a pair in pristine blue terrycloth.

"Finch!" Jonah's mom is coming down the stairs in scrubs—crisp, white, dotted with Muppet Babies. "Jonah said you were coming. So good to see you!"

"Hi, 'Nay." Jonah scoops up Toto, then leans in, kissing his mom on both cheeks. "Need me to make dinner?"

She shakes her head, yanking her dark hair up into a ponytail. "May pinakbet at sinigang sa ref." The *ref*—short for *refrigerator*, I think—catches me off guard. I'm always a little startled by how seamlessly she and Jonah switch languages—mid-sentence, sometimes, or even mid-word. "And I made those peanuts you like," she says, turning to me. "Bowl's over there."

She points through an archway into a living room littered with toys. A bowl of peanuts rests resplendent on the coffee table. It takes all my restraint not to dive headfirst.

"Thank you." I mean it. "*So* much."

"Easy, tiger," Jonah laughs. He sets Toto down, then squeezes my shoulder. "Sharing is caring."

He gives his mom a final hug before she heads out the door, and before we head—not slowly, not calmly—to the living room, just about knocking the bowl off the table in our haste to snatch up salty, oily fistfuls.

"I told you Bailey's allergic to peanuts, right?" Jonah says. "He can never eat these."

"Really?" He must have mentioned it over the years, but I'd forgotten. I feel a funny pang—real, genuine sympathy for Bailey, deprived forever of Reese's Cups, the best of Ben & Jerry's, and Mrs. Cabrera's finest culinary efforts. "Poor guy."

"I can't eat these, either," Jonah says, sighing like a martyr. "Not if I want to kiss him. And *especially* not if I want to . . ."

"Okay, okay." I know where he's going with this, and I can hear Renata and Benjie, Jonah's very little and *very* impressionable siblings, playing with the dog in the next room. "Don't need a blow-by-blow of your S-E-X life."

He grins. Wide. "A *blow-by-blow*?"

I groan and turn away from him and crater my face into the couch's cushions. He laughs. Laughs! The audacity. My face turns redder; I sink further. There's a whole ecosystem down here in the crevices of the couch: abandoned crayons, a bent green Slinky, something that might be a shoe for a doll. I'm just emerging, no longer pink-faced, playthings in hand, when I catch a tiny face peering at me through an open door.

"Hi, Renata!" I hold out my palm, my plastic bounty. "Do these belong to you?"

She wavers in the door, thumb in her mouth.

"You can come in, nenè!" Jonah calls out. "Don't be shy!"

She steps slowly into the room. Her neat black pigtails spring as she moves. "Thank you," she says, in the world's tiniest voice, taking the crayons and toys. Before I can even say "You're welcome," she's turning on her heel, leaping out of the room like I gave her an electric shock when her fingers touched my palm.

"She still gets shy around anyone she's not related to," Jonah says, apologetic. "We're working on it."

I know this, of course. I'm over here a fair bit. So I tell him, "No worries. I'm still shy, and I've got ten years on her."

He laughs, and plops onto the couch next to me before reaching into his backpack for his laptop. "Ready to prep?"

"Hold on." I wipe my hands on my pants. "Don't want to get peanut grease on my keyboard." My computer, unlike Jonah's, is held together by duct tape; I have to treat it with the utmost fragility.

"No worries. I'll start the doc." He opens his laptop and starts to type: "'This House would allow transgender students to use . . .'" What was the exact wording, again?"

"'Transgender students in public schools,'" I correct him, licking salt from my fingertips. "'To use the bathroom facilities of their choice.'"

"Hey." He turns to me. He's stopped typing. "Are you . . . okay? Debating about this, I mean?"

My first instinct, my knee-jerk, is to tell him yes, of course; why wouldn't I be okay with this? I'm a debater. Devil's advocacy is what I do. What we *all* do. This isn't any different from Jonah, with his NUCLEAR POWER? NO THANKS! buttons, arguing for atomic annihilation.

I mean, it *shouldn't* be different. I don't *want* to be different.

Just about everyone at Johnson is clueless about my being trans. Not Jonah, though. We've shared hotel rooms. Shared beds, even. He's seen me late at night, in my pajamas, binder shucked. There was that one weekend he strolled out of the bathroom we'd been sharing, toothbrush still in his mouth, and asked, "Hey, wuff wiff the rubber dick on the towel rack?" I had a whole entire heart attack. Started apologizing. Launched into this frantic speech on the care and keeping of packers. He just held a hand up. "No worrieth," he said, and then stepped away, spat into the sink. "It's a nice dick," I heard him say, over the flow of the faucet. "You've got good taste in dicks."

I've always been grateful for the way he handled that—like it was normal, not something I'd have to apologize for. I'd hate for him to feel like he has to handle me with kid gloves.

"I'll be fine," I tell him flatly. "It's not the first time I've argued for something I didn't believe in."

Jonah falls back into the cushions, chewing hard on his lip. "You remember that one tournament in Tacoma?" he says. "When we had to be anti–gay marriage?"

"Of course I do." I still remember how worried he was when Adwoa read us the resolution, how ashen his face looked. "You talked about boycotting the tournament."

"Right. Because I want to get married, obviously. But then, remember, we started doing research, and we found all those gay activists from the seventies saying, like, 'we don't want a world where it's only okay to be gay *if* you get married.' And I didn't *agree*, necessarily, but I could see where they were coming from, at least. And we used that stuff to build a case I could live with." He shrugs, scratches at the side of his nose. "Do you think there's anything like that for this issue? Like, a pro-trans argument *against* the bathroom thing?"

I shake my head. "I'm not sure."

"Well, what about safety? For trans kids, I mean." Jonah leans toward me. "We could spin it like: Hey, it's not safe for these kids to use the bathroom of their choice, 'cause they might get bullied."

"Huh." For the first time since I read the resolution, I feel that familiar flicker in my chest: hope. "That could work." I reach for my own laptop. "Lots of trans people are afraid to use public bathrooms. I mean, people everywhere. Even in places that don't have these laws."

Jonah's hands go still on his keyboard. "Are you?" he asks, with the tone of someone who regrets what he's saying as he's saying it. "Afraid?"

I open my mouth; I close it. I have no idea how to answer him. We hardly ever talk about my being trans. We *definitely* don't talk about my bathroom habits.

"Not . . . really?" I manage, finally. "I mean, not in the last, like, year, at least."

"Because you, um . . ." His hand works in the air, wrist spinning in circles as he searches for the word he wants. "Because you look like a . . . because you . . ."

I'll put him out of his misery: "Because I pass?"

"Yes. Yeah." There's a nervous flicker in his laugh. "Didn't know if I was allowed to say that."

"Oh, you're not." I laugh, shaking my head. "Definitely don't say 'pass.'"

"Got it." He nods. "I just . . . wanted to know if it made things easier for you."

"Well, sure. I don't get weird looks when I go into the men's room anymore. Although . . ." God, this is mortifying: Who wants to tell their friends how they poop? "I have to use a stall sometimes, and if they're all full—or there's only one, and it's out of order, or whatever—I have to go to the women's room. Which is . . . not ideal."

Jonah winces. "I can imagine."

"Can you, though? You, Jonah Cabrera, strolling right on into a women's bathroom, going, 'Sorry, ladies, the little boys' room was full!'"

He laughs out loud. "Okay, no. I can't actually imagine that. I can imagine the embarrassment, maybe, but . . ."

"Yes! The embarrassment!" I bring a hand down on the couch between us; my palm leaves a crater. "Thank you! This is *the* trans debate, and it's the most embarrassing issue possible. It's not marriage. It's not adoption. It's . . ." I lower my voice—very aware, still, that Jonah's little siblings are playing in the room right next to us. ". . . it's *peeing*."

"God," Jonah sighs, rakes a hand through his hair. "These conservatives were really like, 'Okay, how do we make these people look gross? I know! Let's only ever talk about them in the same sentence as taking a shit.'"

Through the wall, a chorus of giggles: "Jonah said a bad word!"

"Taking a *poop!*" he calls back, but they only giggle harder. Toto joins in, too, barking uproariously. Jonah looks at me, exasperated. "Kids these days."

"They've got a point, you know." I nod to the door, where Renata and Benjie are still howling with laughter. "The bathroom debate isn't just gross—it's *grown-up*. You can't talk about it around kids. You just can't. And that plays into this whole idea of . . . of . . . of trans people, especially women, being rapists, or pedophiles, or . . ."

"Or Buffalo Bill. Right." Jonah taps on his keyboard, scrolls down the doc, all business. "Well, okay. Looks like we've got a good start on the pro-bathroom side. How do we argue against it?"

I stare down Google. I swallow. I've typed *transgender predator* into the search bar. The cursor blinks and blinks. My hands rest on the keyboard. They do not move.

Jonah tilts his head to look at the screen. Sees it. His face goes soft, and he says, in a low voice, "I'm sorry, Finch."

That little flicker of hope I felt before? Gone.

I clear my throat. "It's fine," I tell him, "really," and I can tell by the look on his face, his arcing brow, that he doesn't believe me. Hell, *I* don't even believe me.

"At least the rounds only last, like, half an hour?" There's a hopeful bit of up talk in his voice. Some optimism. "Half an hour's not a long time."

I sit for a moment, silent—chewing on this, chewing on my lip. Jonah is very right. Nothing in me wants to stand up, say that people like me are predators. But it's just half an hour. Just pretend. That's not so bad, is it?

If I want this win—if I want Georgetown—what else can I do?

———————

I'm the first to admit it: I'm not tech-savvy in the least. I'll never understand bitcoins or blockchains, not as long as I live, no matter how many times Roo tries to educate me or calls me a "pleb," whatever that is. But I know enough about computers to understand that my own is on its last digital legs. Tonight, at Jonah's, it stammered and stuttered, shutting down at random. In the end, I gave up—just dictated to Jonah as he typed into our prep doc, swore to him I'd look at it when I got home.

And I can't even do that. The little blue circle is spinning on my screen with no end in sight. What if I stood up, right now, and threw my laptop out the window? I'm weighing this idea when my eye hitches on a symbol low on the screen, a white circle no more than a few pixels wide. It's struck through with something like a screw. A lever, maybe. I move my mouse, hover over the icon: *STEAM*, it says, in that little white bar.

STEAM? Panic surges through me, steals my breath. STEAM is a virus, isn't it? It *is*, it must be; *this* is why my computer's been so slow? Not a second to lose. I open Google and batter my already-battered keyboard: *what is steamcomptr?*

The answer, instantaneous: "Steam is an online platform from game developer Valve where you can buy, play, create, and discuss PC games."

"Roo!" I bellow. "*Roo!*"

I find her on the couch in the living room, fully horizontal. Her dinner—a bowl of off-brand Lucky Charms—sits on the coffee table, the marshmallows consumed and the brown cereal getting visibly soggy. She peers at me over the edge of her laptop like an otter balancing a clam on its stomach.

"What's up?" She tugs out a single earbud. "Wow. You look pissed."

"Why," I seethe, "did you hack into my computer?"

She blinks. "I have literally no idea what you're talking about."

"How did *Steam* get onto my laptop?" I tilt the screen, stab the white icon: *J'accuse!* "Explain how this got here if you didn't hack in."

"Dude, oh my God, Steam is just iTunes for video games." Roo groans, driving the heels of her hands into her eyes. "It's not, like, advanced hacker shit. Jesus Christ, what are you? Twelve years old?"

It's a weird dig coming from a fourteen-year-old.

"Look: All I know is that I didn't install this thing."

"And you think I did? On *that* hunk of junk?"

I click on the logo. A box pops up.

"'Username,'" I read aloud, "'kangarookelly.'"

"Oh." She shoves her fists into the pockets of her hoodie. She does not look at me. "Yeah, that's . . . that's one of my usernames."

"Sorry: *One of* your usernames?"

"Okay. Sometimes, when I'm playing *Civ* on multi-player, I'll use two accounts at the same time." When I look at her, baffled, her voice goes high, defensive: "It makes conquest easier. One less capital to nuke during endgame."

I understand just about nothing she's saying—except this one crucial point: "You've been using my computer to play video games? Against *yourself?*"

"Well, if I'd known you were going to have such a stick up your butt," she huffs, "I wouldn't have done it."

"Roo, I *need* this laptop. For school. For debate. For college stuff." I close it, hug it close to my chest. "It is a very old, very sick computer. It cannot handle video games."

"*Fine*." She sounds angry—why? what right does *she* have?—as she lowers her eyes to her own screen. "Won't happen again."

I'm just about to issue a command: Wipe this Steam nonsense off my hard drive, right now, *or else*. But then I hear these things, in this order: a door swinging open, a pair of heeled shoes clicking on linoleum, and a doorknob hitting drywall, hard. Mom is home.

Along with those familiar sounds, though, I hear a low, ragged hum. It's like laughter, but there's a bite in it, a razor's edge. She's crying, I realize. Mom is crying. But why? I look to Roo. She looks back with the same fear in her eyes.

We move quick, out of the living room, into the cluttered entryway. Mom is still wearing her shoes and coat. She's soaked in gray rain, clutching a cardboard box. I see a snow globe. A picture frame holding our sun-faded faces. The bottle of hand lotion I bought her last Christmas, half-empty now, trembling on top of the pile and threatening to swan-dive.

Mom lifts her head. Every worried line in her face carves itself deeper, deeper.

I swallow, hard. "Is the paper . . ."

"It's over, Finch." She closes her eyes. A few stray tears trickle out anyway. "We're fucked."

chapter five

You'd think I'd have learned, at some point in my seventeen years of life in the glorified mud puddle that is Olympia, Washington, to bring an umbrella with me when I head out into the rain. After hours of tossing and turning, fretting about my future and Mom's, I finally gave up on sleep and set out for Lucy's place. I really thought the coat and boots I threw over my pajamas would be enough for the quick walk over. I was wrong. When Lucy opens the door to find me on her porch, I look like I've just been tossed in a swimming pool.

Lucy scans me up and down, every sopping inch. "Two questions: Who died, and where's your umbrella?"

"Nobody died." I sniffle, but *not* because I'm crying; it really *is* raining on my face. "My mom, uh . . . she lost her job."

"Shit." Lucy lets out a low whistle. "This is normally where I'd give you a hug, but I think I'd better give you a towel instead."

Another sniffle. "A towel does sound nice."

"Well, come on inside, then." She steps back, then stops. "Unless you want to have your mental breakdown out here. We've got a porch swing for that."

"I just want to be dry," I tell her, because I can't even re-member what that feels like, and she leads me in and leaves me dripping on a mat that says *Namaste* instead of *Welcome*.

Lucy lives with her mom in a low-lying split-level house a lot like ours. One crucial difference, though: Where our clut-ter feels ugly, theirs is totally charming. It's all jewel tones, gilt and tin, mahogany Buddhas. Lucy hands me the softest towel I've ever held—it's got to be bamboo, something New Age–y like that—and motions for me to follow her down the hall, into her bedroom. We walk past a tiny gold cat, its paw raised high in greeting. I reach out with a fingertip, pet it be-tween the ears.

"I love your mom's little knickknacks," I tell her.

"Well, you shouldn't," Lucy huffs. "I keep having the Ori-entalism talk with her and she keeps bringing that shit home from garage sales."

I'd honestly like to advocate for said shit—how bad can it be, really, if she bought a Japanese cat in a Japanese family's garage?—but before I can even open my mouth, we're out of the foyer and stepping into Lucy's bedroom, another world entirely, a vintage Lisa Frank notebook in three-dimensional space.

Lucy's strung Christmas lights all along the headboard of her bed, rainbow-colored bulbs sending red and yellow and blue light flickering over the Barbie-pink bedspread where we used to kiss and where we presently hold platonic sleepovers. Every surface in her room is soft. She's got faux-fur rugs in leopard and zebra, beanbag chairs in lime and tangerine, a whole zoo's worth of stuffed animals piled into a pyramid at her headboard.

I fall onto the bed. Calamity strikes. I've dislodged Paddington, and he's tumbling, fast, to the floor. Lucy shrieks, lunging for her British bear, and that's when I see it: a patch of skin, like cracked earth, violently red, just above her hip.

"What *is* that?" I only just suppress a gag.

"What's what?" she asks, cradling Paddington to her chest.

"There, on your hip." I point, wincing. "Were you rolling around in poison ivy?"

"Oh. No. I was trying to give myself a stick-and-poke, actually. Of the Subaru Star. It got infected." She glances down at it, forlorn, and sort of stretches the skin out between two fingers. I look away so I won't barf. "But never mind. We've got more important shit to discuss than my botched tattoo. Like your mom. Who lost her job."

"Yeah. Along with everyone else on staff." It's a miracle I can talk at all; my throat is so, so dry. My eyes, too. I guess nothing—not Mom losing her job, not the shuttering of the paper I've read and loved my whole life—is enough to make the dam break. "No warning. No one's getting severance." Which means even less wiggle room when it comes to paying for college, but I don't say that part out loud. Don't want to come off self-centered.

"Shit," Lucy breathes. "And there's not a ton of jobs for newspaper reporters right now, yeah? Not even in the state capital?"

"Well, no," I sigh. "Because Mom mostly writes music reviews. Covers art shows. Things like that. She's talked to some local politicians about, like, state funding for glee clubs and school musicals, but . . ."

"But politics isn't really her beat. I get it. Is she going to, like . . . write for other places? Magazines? Or just start a whole new career?"

I can't answer her. I can only plant my face in the soft belly of a Care Bear and scream like my Celtic warrior ancestors.

"Attaboy, Finch." Lucy reaches into the pile of stuffed animals to stroke my head. "Abandon the spoken word. Regress to cavemanhood."

After maybe my fourth scream, there's a knock at the door: "Lucy? Sweetie?"

I lift my head. My hair falls damply into my eyes, and through the reddish fringe, I can see Lucy's mom stepping through the door. Her curls have turned pink in recent months, but a darker sort of purply-pink, nothing like the cotton-candy hue Lucy's trademarked.

"I brought tea," she says, and lifts a long wooden tray. I see a blue ceramic kettle, a sticky jar of honey, and three lovingly chipped mugs. None of them match. "South African honeybush. Uncaffeinated, naturally sweet, *and* proven to inhibit the growth of tumors in rats."

"Thanks, mamacita." Lucy takes the tray. "We needed this."

She fills the mugs and hands me one from the gift shop at Mount Rainier—sturdy, painted with snowy peaks. Little brown rings tell tales of tea parties past. I close my eyes and take a sip of honeybush that warms me from the inside out. I want to cry: Lucy's mom really got up in the middle of the night just to boil water, to make tea, to assemble her most stalwart mugs, all for me. And for a second, I think I really *might* cry—the feeling's there, that tight heat behind my eyes. But when I lower my mug, no, nothing; drought.

Lucy's mom takes a seat at the foot of the bed as we settle into place against the stuffed-animal pyramid. Lucy throws an arm around my shoulder. I'm grateful for it. For her.

"So," Lucy's mom starts, her dark pink eyebrows arcing up, "you two back together?"

"Nah." Lucy shakes her head. "He just needed a cuddle."

"I got some bad news tonight," I explain.

"Really bad," says Lucy. "He ran all the way over here without a dang umbrella."

"Do you want to talk about it, Finch?" says Lucy's mom. "I'm a licensed hypnotherapist, you know."

"Oh, no. I . . . I'd rather not be hypnotized." I shake my head, smile, try not to look *too* freaked out. "Thank you, though. For offering."

"Finch's mom lost her job today," Lucy says. "The *Mountain*'s owners shut it down. Fired all the reporters."

"Oh, Finch, honey." Lucy's mom reaches out, squeezes my knee in sympathy. "What goes around comes around. Just remember that."

I laugh, bitter. "I sure hope so."

"Now, your father," she says, speaking slowly, cautious, "he's not working, either, yes? Do I have that right?"

It kills me to nod. "I mean, he's been looking for a job for a long time, but . . ."

"I understand, sweetheart." Lucy's mom smiles. "You know, if you ever need a distraction, we've been doing some volunteering with the Alice Brady campaign. She's just incredible. They've got a ton of resources that could help your family."

Lucy brings a fist to her chest, pounds the place over her heart. "Mutual aid!"

"Thanks," I say, "that sounds really neat," but I don't ask Lucy's mom what she means by "resources," or how Lucy thinks "mutual aid" is going to keep my family from the brink. The Newsomes aren't exactly in the one percent, but I'm not sure they know what it really is to be broke. There's real money in hypnotherapy and vegan food. Gwyneth Paltrow's built an empire on it.

"And if you've already submitted your financial aid applications," says Lucy's mom, "you'll want to get in touch, tell them what's changed."

"That is . . . a *really* good idea." Just for a second—a gorgeous, guilty second—I wonder if this could be it, my ticket into college: not one, but *two* jobless parents. Could this actually . . . *help* me?

No, no—what am I thinking? Being broke isn't going to *help*. There's a reason that Ari Schechter got into Georgetown early and I didn't. Forty million reasons, actually.

"You're still aiming for D.C., right?" says Lucy's mom. "Not anywhere nearby?"

"He doesn't want to go to Evergreen, Mom," Lucy cuts in, before I can speak. "I've already given him the pitch."

"Oh, but Evergreen's an incredible school," she says. "You

know, when I went to Evergreen, I dated a girl who dated Carrie Brownstein."

"Mom!" Lucy squeals, rocking forward onto her knees. "Why didn't you tell me? Am I really two degrees of separation from lesbian royalty?"

"Who's Carrie . . ." I begin, but Lucy's mom is already moving on, resting her hand on my knee again.

"We'll be crossing our fingers for you," she says. "Whether you stay in this Washington or move on to another one."

I feel a smile, a real one, flicker across my face just for a moment. At least *someone* believes I can still make it there, to that other Washington. "Thanks," I manage. "That means a lot."

She smiles back. Her hands return to her own mug, and she takes a long, slow sip.

"Well, I guess I'll be going back to bed," she says, as she rises, pats the foot of Lucy's bed. "You guys be safe. I've got a few dental dams in the . . ."

"Oh my God, *Mom*," Lucy cries out. "I literally just told you we're not dating anymore."

"Whatever you say!" She smiles—clearly not convinced—and makes for the door. "You two have a nice slumber party, now."

She's barely closed the door before Lucy and I collapse into each other, waves of laughter washing over us.

"She wants us to get back together," I giggle, "*so* bad."

"Oh, yeah. She ships us hardcore." Lucy leans away from me, grabbing a stuffed elephant the color of cream soda. "She thinks you're a good influence on me, even though . . ." She taps the elephant's soft snout against my own. "We all know that *I* am the good influence on *you*."

"You don't think our sleepovers are weird, do you?" I ask, idly stroking the elephant's velvet ear. "I mean, we've been broken up for years, and I still come to your house in the middle of the night."

"No. Not weird at all." She's emphatic. "Best friends sleep over all the time."

"Even girl and boy best friends?"

"How very Mike Pence of you." She tosses the elephant at me. "Look, I'm not even into boys. And you're probably not even into girls, although you . . ."

"Lucy . . ."

". . . Continue to deny it."

I give her the finger. She rolls her eyes, then rolls off the bed, making her way to the closet.

"What are you doing?" I ask.

"If you're staying over, you should get changed," she says. "You can borrow some pajamas from me."

She finds some old sweatpants for me, and a worn-out T-shirt from a concert at the Showbox in Seattle. I take them to the bathroom, and when I come back, free of my binder and swaddled in Phoebe Bridgers merch, the Christmas lights are out in her room. I have to squint through the dark to climb under the covers with her. She wraps her arms around me, burrows her nose into the back of my neck.

"I'm sorry about your mom," she murmurs. "And her job."

"Thank you."

She's quiet a second, and then, softly, she says: "You'll get through this, you know. You and your family."

I turn, search her face in the dark. "What do you mean?"

"I mean, yeah, your parents fight all the time and shit. Un-employment's definitely not gonna make things any easier. But, like, they've got each other's backs, you know? Nobody's gonna split."

Her voice cracks on that last word, *split*, so I ask her: "Did your dad . . ."

"Yeah. Two days ago. Another fucking pathetic e-mail. He started going to church again, he's praying for me and my mom, will I stop being such an ungrateful little bitch and write him back, blah, blah, blah . . ."

"I'm sorry, Lulu."

"Don't be. I don't give a fuck about him. I've got the best mom in the world."

"You really lucked out, you know?" I mean it. "You two just . . . you *like* each other. You really, honestly like each other. And you are so much better off without him."

She moves closer to me, 'til we're nose to nose. "You ever wonder why people get married?"

"I mean, financial security. And there's all this stigma against single parents, too. Our whole society is basically built to lock out anyone who isn't part of a nuclear family. There's this guy Michael Cobb who wrote a whole book on—"

"Okay, I love a political diatribe as much as you do," she says, "but that was *not* an invitation to go full debate champ on me."

"Sorry. I probably deserved to be interrupted."

"I'm just saying—sometimes I'm glad my dad walked out, you know?" She blinks; I feel her lashes up, down on my cheeks. "Like, if he'd stuck around? If I'd spent the last decade actively dealing with his shit? I would be way, way worse off than I am now."

"I think there are lots of people who are just happier not being married." I pause. I can feel my voice shifting, going small, timid in my throat. "But if you really love someone, and they really love you, and the two of you take good care of each other . . ."

"What the hell?" Lucy laughs, kicks me lightly in the shin. "Since when are you a hopeless romantic?"

"I'm not!" I squirm away from her—her, and her icy-cold feet. "I swear!"

"I know, dum-dum. I dated you."

"I really don't know if I'll ever date anyone ever again."

It's the kind of thing I wouldn't say to anyone but Lucy. Wouldn't say to anyone at all if the lights were on. If I weren't already so sad.

Lucy's sigh feathers my face. "Don't do this," she says. "You're always doing this."

"Doing what?"

"Cockblocking yourself," she says. "Or, like, clamjamming."

"I . . . *clamjamming*?"

"I'm trying to respect your anatomy!" She twists away from me; I'm trying, hard, to land a kick of my own. "Leave me alone!"

"*Clamjamming* is the worst thing I've ever heard in my whole life."

"Okay, fine. I'll never say it again." She crosses her heart, and we settle back into place, both giggling unstoppably in that stupid, sleepover-giddy way. "I just wanted to stop you before you went into one of your self-hate-y spirals."

"I do not *hate* myself," I scoff. I don't. I really don't. Well. I don't *think* I do. "It's just . . . hard for me to date anyone, you know? Especially 'til I have my surgery."

She snorts. "*I* dated you."

"Yeah, but you *like* clams."

"Only if the clams are attached to girls," she says. "And, for the record, I like all kinds of girls. Girls with clams, girls without . . ."

"But not everyone's like you! Most girls . . . they wouldn't even think about dating a guy like me. And that's . . . you know, whatever. Fine. To each their own."

Lucy's silent for a second, staring up at the ceiling. Her quiet feels heavy, loaded.

"You know," she starts, slowly, "I spent a long time wondering why my dad walked out."

This feels like a non sequitur. "Where are you going with this?"

"Well, like, I spent a lot of time asking myself, 'What's wrong with me? What did I do? Why doesn't he love me?'"

"Lucy." Something in my stomach sinks like a stone. "You *know* it wasn't your fault."

"Exactly. His rejection of me? It had *nothing* to do with me.

Fuck-all. He didn't know me. Didn't *want* to know me. He just wanted out of my life. And that was a *him* problem, not a *me* problem." She tilts her head onto my shoulder, kisses my cheek, makes sure I'm listening. "So, like, don't go through life thinking you're the problem. The girls—the *people*—who can't look past your body? *They're* the problem. Not your chest. Or your clam."

"I will pay you real human money if you never say 'clam' again."

She laughs, leans away, blows me a raspberry. "You'll find someone, Finch."

"Are you sure?"

"Positive. Now, go to sleep."

And somehow, in spite of everything, I do.

I manage to show up at school the next morning even though all I want to do is curl up in Lucy's bed and sleep the day away beneath her mountain of stuffed animals. I sleepwalk through my first few classes. By lunch, I'm beyond bleary-eyed, nodding into my locker while I search the clutter for the student ID I'll need to breach the cafeteria. I'm so sleepy that it takes me a second to register the hand on my shoulder. I turn around, look up: It's Jonah, giving me a big, easy smile.

Behind him, a few feet away, Bailey doesn't look up from his phone. He seems very absorbed. I don't know what he's looking at, but whatever it is, it must be fascinating.

"Did you get my message last night?" Jonah says brightly.

"There was this article in the *Atlantic* about a school that had a big blow-up over a trans kid wanting to use the bathroom. They were talking about like, single-stall bathrooms, and I thought maybe we could . . . Finch? You with me?"

"Totally." I've absorbed maybe half the words he's said. "Sorry, I didn't see the . . ." I break, yawning wide. ". . . the article. Didn't check my e-mail last night."

"Whoa. That's a first."

"Yeah." I let out a limp laugh. "Kind of an intense night."

"Aww, I'm sorry, Finch," Bailey says, a sympathetic glimmer in his eye. "I have to steal Jonah now, but if you guys wanted to catch up later . . ."

"Actually, Bee?" Jonah turns to Bailey. "Could you give us a minute?"

"Sure." Bailey's smile seems oddly tight, tense. "No problem."

He rolls his eyes as Jonah turns back to me. Jonah doesn't see it, but I do. It's a rude, luxurious circle, arcing up to the ceiling and ending where it began: the screen of his phone, emitting a low, sugary bloop. *Candy Crush*. Unmistakable.

"You said you had an intense night?" Jonah lowers his voice, just a little: I can hear him, but Bailey can't. "Intense like how? Good intense, or bad intense?" He sounds truly concerned. "Please don't say bad intense."

"Intense like, um . . ." My throat pinches every word on the way out. "My mom, she . . . she lost . . . lost her job."

"Oh my God." Jonah's hand; my shoulder. "Finch, I'm so, so sorry."

The look on Jonah's face is genuinely devastated—like he's

the one who got the bad news, not me. It sears me, seeing it. I can't meet his eyes, so I lower my own to the floor. Even his sneakers are the color of a bruise.

"I mean, we've known it was coming for a while." I want to say something to soften the blow, to wipe that sad look from his face. "It's not really a surprise."

His arm around my shoulder now, he's steering us down the hallway. There's an alcove here, a bench welded to the wall. It's quieter. We perch.

"Are you okay?" he asks. "Can you tell me more about what happened?"

I'm about to give him an answer—a long one full of sound and fury about the venture capitalists who picked the bones of our local paper—when Bailey, suddenly, appears in front of us and lifts his phone. A clock goes *tick-tick* on the screen.

"Hey, sorry," he says, "but lunch is over in half an hour, and we're going to get stuck in the lineup at the boba place if we don't—"

"*Babe.*" A flicker of real anger rolls through the word. It's something I almost never hear in Jonah's voice—definitely not when he's talking to Bailey. "Finch's mom just lost her job."

"Oh, Finch, *honey.*" There's that sympathetic look in Bailey's eyes again; this time, I trust it less. "That *sucks.*"

"Yeah," is all I can manage to mumble. "It really does."

Talking is hard when I feel like this: funny, foggy, like I'm floating out of my body. It's only when Jonah presses into me, his arm like an anchor, that the world filters once more into sharp focus.

"Do you want to grab a bite with me and Jonah?" Bailey asks. "I mean, unless you're not feeling up to it."

"Bailey. Come on. This is kind of a crisis." Jonah cuts in stern, like he's addressing an unruly Renata or Benjie. "You and I can just get coffee after school instead."

"But we're meeting at the Green Bean after school," I pipe in. I don't want to be a pain; I also don't want him to forget. "We have to prep with Adwoa."

"Right." Jonah purses his lips, blows out. "Okay! We can have a lunch date tomorrow, then, Bee. Does that work?"

"KIRO-7 is interviewing me tomorrow at lunch. Remember?" Bailey lifts a hand, crosses his fingers. "Hoping to drum up some press before my callback at Juilliard." He sings this last word, really draws it out: *Juuuuilliaaaard*.

"Well, we'll just . . ." Jonah thinks for a second, then gives up, sighing. "We can go out some other time."

Bailey throws an arm over his forehead, going for a Southern belle–ish swoon. "I'll just grab lunch by my lonesome, then."

Before Jonah can say anything more, Bailey's spinning on his heel, striding down the long, blurry stream of the busy hallway. I look at Jonah. He's wincing with his whole entire body.

"Are you sure *you're* the one who should be comforting *me* right now?" I ask him. He tries to give me a reassuring smile and misses the mark so badly that I burst out laughing. "Seriously, Jonah, he's being kind of a jerk today. Is everything okay with you guys?"

Jonah squeezes me around the shoulders again. "Finch,

trust me: That had nothing to do with you," he says, even though that wasn't what I'd asked. "Bailey's just stressed out. His Juilliard callback is this weekend. The musical opens next week. We're still sorting out the whole long-distance thing. He's on edge, and it's seriously not your fault. Like, if anything, it's *my* fault."

I lower my voice, lean in. "You *still* haven't told him about UDub?"

"I'm going to," he says, wincing only slightly this time. "When he's in a good headspace, and he's ready to hear the news, I will." Jonah's arm falls from my shoulder. And, wouldn't you know: I miss it! It's that same thing I felt last night, curled up between Lucy and her stuffed animals. I want it back. "Don't worry about me, Finch. You've got enough to worry about these days."

I look up at him, at the look on his face, hopeful and sad all at once.

And I can't help it: I worry about him.

We really should've known better than to book a sit-down at the Green Bean right after school. Shoulder to shoulder with Jonah and Adwoa, I scan the crowded dining room, a wide sea of squalling babies and squalid co-eds, for a free table somewhere, anywhere.

Adwoa's the first to lift her hand: A cluster of silver-haired men are rising—very, very slowly—from a rare four-top. She bounces on her toes briefly before charging forward.

"Finch! Help me colonize that table." She tosses a crisp petty-cash twenty to Jonah: "Cabrera. Drinks?"

"On it." Jonah veers for the counter. "Your poison?"

"Black," says Adwoa. "Zero cream, zero sugar."

We branch a little through the crowd. Jonah calls out, "Finch?"

"A hot lemonade? With some honey, maybe?" Something flickers across Jonah's face, a startled kind of squint. Does he think I'm being finicky? "Sorry!" I call out. "I know it's weird, but I don't want to lose my voice, and . . ."

"No, no. Not weird at all." Jonah pulls away from us, telegraphing two thumbs-ups. "One black coffee and one hot lemonade, coming right up."

Then we really fork—Jonah angling all the way to the counter, me and Adwoa booking it to the four-top to drape parkas, scarves, bags over the seat-backs. Adwoa drops her purse into her chair, and I laugh.

"Your bag needs its own seat?"

"Uh, yeah," she says. "It's a Telfar. Alexandria Ocasio-Cortez has one."

"Oh. I don't know much about fashion, but I do know that I'd die for her."

Adwoa laughs, sweeping her braids up into a low ponytail. "Hey, have a seat, would you? I wanted to see if you're okay with this trans resolution. Since it's personal for you, and all."

"But isn't every resolution personal?" I take a cautious seat; I don't love being singled out like this. "You're always saying the personal is political."

"Well, sure. But there's a difference between, like, 'this affects all of us' and 'this one affects *me*,' you know? Like, we all worry about gun control, right? We *don't* all worry what bathroom to use."

"They make Muslim girls debate about hijabs," I tell her. "They make Catholic kids debate about abortion."

"You've got a point," she says, thoughtfully. "God knows I debate police abolition all day every day with any white guy on campus who opens his mouth about this 'Blue Lives Matter' garbage."

"I honestly don't know how you do it." I can hear awe sneaking into my own voice. "I never have the energy to engage with people like that."

"Well, I have to 'engage' whether I like it or not," Adwoa says, sighing. "It could be me one of these days, you know? Like . . . God, I don't want to get too heavy, but Sandra Bland? She looked *just* like me."

A wave of sudden, total guilt swirls through me. I've seen a lot of headlines about murdered trans people; I've never seen a victim who looked like me. They seem more like Adwoa, if anything: almost always girls, almost always black. Sometimes, they're sex workers. Their lives are so much more dangerous than mine. So why am I quailing about this debate? What do *I* have to lose, anyway? If I've got all this privilege, shouldn't I be body-checking terves every second of every day?

I square my jaw. "I'm okay with this resolution, Adwoa," I say. "I *have* to be."

". . . Okay," she says, skeptically. "That's . . . good to hear. Let's just make sure you're taking care of your . . ."

Before she can finish her sentence, Jonah's back, heavy tray in hand. "For the lady: tall, dark, and handsome." He hands her a pristine ceramic mug—no paper or plastic at the Green Bean, ever—full of black coffee. "And for the gentleman: hot lemonade with honey and just a touch of ginger."

I take the mug from him. *Ginger*, I think, *that's new*. I take a cautious sip; the flavors bloom on my tongue. It's *so* good. I surprise myself by sighing out loud.

"Did I get it right?" he says, sounding worried.

Was it the sigh? Did he mistake it for, I don't know, dismay?

I set the mug down. "No, no," I hurry to tell him. "It's perfect. Thank you."

"Another satisfied customer," he says, his shoulders falling in relief. He shifts Adwoa's coat and slides into the chair next to her, kitty-corner to me. Then he reaches for the tray again. His drink of choice is an iced coffee housed in a glass the size of a car battery. At least, I *assume* it's coffee. It's . . . pink? Can coffee even *be* pink?

Adwoa says exactly what I'm thinking. "What *is* that? A strawberry milkshake?"

"This is an iced raspberry white chocolate mocha with soy milk." Jonah, saving the turtles, takes a long slurp from the metal straw he brings everywhere. "With rose petals on top."

"I see." Adwoa pauses. "May I say something low-key homophobic?"

Jonah laughs. "You may *not*." Defiant, he stirs the rose

petals into his admittedly very pretty drink. "Anyway, tell me: What did I miss while I was getting drinks?"

My eyes meet Adwoa's. She nods—*go ahead*—so I do.

"We were, um, talking about the resolution," I tell him. "Whether I'm comfortable with it."

"Oh!" Jonah snaps his fingers. "Same talk you and I had at my place, right?" I nod at him; he nods back. "And you're still cool with it? You don't want to skip this one?"

. . . *Skip this one?* "No!" I yelp. "No way. This is the national championship we're talking about."

"I know. I know. I'm just saying: I wouldn't blame you if you didn't want to debate about something so close to home." He sighs, shrugs: "I mean, I skipped the musical this year, pretty much for the same reason, so . . ."

"Wait." I blink at Jonah, confused. What "reason" is he talking about, exactly? "I thought you just wanted to focus on Nationals."

"It's honestly no big deal," says Jonah, with an odd heaviness that tells me, yes, this is an absolutely tremendous deal. "There's a big role in the musical for a Chinese man. And since I'm the most experienced Asian guy in the club, that's probably where they would've put me. Bailey really wanted me to do it."

"So what's the problem?" says Adwoa. "I mean, I'm glad debate's got your undivided attention right now. But this musical sounds made for you."

"Yeah, but it's like . . ." Jonah sighs heavily, slumping chin-to-palm. "This show isn't the *most* woke?"

His shoulders are all tense, hunched up around his ears, the way they get when we're about to walk into a big round on ten minutes of prep time. Wow. He *really* doesn't want to talk about this. I'll just change the subject. Easy.

"Shouldn't we start prepping?" I say, setting down my lemonade.

"Nuh-uh," hums Adwoa. She leans closer to Jonah. She's *very* interested. "What's wrong with the musical, Jonah? Spill the tea."

"Fine." Jonah forces out a breath. "So, basically, the main character moves into a hotel run by this Chinese lady." He pauses; another frustrated huff. "But she's actually a white lady in disguise, so . . ."

"So, yellowface," Adwoa says, flatly. "Okay. We're talking yellowface."

Jonah looks down, sighs, addresses the tabletop in a low mumble: "She does an accent, and she squints, and she wears this, like, white pancake makeup." He lifts his head, sighs again, and says, "But, I mean, she's the villain, so it's not, like, condoning . . ."

"Oh, no." Adwoa's eyes are almost popping out of her head. I don't have a mirror handy, but I bet I look just as shocked. "I think it's condoning *plenty*."

Jonah doesn't answer. His eyes, again, are on the tabletop. I reach out, lay a hand on his arm.

"I can see why you wouldn't want to be part of something so . . . so . . ." I look for the right words; I don't find them. ". . . Something like *that*."

"There's more." Jonah takes his longest, weariest breath yet. "There are these Chinese henchmen—like, actual Chinese guys, not white people in disguise. And they kidnap girls from the hotel. White girls. And uh . . ." He pauses, cringing. "They sell the girls. Into, uh . . . sex work. In Hong Kong."

There's a long, stunned silence. Adwoa's mouth actually falls open, just a little. When I finally manage to open my own mouth, all I can say is ". . . *Wow*."

"Yeah," says Jonah, glumly—and this, I guess, is the thing that sends Adwoa careening once again into lawyer mode, because she brings her flat palm down on the table and says, "I'm sorry. I'm sorry. *Kids* are doing this? For a school play?"

"Yeah. All over the country. It was a smash on Broadway back in 2002. Won a bunch of Tonys. So there must be *something* appealing about it. I don't know. Some of the songs are all right."

I've never seen shame on his face before, and seeing it now—the soft, low arc of his bottom lip, the gleam in his eyes gone dull—it's enough to make my stomach ache. How much does it hurt, I wonder, to defend something that hurts *you*?

"Have you talked to Bailey?" I ask him, quietly. "Does he know you've got issues with the musical?"

Jonah's quiet for a long moment, stirring his drink. Fat pink petals sink through the pale cream at the top.

"The show is a *really* big deal for Bailey," Jonah says. "I mean, playing this iconic role? As a boy? Making it into a gay love story? I wouldn't want to get in the way of that." There's some real optimism sneaking into his voice now. "I'm probably just overreacting. I mean, I've definitely done stuff that would make Bailey mad, so . . ."

What is he talking about? What could Jonah possibly have done that would . . . Oh. *Oh.* College. Jonah still hasn't told his boyfriend about UDub. Bailey still fully believes Jonah's following him to Manhattan in the fall. Is *that* why Jonah's keeping quiet about the musical? Is he just steeling himself for another, bigger fight?

I can't ask Jonah about any of this. Not just now. Adwoa's already got him on the stand. "*Overreacting?*" she's saying. "You're 'probably just overreacting'?"

"Well, maybe," Jonah says. "I don't know."

"You are *not* overreacting," she insists—one hand a tight fist. "Look at me. Listen. Everyone else with a hand in this racist circus is *under*-reacting." She loosens that fist, loops a finger around the fury on her face. "*This* is the appropriate reaction."

"I'm not *condoning* it, Adwoa," Jonah answers. "I just don't want to wreck this thing that Bailey's, like, living for."

"Okay. Listen." Adwoa lays a hand on the table, right in front of Jonah. She's quieter now, her voice more level. "As someone who also dates white boys from time to time?" She presses her hand to her heart, levels a dead-serious gaze at Jonah: "I have let *plenty* slide over the years. And I can't tell you how bad I wish I could go back to every time I was like, 'Just be cool, don't rock the boat, it's no big deal.' If I could do it all over, I would've said no to so much racist nonsense." She sighs, drops her hand to the table. "I just want better for you, Jonah. It's what you deserve."

"I'm not saying the musical *isn't* racist. Like, it is. It really, really is. But I don't think Bailey's a monster, either. And I don't think this is a big enough deal for me to, like, pick a huge fight over." He stops here—probably sees Adwoa reeling up for a rebuttal—and begins to plead: "Sorry. Can we just move on?" He turns, appeals to me: "Finch? We should probably start prepping, yeah?"

Should we move on? *Can* we move on? I feel betrayed, and Bailey's not even my boyfriend.

"I'm sorry," I tell Jonah. "I'm really, *really* sorry you have to deal with this."

"It's all good," he lies brightly, and opens his laptop. "Anyway! Less than three weeks 'til Nationals!"

I want to say more—so, I can tell, does Adwoa—but Jonah is moving on. What can we do but follow him?

chapter six

The next day is a rare one: After school, I'm free. No debate club meetings. No Green Bean prep sessions. My only job is to ferry Roo home on the bus—and make sure she at least attempts to start her homework before descending into a video game fugue state.

I find her in the library—earbuds in, laptop open, screen a maelstrom of war and ruin. She doesn't turn around. She doesn't say hello. In the world of her screen, everything is copacetic. There are fights, sure, but they're fights Roo can win. She's retreating into a landscape she can control.

"Hey, Roo." I pull up a chair, speak to her gently: "You're playing, right? How's it going?"

"Bad," she says, scowling.

"Oh, no. What's going on?" I lean closer, peering at the screen. Mom and Dad give her a lot of shit for gaming; I try to show a little interest, every now and then. "Is some despot giving you a hard time?"

"So *Gandhi*"—she spits his name like she's swearing— "finished the Manhattan Project before I did, and now I'm paying off the city-states to score a diplomatic victory. But he is *not* having it. One of my spies slipped me the intel that he's plotting to bomb my capital." She stops, double-clicks on a patch of tundra. "So I'm gonna stockpile giant death robots next to the Kremlin I built in Sparta and hope for the best."

I blink. It's a lot to process. The Kremlin stockpiling giant death robots? Sure. I'll buy that. But in Ancient Greece? And to fend off a nuclear strike from *Gandhi?*

"Isn't he a pretty peaceful guy, Gandhi? Would he really go for nukes, you think?"

She snorts. "You don't know *shit* about Gandhi."

"Evidently." I nod. "Care to teach me?"

"He's a menace," Roo glowers. "Him and his little round glasses and the—oh, no!" Her voice leaps up an octave: "No, no, *no!*"

My eyes dart to the screen just in time to see it: a mushroom cloud billowing over the emerald isles of Roo's queendom.

"Dammit!" Roo shouts. "I thought I had two more turns to . . ." Another bomb falls, dousing Athens in smoke. "*Fuck!*"

"That's it, Ruby Kelly! Three strikes!"

I whirl around: Mrs. Rubin, the librarian, is marching at us. Roo yanks her earbuds out of her ears.

"I'm so sorry," she pleads. "Gandhi just dropped a nuke on my capital, and—"

"I don't give two shakes of a little lamb's tail what Gandhi is up to," she says—and it's shocking, really, how menacing *little lamb* sounds coming out of her mouth. "You will not use *that* language in *my* library."

Roo doesn't even bother to save her game. She snaps her

laptop shut, shoves it into her bag, and flings it over her shoulder. Mrs. Rubin is at our backs all the while, bellowing about *that* language in *her* library. We escape to the foyer with our lives, but only just.

"So, are you coming home tonight?" Roo says as we cut through the after-school crowd. "Or do you live with Lucy now?" She sounds snide, and sad, and hurt—hurt by *me,* I realize, and rush to catch up with her.

"Wait. Are you mad at me, Roo? Because I went over to Lucy's the other night?"

"Could've used some time in the blanket fort after Mom's shocker." We reach the door and she kicks it open. "That's all I'm saying."

"I'm sorry, Roo. I just wanted to be with my best friend." We spill onto the stairs of the school. The cool air smells like rain; I am, once more, umbrella-less. "I felt really overwhelmed after Mom told us, and—"

"Join the club." Her messenger bag swings as she descends the stairs, smacking some poor kid in the back of the head. "I had to lie awake all night, by myself, dealing with this bomb Mom just dropped."

"I don't know how much help I would've been," I tell her honestly. "I'm dealing with a lot right now."

"Right, like your college apps." Roo is still a few steps ahead, striding up the sidewalk. "And how you'd rather glug toilet water than stay in Olympia 'cause you don't give a *shit* about me."

"Roo, *what?*" The bitterness, the hard-bitten swearing—

where is this coming from? I catch up to her, finally, and take her gently by the shoulders, spinning her 'til she's facing me. "What are you talking about? Why do you think I don't care?"

She shakes her shoulders to rid herself of my hands. Other kids cry when they get emotional; not Roo. She is *seething*. I can hear her grinding her teeth in her closed mouth, one row scraping against the other.

"You're *always* dealing with a lot," she spits. "You only ever think about yourself."

People are staring. I'd rather they didn't. "Hey, come on," I say, in a voice as gentle as I can make it. "Let's find a quieter spot."

She hesitates, but she does follow me—off the sidewalk, through a narrow line of withered brown trees, and into a poured-concrete courtyard. There is a bench here, made of a stiff ridged metal and bolted to the ground. We sit down. Roo brings her knees up to her chest. She stares ahead in profile, her black hair fluttering freely in the wind.

"I love you, Roo," I say to one acne-pebbled cheek.

"But like. Next year. When you're away at college . . ." She sighs; her hands retreat into the sleeves of her hoodie until only her fingertips poke out, like turtles' heads. "I mean, I'm gonna miss you. But I don't know if you're gonna miss me the same way."

The words land like a fist to the gut.

"Roo, no," I manage, finally. "Of course I'm going to miss you. Next year, when I'm in my dorm, and I can't sleep, and you're not around to help me build a blanket fort . . . I mean, what am I going to do?"

She lifts her sleeves to her face. She's quiet for a long time. When her hands finally fall into her lap, I can see tiny patches on her sleeves, darker than the rest of the fabric—places where she caught the tears before they could fall. How did I miss this? How long has she felt this way? Like I've got one foot out the door, like I can't wait to get rid of her.

"But you'll have a whole new city," she says, and sniffs, "and friends, and school, and I'll just have . . ." She sweeps her arms across the damp concrete nothing that surrounds us. "This. Minus you."

"You *will* still have me," I tell her, emphatic as I can. "You can pick up the phone any time, any hour of the day—or the night—and I'll be there."

"Exactly," she says. "You'll be *there*."

She sits with her knees to her chest, silent, like she's waiting for me to prove her wrong. I don't know what to tell her, don't know how to make this hurt less. There are so many things pushing me out of this town, pulling me toward D.C. She isn't one of them. She makes me wish I wanted to stay.

"I'm here now, though," I tell her. "And I love you. And I'm not going anywhere. Not yet."

She's not all the way satisfied with this answer—opening her mouth, then hesitating. She plays with her damp sleeves, one thumb rolling over the other in her lap.

"Could we do something together?" she says, after a brief quiet. "Like, right now. Go somewhere?"

"Yes." I can't say it fast enough. "Absolutely. Anything you want. GameStop?"

"That's not a bad idea," she says, and lifts her head, giving me a hard-won smile. "But I was actually thinking more like . . . ice cream?"

My turn to smile. "You got it."

It's after our trip to Baskin-Robbins, kicking off our rain boots in the mudroom, that I notice something odd: Our house smells utterly unlike our house. It smells . . . dare I say . . . *good?* That mysterious wet-dog odor is gone. In its place, there's a kind of Olive Garden bouquet, all rosemary and garlic and olive oil. A tiny bead of drool slides from my open mouth and lands, a wet dot, on my chest—that's how hungry I am, even post ice cream.

"Gross!" Roo giggles, just as Mom steps into the entryway, her apron flecked with red sauce and redder wine.

"Welcome home, kiddos," she says—and then, more stern: "Roo? Is that chocolate ice cream I see on your cheek?"

"It is," says Roo, then licks the back of her hand, and rubs at the sticky residue with it, the same way a cat uses a paw. "Sorry."

Mom lifts a hand, brushes some rain-damp hair out of my eyes. "You guys went out for some sugar therapy, huh?"

"I hope that's okay." I'm a bit suspicious. When was the last time I came home to dinner on the stove? Hell, when have I ever come home to anything but a fight? "It's just been . . . you know, a rough week."

"Sure has been." Mom sighs, weary. "We've got a lot to talk about. Come on in. Dinner's almost ready."

Her hand on my back, she steers me into the kitchen, where Dad is rolling up meatballs and dropping them, one by one, into a sizzling pan on the stove.

"There's my man!" Dad gives me half a hug, his hands covered in raw pink beef. "How you doing, champ?"

I don't know what to tell him. I don't understand what I'm seeing. We are not, ever, a spaghetti-and-meatballs family. We are a Wonder Bread family. A Campbell's Ready-to-Serve family. Even, occasionally, a cereal-for-dinner family. Did someone get some good news today? Did Dad get a job? Did Mom, by some miracle, get hers back?

But when we sit down at the table, hold hands, say grace—blue-moon events, all three—I know that there's no good news coming. Mom prays for guidance as she "embarks" on a "new chapter" in her life. Dad prays, more directly, for a job interview. And then he doles out the pasta, and Mom doles out the sauce, and I'm dispatched to the kitchen to retrieve garlic bread from the oven and dole that out, too. We pass around pepper, salt, paprika. Nobody speaks 'til the plates are half-empty—or, well, half-full, but I've never been much of an optimist.

"So." Mom lifts her head, clears her throat. "Yesterday was my last day at the *Mountain*. The last day of the paper, too."

Dad cuts in: "And we've got a lot to talk about as a family."

Mom takes a deep breath. She doesn't snap at Dad for the interruption. Not yet, anyway. "The good news," she says, "is that we all have 'til the end of the month on my health insurance."

"Wait." The fork falls out of my hand, hits the plate, hard; *kertwang*. "The end of the month? But . . . this summer . . . my surgery . . ."

"I know, Finch." Mom reaches out, squeezes my hand. "It's going to be a hard few months. Maybe longer. We're all going to have to sacrifice some."

Everything I've just eaten threatens to come back up. "But I *need* surgery. It's not something I can . . . can just . . . *sacrifice*."

"Kid, listen." Dad sets down his own fork. "This operation you want? We're talking thousands of dollars. You know we don't have it like that."

"But it's not . . . I'm not asking for . . ." I stammer, struggling for the right words: "I *need* this. Or else I'll go to college this fall and . . . and I . . . I still won't be able to go out when it's hot, or . . . or run, or go swimming, or . . ."

Mom's hand in my own, heavy, presses harder. "I know, honey," she says. "And I'm so sorry. But there's nothing we can do. You're just gonna have to stick it out a little longer."

"Yeah, and like," Roo says, mouth full, "you don't really do much running or swimming anyway."

"Because I *can't*!" I bring a fist to my chest, my heart, feel the sleek constricting fabric under my shirt. "With this thing on? I'd be risking my life!"

"'Risking my life.' Jesus." Dad snorts. He wipes his mouth, tosses the napkin down, stains blooming all over it. And then he turns to me, points a finger: "Listen. You? You're not in danger. This house is in danger. Our mortgage. Your tuition. *That's* in danger."

My body *is* my house, I want to tell him. It's where I live. I haven't felt safe in it for a long, long time. And I'd give up anything—give up Georgetown, even—to finally, finally have a home of my own.

"No one's saying you can't have the surgery," says Mom, playing good cop. "Only that you'll have to wait."

"But . . ."

"No *fucking* but." Dad brings his hand down, flat, on the tabletop; the whole room shakes. "It's not happening. Nothing we can do. You're just gonna have to live with this. Can you do that?"

Well? Can I? I've made it seventeen years in this body. What's one or two more? I don't want to go on like this, but I *have* to go on like this. What other choice do I have? Working part-time jobs between my classes next year? Just working next year, period? Setting college completely aside?

My breath is growing short. My pulse racing. My head swimming.

"Can you do that?" Dad repeats.

I nod. There are some arguments even I can't win.

chapter seven

I'm curled fetal on my bed, knees to the chest I hate, when Jonah's ringtone peals through the room. It bears mentioning that he chose it himself: "Squidward Nose," by the rapper Cupcakke, her special euphemism for a certain piece of genitalia. It is extremely funny, highly inappropriate, and *deeply* jarring in my present catatonia. I startle so hard that my knee collides with my nose. The first thing I say to him when I pick up the phone is "*Ow.*"

"Are you okay?" He hesitates. "Should I call you back?"

"No, no, no." I might be bleeding, but Jonah doesn't need to know that. "Just bonked my nose. I can talk."

". . . All right," says Jonah—not believing me, clearly, but not wanting to pry. "I just wanted to check in, you know? After that talk we had the other day? About your mom?" He sounds tentative. "How are you holding up?"

"Honestly?" I wince at the new pain when I inhale. *Am I* bleeding? "I am holding up very, very badly."

"What happened?" He pauses. "I mean, besides everything with your mom and the paper?"

"Let me see. Where do I start?" My nose still hurts, but

when I lift my fingers, swipe experimentally, there's no blood. "Well, we might lose the house, and we *will* lose our health insurance, which means I'm not getting surgery this summer, unless you've got a spare ten or twenty thousand dollars lying around."

"Wait. Surgery?" Jonah sounds confused—and a little fearful. "I didn't know you were having surgery."

"Oh, don't worry—it's nothing life-threatening." I don't know if this is, actually, strictly true. "It's . . . what's the word? Elective. An elective surgery."

"Oh," Jonah says, confused—and then the transgender penny drops: "*Oh*."

"Yeah. That kind of surgery."

"Why didn't you tell me? I could help you set up a fundraiser online. My dad could put a link in the church newsletter. It goes out to, like, a thousand people a week."

I know I should feel grateful for Jonah's help, but I only feel ashamed. He's really offering to fundraise, for *me*, among his father's congregants, at a church I don't even belong to. These are people with their own rent to pay, their own families to feed, their own prohibitively expensive medical bills to weep over.

"Jonah. Please." My throat feels tight. "You don't have to do that."

"Sorry," he says, sounding stung. Was I too forceful, just now, turning him down? Did I hurt his feelings? "I just . . . want you to have this surgery. If you need it. Which it sounds like you do."

The silence feels heavy—with my embarrassment, with his. I'm grateful that he, clearing his throat, breaks it first.

"So, uh, Nasir texted me. He was wondering if you wanted to drive up to Seattle this Saturday. Run a practice round."

My first answer is a knee-jerk: no. "Absolutely not. Treat our sworn enemies to a taste of our cases right before Nationals? No. Never."

He laughs. "They're not going to steal all our points, Finch. They're better debaters than that. Besides, when are we going to have another chance to practice with a team of their caliber?"

Jonah's got a point. We'll run a few rounds in debate club, of course. But even Jasmyne, our heiress apparent, can't sharpen my steel the way Ari would.

"Just the one round?" I hedge. "This Saturday?"

"Just the one," he repeats. "Are you in?"

"I'm . . . *tentatively* in."

"Awesome," he says, and I can feel a smile, some relief, moving into his voice. "I have to drive Bailey up to SeaTac on Saturday morning—to his Juilliard callback. I figured we could drop him off, then drive to Annable."

I sit up straight. I did *not* consent to spend my morning in a compact vehicle with Jonah and Bailey and all their simmering tension.

"What about his parents?" I'm desperate. Is it too late for me to get out of this? Or, at least, get Bailey out of this? "They can't drop him off?"

"Nah. They work weekends at Amazon. Brutal hours, apparently."

"I bet." I feel an immediate flood of sympathy for Bailey—and, God, for his parents. Visions of windowless warehouses, churning assembly lines, and Jeff Bezos's bald pate dance in my head.

"Besides, Bailey really wanted me to see him off. Gotta give him a kiss for good luck before he gets on that plane, you know?"

"So you guys are doing better?" I ask, dubious. "You talked about the musical?"

"Oh, no. There's no point, really." He laughs; there's a false note in it. If he were here next to me, he'd give me an equally false shrug, I bet. "I'm over the whole thing. Honestly."

I'm deeply unconvinced. ". . . Okay, Jonah."

"Seriously, Finch, he and I are totally fine." He laughs again. "It's amazing what a good make-out session will do."

I wince. "Maybe I should find my own ride to Annable, then." One last attempt to get out of this third-wheel arrangement. "Wouldn't want to take up the backseat if you need it for more important things."

"And *what* are you implying, Finch Kelly?"

"Nothing! Nothing at all!"

Jonah snorts. "Pick you up at seven?"

"I'll set my alarm," I say.

I hang up. I chew on a hangnail. It'll be fine, won't it? This ride up to Seattle? Jonah and Bailey haven't exactly been on the best terms lately, but if Jonah says they kissed and made up, I guess I have to take him at his word. They haven't had the fight about the musical. Or the fight about college. Not yet. And, God willing, they won't have those fights on Saturday. Not with me in the car.

I think.

I hope.

When Jonah told me Bailey would be flying to New York this weekend, I assumed one suitcase. A suitcase and a carry-on, tops. I was absolutely not anticipating every seat in the back of Jonah's car, middle sliver included, to be filled with luggage, each piece carefully buckled in. Safety first, I guess.

I tap on Bailey's passenger-side window. His hands are occupied with his phone, so his elbow goes to work, pressing on the side-dash button to bring the glass down.

"Hey." He doesn't look up from his screen. "What's up?"

"Should I balance one of the suitcases in my lap?" I ask. "Or, uh . . ." I don't actually know what the "or, uh" would be, here: riding on the roof like Mitt Romney's poor old diarrheic Irish setter?

Jonah looks over his shoulder, apparently for the first time. "Bailey! Where's Finch supposed to sit?"

Bailey, finally, lifts his eyes from his phone, and follows Jonah's gaze into the backseat. "Oh!" He sounds like he, too, is seeing this mountain of luggage for the first time—even though he's the one who put it there. "Oops! I totally forgot you'd be riding along."

Jonah laughs, opens his door, steps out. "I'll clear a seat for you, Finch."

"I am *so* sorry," Bailey says, more to Jonah than me. "My brain is soup this morning."

His brain's sharp enough to call out careful instructions when we start to move his luggage, though. "Be careful with that duffel! Don't let it drag on the ground. If the mud soaks through and stains the Xylophone, that's, like, a forty-dollar dry-cleaning job."

I'm about ready to drag Bailey out of the car for some decidedly non-stage combat. But Jonah, ever the diplomat, manages a lighthearted joke: "Of course, babe. You know how much I value your sequins."

Duffel unmuddied, we finally make it to the trunk. Shocker: It's completely empty back there. Nothing but a light sprinkling of pine needles from Jonah's last camping trip. Or fir needles, maybe. I can't say for sure. Jonah's the outdoorsman, not me.

We look at each other, our eyes asking the same question: Why didn't Bailey just put his things in the trunk? Did each piece of luggage really need its own seat belt? We're dangerously close to bursting into laughter, so Jonah presses a finger to his mouth—*shh*—and motions for me to slide the duffel into the empty space.

And then it's done. We're off. We have ninety minutes ahead of us, and fifty miles of tree-lined highway. I've got a new *Economist* to keep me busy; Jonah's got the radio. Bailey, bleary-eyed, tilts his head against the passenger-side window and sighs out loud.

"Can you believe that the first callback is at eight tomorrow? That's *five o'clock* our time. I'm going to be jet-lagged as fuck." Another sigh; another white moon of breath on the window. "And the air on the planes is always *so* dry. God, my poor vocal cords. I'm so glad I remembered to pack a steamer."

"What's a steamer?" All I can think of are ocean liners, the *Titanic*-y ones. That can't be what he's talking about.

"It's a humidifier for your vocal cords." Bailey lifts a hand, taps on his throat. "Soothes all the muscles so you don't lose your voice."

"Wow, sounds handy," says Jonah. "Mind if we borrow it for our next tournament?"

"Why?" Bailey laughs. "You do a lot of singing at debate tournaments?"

"Well, no. But we do a lot of talking, and, uh . . ." His turn to tap on his throat. "Same muscles."

"Oh, duh." Bailey claps the heel of his hand against his forehead. "Ignore me! Like, I said: Brain equals soup. I'm an idiot."

"You're not an idiot," Jonah says fondly. "You're just under-caffeinated."

So far, this ride is not at all the parade of awkwardness I worried it would be. Jonah starts a sentence; Bailey completes it. They trade jokes, private ones, you-had-to-be-theres that fly way over my head. We stop at an intersection, and Bailey's hand reaches across the divide to squeeze Jonah's. The bitchy boyfriend I'd glimpsed in recent days is gone. This is Bailey the devoted partner, the guy who looks at Jonah like he hung the moon. I feel a bit like a little kid, pressed into the backseat, but I don't even mind it. The feeling is safe, cozy.

So cozy, in fact, that I'm nearly asleep, my head tilting on the pillow of Bailey's backpack, when I hear Jonah's voice spike: "No! Really? This close to the opening?"

"Right? Eddie Wong just up and quit the show! Zero warning! And now this freshman has to step in and learn Ching Ho's entire track in a week."

"In a *week?*" Jonah lets out a low whistle. "Wow. I hope he pulls it off. Damn."

"Now, see, if you'd auditioned, none of this would've happened. Ching Ho would've been yours. Sewn up."

"Man, it's really too bad the musical is so close to Nationals this year." Jonah steers us into the curve of a roundabout. "Would've been impossible to do both."

"But you're still coming to see it, right, babe? Opening night?" Bailey doesn't wait for an answer—he turns, instead, and looks at me over his shoulder, like he's just had a brilliant idea. "You should come, too, Finch! Take a load off before your big debate!"

"Oh, no, thanks." I smile, aiming for polite. "From what Jonah's told me about the musical, it sounds a little . . ."

That's as far as I get—*a little, dot dot dot*—because Jonah's eyes flash in the rearview mirror, begging me, without speaking, to stop talking. But it's too late: Bailey has turned his head. He's caught the look on Jonah's face.

"A little *what?*" he cries, clearly wounded. "I thought you loved *Millie!*"

"I do! I do!" Jonah insists. "I sing along whenever you play the soundtrack, don't I?"

"The *cast recording*," Bailey corrects him. "When I play the *cast recording*."

"I just like some of this new-school musical theater more, you know?" It's a weak excuse, but Jonah does his best to sell it. "Like, I'm counting down the days 'til Lin starts letting high schools do *Hamilton*."

"God, yeah, can you imagine? I'd be King George, obviously, and you . . . hmm, who *would* you be, Jojo?" The question floats in the air as Bailey reaches for the glove compartment. "Is the aux-cord in here? We might need to have a sing-off to figure out which role fits you best."

Jonah's diversion has worked. Perfectly. Bailey is rummaging through the dash, yammering about this founding father and that one. The issue of *Millie*, and the show's being *a little* . . . has been wholly forgotten.

Well, forgotten by Bailey, anyway. There's a tense set to Jonah's jaw, an emptiness in the answers he gives Bailey. He's not really listening. I know he doesn't want to confront his boyfriend—but me, I have no such qualms. And I'm starting to get angry. Angry at Bailey, yes, but angry *for* Jonah, too. If Bailey doesn't notice, or doesn't care that he's hurting Jonah . . . well, shouldn't I say something? I could take the blows for Jonah. I could help.

"Hey, Bailey?" I begin bluntly. "Is it true that there's a character in *Millie* who dresses up in yellowface?"

". . . Yellowface?" Bailey sounds baffled, like he's hearing the word for the first time ever. "What, like blackface?"

Jonah cuts in, quick: "We don't have to talk about this right now."

"Actually, Finch, since you asked," Bailey says, sort of waving Jonah down, "there is a character who sort of disguises herself as a Chinese lady, yeah. But she's the villain. Everything she does is evil. Including the disguise. It's not, like, *endorsing* dressing up like a Chinese person." He throws his hands up, casting a helpless look at Jonah. "I mean, Jonah, if I'm saying anything problematic here, please, by all means, call me out, but—"

"Really, Bailey? You need Jonah to tell you what's 'problematic' about a white woman doing yellowface?"

". . . Whoa. What the hell?" That porcelain face of his is turning pink, indignant. "*What* is your problem, Finch? Why are you attacking me like this?" I roll my eyes and open my mouth, but he doesn't wait for my answer. He's already swiveling back to Jonah. "God, what is this, Jonah? Did you go behind my back and complain to Finch?"

"I . . . I mean . . ." Jonah stammers. "You have to admit, Bailey, there's a *lot* of stuff in *Millie* that's, like . . ."

"Are you serious?" Bailey looks shocked, like Jonah just leaped across the divide and smacked him in the face. "You *know* how much this musical means to me!"

"Which is why I didn't say anything!" Jonah's brown eyes are bright, frustrated. "I didn't want you to feel like I was accusing you of—"

"So I'm a racist," Bailey interrupts. He turns away from Jonah, pulling in a shaky breath that paints the passenger-side window white. "*Wow.* I'm racist, and I hate Asian people."

"Nobody's calling you a racist, Bailey," I say, firmly. "All we're saying—"

"Finch." Jonah's voice is hard. The narrow glare he gives me is harder. "Please?"

"Me?" I squeak. "What did *I* do?"

Jonah doesn't answer, too busy pulling into a parking spot. I dig my fingertips into the flesh of my thighs, newly anxious. Up front, Bailey's still sniffling.

"I am *not* a fucking racist," Bailey mewls, his voice thick with phlegm and tears. "And I do *not* hate Asian people. I've been dating *you* for two years, Jonah. Like, hello? You're fucking *gaslighting* me."

The Seattle-Tacoma International Airport looms outside the window, a wall of hard gray concrete pillars leading to the departure gate. Bailey will be leaving now. Thank *God*.

But I've got the feeling this fight isn't over. That glare, that *Finch, please*; Jonah is *not* happy with me. Even though I'm on *his* side.

"Look, Bailey, I'm sorry." Jonah's voice is quiet. He turns the key in the ignition. "I didn't want to upset you right before your big Juilliard callback."

"Too late!" Bailey throws his hands up. "I'm upset!"

"Let me help you with your bags, okay?"

"Fine," Bailey answers curtly. He pushes his door open, steps out, and closes it with a slam that shakes the frame.

Jonah opens the door to the backseat. He removes Bailey's bags. And he gives me nothing—not a word, not even a look—before closing the door. I'm left in the newly frosty air of the empty car, alone. Feeling rattled, I pull my phone from my pocket.

FINCH KELLY: Really bad fight with Bailey just now

LUCY NEWSOME: omg whats he doging??????

LUCY NEWSOME: *doign

LUCY NEWSOME: *doing

FINCH KELLY: Defending the school musical. Google Thoroughly Modern Millie.

A few seconds pass.

LUCY NEWSOME: WHAT

LUCY NEWSOME: the FUCK

FINCH KELLY: Yeah. Bailey threw this huge temper tantrum and said it isn't racist and also he isn't racist because he's dating Jonah

LUCY NEWSOME: holy shit

LUCY NEWSOME: what did jonah say???

I look up, out the window. Bailey and Jonah have made it to the sidewalk. I expect to find them arguing, but they're not. They're holding each other, standing still in a flood of travelers. Bailey speaks a word that I sure hope is *sorry*; Jonah smiles as he says it, and smiles again when Bailey kisses his forehead. He pulls back, but only far enough to tuck a curl the color of cornsilk behind Bailey's ear.

I want to feel disgusted, watching this reconciliation. I know that Bailey has done less than nothing to earn it. Instead, from my place in the backseat, I feel, once more, like a little kid. Like I'm looking into a world I'm years too young for. In this world, their world, you might fight with your partner, but you make up. You forgive one another. You've got your flaws; they've got theirs.

Then again, one of Jonah's flaws may be this: He's way too quick to forgive.

FINCH KELLY: He's in love with Bailey, and I understand that, I do, but he lets Bailey get away with murder

FINCH KELLY: Bailey was being so rude and so racist, you wouldn't believe it

LUCY NEWSOME: wow that sucks

FINCH KELLY: And then when I tried to jump in and defend Jonah, he got mad at ME? And I have no IDEA why

LUCY NEWSOME: i mean like

LUCY NEWSOME: maybe jonah didn't want you to fight his battles for him?

LUCY NEWSOME: like i know you have a boner for jonah but that doesn't mean you can just like. go in there and white knight and try to solve all his problems. ykwim

My breath hitches in my throat. Is Lucy right? Was I white-knighting for Jonah just now? Fighting his battles for him?

These are valid questions, but they're quickly eclipsed by a more pressing one: Why does Lucy keep insisting that I'm in love with Jonah? I'm not! I'm not even gay! I'm definitely not driving a wedge between him and his boyfriend out of love-lorn jealousy.

Even if that boyfriend happens to be kind of a racist jerk.

FINCH KELLY: Okay, let's get this straight: I do not have a "boner" for Jonah

FINCH KELLY: Technically speaking I'm incapable of truly

having a boner for anyone until I get phallo. Or at least meta.

LUCY NEWSOME: lmaooooooooo you KNOW what i mean

LUCY NEWSOME: i don't meant to put you on the spot here it's just honestly like

LUCY NEWSOME: i've noticed this for a while! you're like! weirdly jealous of bailey and jonah's relationship!

LUCY NEWSOME: and now you're jumping into their fights and getting super mad at bailey!

LUCY NEWSOME: i mean maybe for legit reasons but still!

I frown at her last message. I wonder: Does she have a point? And even if she does—even if I *did* stick my nose in a fight that was none of my business—doesn't that pale next to what Bailey did? What he said?

FINCH KELLY: Look. Jonah is my friend. And I think he deserves a lot better than Bailey.

LUCY NEWSOME: oh hell ya i agree w u there

I lift my head. Jonah's walking back to the car. He's got his hands in his pockets, his head down, eyes on the pavement. It's impossible to see his face. Impossible to tell if he's happy, sad, angry. If he's going to ream me out or tell me to just forget the whole ordeal.

Keeping my phone in my lap, I type:

FINCH KELLY: Gotta go. Jonah's back. We are blissfully Bailey free for the rest of the day.

LUCY NEWSOME: good. crossing my fingers he dtmfa

FINCH KELLY: dtmfa?

FINCH KELLY: Was that a typo or does it stand for something?

LUCY NEWSOME: DUMP THE MOTHER FUCKER ALL READY

I smother a laugh and shove my phone into my pocket as Jonah opens the door on the driver's side and sits down. "Hey. You okay?"

He doesn't start the car. His hands are on the wheel: tight grip, white knuckles. "I need a minute," he says, his voice tight.

". . . Sure," I say. A flicker of fear burns through me. He's angry. That much is clear. But is he angry at Bailey . . . or at me? "I'll wait. Take your time."

"And come up here." He points a thumb at the passenger's seat. "I'm not your Uber driver."

My breath's shorter, my posture stiffer than usual, as I step out of the car and take my new seat. I can't quite bring myself to turn my head and look right at him. I click my seat belt into place, sweaty fingers fumbling on the buckle.

"I told you I didn't want to talk about the musical."

"I know, but I couldn't just sit there and let him—"

He lifts a hand: *Quiet, Finch.* "I didn't want to argue about the musical," he repeats. "Two reasons. One: I didn't want to upset him right before his big audition." He turns the key in the ignition, begins to steer us back into the flow of departing cars. "And, two—as you know—he really wants me to go to NYU with him, and I'm . . . I mean, I already said yes to UDub." He sighs. "And I know he's going to be mad when I tell him, so, like, in the meantime . . . I don't want to give him *more* reasons to be mad at me, you know?"

"I wasn't trying to make him mad!" I insist. "But then he started defending yellowface, and I *knew* he was hurting your feelings. I thought if I could show him how racist he was being, then I'd help you."

"Help me? Help me do *what?*"

"I don't know!" I'm wringing my hands, a pathetic nervous tic. "Win the argument!"

"It's not about *winning*, Finch." Frustration flickers in his voice. "Bailey's not Ari or Nasir. He's not some enemy we're trying to obliterate. He's my boyfriend. I have to think about his feelings."

I bring my palms down against my knees, forceful. "But he's not thinking about *your* feelings!"

"And *you* are?" He looks at me, a challenge in his eyes. "Like, I get that you want to help me, Finch, but it's not your life. You don't get to decide what's best for me." He turns away, laughing. "You *literally* don't have any skin in the game."

For the first time since Jonah started talking, I actually hear him. I lean against the window—queasy, suddenly—and think hard about how I'm coming across. How I must have come across during that fight with Bailey.

"I'm sorry," I say, voice quivering, and swallow. I've never been carsick in my life. This would be a *terrible* time to start. "I wasn't trying to talk over you."

"Yeah, but . . . you did," he laughs. "And you didn't help. Like, it's so hard . . . it's *so* hard, Finch, to talk to white people about this." He lifts a hand, flicks his fingers between us. "You included. Right now. *This* is hard. I don't want to be harsh, but . . ."

"No, no." I turn my head, look right at him. "Please. Be harsh. I deserve it."

"You really kind of do, man." He pauses, taking a deep breath. "From now on, just . . . only help if I ask you to help. Got it?"

"Loud and clear," I tell him, and then I tilt back to the window, grateful for the cool glass; my skin is burning with embarrassment. "I'm really sorry, Jonah," I murmur to his reflection. "I swear. It won't happen again."

"I know you are," he says. "And I know it won't." One more deep breath; he holds it for a moment, and then he blows it all out. "All right. We ready to crush Ari and Nasir?"

He offers me his fist. With profound gratitude, I turn to him and bump it.

"Let's do it," I tell him. "Let's crush them."

At about half past nine, we park on the street outside Annable. Well, one of the streets outside Annable, anyway. The campus is a monster, sprawling across ten acres of verdant greenery in a rich-as-piss Seattle suburb. The buildings are all a hundred-plus years old, but there's some architectural magic at work in these old schoolhouses. On the outside, the Schechter Library is all weather-beaten brick and homey mansard shingles; inside, it's as glassy and sleek as an Apple store. Wide-screened computers line one wall. Silver e-readers charge in docks against another. Rows on rows of real books in glass cases look like they've never been touched by human hands.

"You're late," says Ari, with a puff from her Juul. She's seated with Nasir behind a glass desk cut in a funny modern-art shape. "We were supposed to start at nine."

"Sorry, Ari." Jonah drops his backpack at the northern foot of the amorphous glass blob. "We had to drop Bailey off at SeaTac."

"Ooh, who's Bailey?" says Nasir, clad in a Supreme hoodie, a Supreme bucket hat, and—well, no visible logo on those sweatpants, but I'd be willing to bet: Supreme. "She hot?"

"She's my boyfriend," Jonah says. "And, yeah. Smokin'."

"So, what," Ari goes on, blinking through purple vapor, "you *had* to drop him off? He *had* to make you late? He couldn't just take an Uber?"

I squint at her. "All the way from Olympia to SeaTac?"

"God. Sorry." Ari rises, rubbing at her temples. She's wearing her school uniform—I mean, the whole ensemble: the blazer, the necktie—even though it's a Saturday. "I always forget you guys don't live in the city."

"Well, even if we did, we can't afford to hire private drivers whenever we want," I say. And, because I'm trying to get back in Jonah's good graces, I add: "Bailey's folks work weekends packing boxes at Amazon just to—"

"What?" Jonah's surprised. "No, they don't."

I blink at him. "But you told me the other night that his parents work weekends at—"

"I mean, yeah, but his dad's a programmer," Jonah says,

"and his mom's a graphic designer."

"And they have to work on Saturdays?"

"Apparently, yeah. Some big Prime Video overhaul?"

. . . *Why* did I think Bailey was one of us? He doesn't dream of Broadway—not the way I dream of a seat in Congress, not the way Jonah dreams of cleaning up the oceans. He doesn't even have to dream, probably. He just wants, and he receives. Must be nice.

"Well, anyway, you guys are late." Ari pockets her vape and cuts a quick glance at her glossy watch. "So can we get started? Please? Get a move on? Flip a coin?"

When the dime landed on Roosevelt's gleaming head, I felt total relief. We'd be arguing *for* my right to pee, not against it. I wouldn't have to sacrifice any of my principles, not even in the name of practice, not today.

See, we were very deliberate when we built our affirmative case. Very careful to guard against any transphobic tirades. Guess how many times Jonah says the word *transgender* in his opening?

Once. Up top, reciting the resolution.

The rest of the speech he devotes to simple, practical questions. "How would anyone enforce a ban like this, anyway?" he asks. "Would police deploy to high school restrooms? Carry out strip searches? Ask for papers? Or maybe go the biometric route, embed a chip in the hand of every child, have them scan their palms at the locker-room door?"

By the end of Jonah's eight minutes, this is no longer an argument about sex or religion or anything spicy. It's about money. It's about enforcement. It's about the plain fact that there's no way—cost-effective, or constitutional—to divide a student body into phallus and pudenda and funnel them toward specially segregated toilet bowls. That's it. Bullet-proof. Refute us with some rant about the sanctity of human dimorphism, and you're cruisin' for a losin'.

But we should've known Ari would be too smart to take our boring bait.

And *I* should've known that it would hurt just to hear her.

"My opponent stood at this podium, Mr. Speaker, and pre-sented apocalyptic scenarios, dystopian ones," Ari says—even though the podium is just an *Infinite Jest* stacked on a *War & Peace*, and the closest thing we've got to a Mr. Speaker is the custodian mopping up mud in the hallway. "Mr. Cabrera would have you believe that this common-sense legislation is unen-forceable. He proposed armed police carrying out strip searches in high schools. Biometric chips in forearms!" She performs a laugh, then straightens her face. "In actuality, of course, en-forcement is neither costly nor draconian. Every human being is born with their own enforcement tool, free of charge." She taps at her temples: "A pair of eyes, Mr. Speaker."

She is less than a minute into her speech. I should defi-nitely remain in my seat. I should definitely *not* rise up on a hot, bodily wave of anger and throw out my arm, and shout, "On that point, madam!"

But it's done. It's done, and I'm standing, and Ari's looking at me like I've got three heads.

"I've only been talking for, like, ten seconds," she says, in her civilian voice. "What are you doing, Finch? Sit down."

I don't want to sit down. I want to physically fight her. It takes all the willpower I've got—including some from Jonah, tugging on my sleeve—to plant my butt back in my chair.

"Thank you. Jesus." She turns her head; she goes on: "My opponent talks about gender like it's a game of four-dimensional chess. But gender is simple. It's easy to visually verify. And—"

I leap to my feet—"On that point, madam?"—and, shocker, she waves me down again.

"In virtually all cases," she says, visibly pissed to have been interrupted so soon, "it's possible to glean a person's gender merely by looking at them, and—"

This time, leaping up, I don't even bother with the formality: "So prove that you're a woman."

She lets out a shocked sound, half a cough. "Excuse me?"

"Prove to us," I repeat—on a roll, knowing it—"that you're a woman."

"Well, for one, I was born with a vagina, and thus 'assigned female at birth,' so—"

"Well, we don't have the tapes from the maternity ward," I say. "We have no idea if you're telling the truth."

"Sit down, Finch," she says, through gritted teeth.

"No, no. This is the burden of proof you've established: You need a vagina to enter a women's bathroom, because having a vagina makes you a woman." I lift my hands, smile, and go in for the kill: "So prove to us that you're a woman."

"Finch, if you ran this line of questioning in a real debate, I'd report you for sexual harassment."

Jonah raps his knuckles on the table. "So you admit that interrogating people about their junk is sexual harassment?"

Nasir laughs; Ari cuts her eyes at him. "You're supposed to be on *my* side, Nas."

"I'm waiting for my answer," I say, feeling smug now; I've got her cornered. "Please, Ms. Schechter, go ahead: Prove to everyone here that you're a woman."

"Well, no, Finch, I'm not going to lift my skirt and flash a roomful of teenage boys," she says, "even though I'm sure you'd all love that."

"I know I would," says Nasir.

She moves to slap him. He just barely dodges her open palm.

"But you said, and I quote, 'Gender is simple, and easy to visually verify.'" I can see her squirming. "I've *got* her. "But the people who experience the most harassment in bathrooms are women like you. Women we might call 'butch.' Who look masculine. And you—you've got a man's haircut"—and it really is shorter than it was when I saw her last, more Maddow, now, than Rodham—"and you're wearing a very manly blazer, and a very manly tie, and—"

"Okay, okay, you've made your fucking point," she says, water beading in the corners of her eyes. "And you could've made it without telling me that I look like a fucking man."

"Ari, that's not what I—"

But she's clapping a hand over her mouth, and letting out a sound like a small animal drowning, and spinning on the heel of her Gucci loafer. Before I can blink, she's sprinted out into the hall, moving so fast her body blurs.

. . . And that makes *two* people I've brought to tears today.

". . . Well," says Jonah, after thirty seconds or so of shared, stunned silence. "That could've gone better."

"No shit," Nasir says.

I want to say something like, "Yeah, well, *she* insulted *me* just as much," but I can't. Nasir is in the room. Why would I tell him I'm trans? He's a living, breathing episode of *Family Guy*.

"You'd better go apologize," says Jonah.

"You're probably right," I answer.

I find Ari perched on a bench in the hall, mouth locked around her vape pen.

"Hey," I begin, gently, because I can see the red rimming her eyes. "About that whole thing just now . . ."

"Go fuck yourself."

"On school property? People have gone to jail for less."

She snorts; purple vapor billows from her nose.

"Oh, goddammit," she says. "That was a good one."

"Thanks." I start forward; I stop. "Can I take a seat? Do you mind?"

"Go ahead." She angles her thumb at the empty space on the bench. "Just don't fucking touch me."

"Okay." I place myself down, carefully, as far from her as possible. "So. Things got heated in there."

"Sure did."

"I shouldn't have said all that, Ari." I reach for her, then remember what she said about no fucking touching. I settle for patting the bench instead. "You don't look like a man."

"*Ugh*," Ari grunts. "That is *so* not the fucking point." She screws her eyes shut, rubbing at her temples with both hands. "Like, yeah, whatever, I don't look like a girl. But I don't *want* to. There's all this pressure for me—I mean, for Jewish girls, period—to iron out our curls and wax our mustaches and contour our noses into little ski slopes. And that's on top of . . . like, you know, I'm not exactly sample size." She sighs, sweeps a hand over her body. "Whatever. I'm rambling. Sorry. I just don't care about that shit. Like, at all. I could spend all my time starving myself and straightening my hair, or I could, like, actually do something with my life."

"I'm *really* sorry, Ari," I say, again. I mean it. I've been where she presently is: facing a lifetime of waxing, wincing away from it. "I obviously struck a nerve in there, and . . ."

"Okay, okay. That's enough. I just need to grow a backbone." She lifts her head, opens her eyes. "You too, by the way. I don't know why you got so angry in there just now, but it's super sloppy to go ad hominem like that."

"I can't really help it." God only knows why, but I'm feeling tenderly toward Ari. I can see some of my former self in this anxiety she's got, this fear that she's not girling right. So I'm a little more honest, maybe, than I'd usually be. "This resolution *is* ad hominem for me."

She gives me a sidelong squint. "What do you mean?"

I look at her, take in her confusion, her curiosity. She just bared her soul to me, didn't she? Don't I owe her the same? Maybe we have more in common than I thought.

So I breathe in deep, and I say it: "I'm trans."

She doesn't answer me. Not at first. Her eyes go wide, and then narrow, and then she sort of scans me, up and down. Like she's confirming that I'm speaking English. That I really said what I just said.

And then, suddenly, there's a click of comprehension in her eyes.

"Oh, shit," she says, her voice softening. "Who else knows? Jonah? Nasir?"

I shake my head. "Jonah knows," I tell her. "Nasir doesn't. Obviously."

She snorts. "Yeah. I wouldn't spill my guts to Nasir, either." She jams her vape into the pocket of her blazer, and then turns, placing her broad hands on my knees. "Also, like, I hope you know that everything I said in the round just now . . . I don't actually believe that shit. It's just the case we're running." She pauses, squeezes my knees. "I've been doing a ton of research, and I know it's not easy for . . . for people like you. So, like, thanks for trusting me with this."

". . . Thank you?" Where was *this* girl in that round? And if she doesn't believe what she was arguing, what *does* she believe? "You can see why this debate brings up a lot of painful stuff for me."

"Right. Of course. It must be really hard." She nods, and lifts her hands. "So, what do you want me to do about the pronoun thing? Just keep using 'he' and 'him' for you? Like, in public? Until you're ready to come all the way out?"

"Uh. Yes?" She blinks at me, mystified. Oh, God. Time to spell it out, clear as I can: "I'm a *man*, Ari. A transgender man." Still nothing. I sigh. "Female to male? Assigned female at birth?"

". . . Wait." Ari pulls away, her hands falling back into her lap. She rakes her eyes over the length of my body again. And then she snorts. "*No* way. Bullshit. I've literally seen you with fucking beard stubble on tournament mornings."

"Yeah, because I take testosterone." I reach up, draw a demonstrative little loop around my chin. "It gives me facial hair. Makes my voice deeper. Moves the fat in my face around."

"Really?" She's squinting, hard, her brows almost meeting in the middle. I can practically see the math equations dancing around her curly head. "You really were, like . . . I know I shouldn't say 'born a girl,' but, like . . ."

Part of me wants to fight her on this "born a girl" business. Another part of me—the bone-tired part—doesn't want to prolong this conversation even a second longer than I have to.

"That's right." I say it slowly, like I'm speaking to an infant. "Born a girl."

"And do you, like, tape your, uh . . . your chest down? To make it flat?" She lifts a hand, draws a flat line across her own round chest. "Or did you have surgery to . . ."

Nothing I love more than getting grilled about my medical history. "I'm leaving now," I say, as I rise—can't do it fast enough—and turn, and start to walk, brisk, back down the hall to the library.

"Wait. Wait! I'm sorry." She's leaping to her feet, hurrying after me, tugging on my arm. "It's just, I've never met anyone, like . . . anyone trans, and you look so . . . I mean, you seriously look *exactly* like a guy."

I lift my arm, shake her loose. "I *am* a guy, Ari."

"Yeah, but it's not like . . ." She hurries after me, eyes bright, excited. "Not like Hilary Swank in that one movie. Like, you *really* look like a guy."

Hilary Swank? I stop in my tracks, turn to the wall, and plant my forehead firmly against it. "Fuck. I should *not* have told you this."

"I won't tell anyone," she says.

"Oh, God." Terror rolls through me. I turn to her, eyes wide. *"Please* don't tell anyone."

"I won't!" she chirps, and mimes the zipping of her lips. "I swear. Your secret is so, so safe with me."

I don't trust her. Not one iota. But the cat is well and truly out of the bag now, flailing around with its sharp little claws. Ari knows. She knows because I told her.

And there is no way for me to walk my words back.

chapter eight

The rest of my weekend drags by on its knuckles. All I can think about is getting to Monday, to debate club. After the twin catastrophes of Saturday—launching World War Three between Bailey and Jonah, outing myself to Ari—I'm looking forward to some normalcy. If I can just stand next to Jonah, soak up the glow of his easy smile, then I'll know that we're okay. That we're united, still. That we've got what we need to take Nationals.

Jonah's locked in a small circle when I walk in. Listening to the freshmen, the sophs, the juniors, all talking over each other about their weekends. If he sees me enter, he doesn't show it. I wonder if I should tap him on the shoulder, say hi, but he seems absorbed: Ava ate charcoal ice cream yesterday, for the first time ever, and it tasted *so* weird; Jasmyne caught up on *Riverdale*, and the plot makes less sense with every passing episode; Tyler saw a production of *Grease* at Evergreen, featuring an all-female cast, and the young woman who played Danny Zuko was, reportedly, "hot as fuck."

Jonah says nothing about his weekend, our weekend. I try to meet his gaze, more than once, but every time, he's got his eyes on someone else. I don't know if he's doing it deliberately, but I feel this funny ache, still—a flower-to-sun hunger every time he turns away.

"All right! Ten past! Let's get started!" Adwoa brings her fist down like a gavel against the history teacher's desk. "First item on the agenda: Finch and Jonah went up to Annable this weekend for a pre-Nationals friendly! You guys wanna debrief? How'd it go?"

"Great!" says Jonah brightly. You can really hear the exclamation point there: *great!*

But I've seen him on sunny days and gray ones—that time we flew to Junior Nationals in Tampa, for instance, and Delta lost all of our luggage, and Jonah dropped his phone in a toilet at the airport. I know his moods, is what I mean. And this? It's not an especially good one.

"Okay. So it was great." Adwoa spreads her hands. "Can you give us a little more than that?"

He gives Adwoa a look equal parts miserable and apologetic. And so she turns to me. "Okay. Finch: How did the round go?"

But I'm also at a loss. How do I talk about the round without mentioning my fight with Ari—or the subsequent outing, which I regretted so deeply that I never even told Jonah about it?

"Okay. Looks like I need to talk to Jonah and Finch out in the hall." She lifts her hand, points at the door, even snaps her fingers for good measure. "Boys? Out. Jas, run through this week's *Slate* quiz while I'm gone."

We follow her into the hallway. She closes the door behind us, crossing her arms. "Okay, no more of this nonsense," she says. "Tell me exactly what went down this weekend."

". . . Maybe not while everyone's looking?" Jonah angles a thumb through the plate of glass in the door. A cluster of kids have gathered there. Ava's wobbling on curious tiptoe. They struggle—well, fail—to disperse as Adwoa glares daggers.

"Fine. Let's move. She plants a gentle shove between my shoulders, and then between Jonah's. She guides us up the hallway, into a lower-traffic corner. As we walk, she asks again: "This weekend: What happened?"

"Nothing," I say, just as Jonah says, "Not much."

"Okay, what the hell is going on?" Adwoa looks at us, suspicious. "Did Nasir say something hateful? Is that it?"

Well, yes. But his comment about Jonah's smokin' hot girlfriend, Bailey, was really only the tenth or eleventh most screwed-up thing to happen this weekend.

"Bailey and I got into a huge fight on Saturday morning," Jonah blurts, suddenly. "I had to drive him to the airport for his Juilliard callback, and we started arguing in the car, so I was off my game at Annable and then, just . . ." He sighs out, plainly frustrated. "I've been going back and forth with Bailey all weekend—and all day today, actually—and I'm really tired, and really out of it, and . . . Yeah. That's it. I'm sorry."

"All weekend?" I ask him quietly. "But I thought you two . . . at the departure gate, you kissed . . ."

"Kissed, maybe." Jonah shrugs. "Didn't make up."

Listening to him, feeling the fatigue in his voice, I feel a

sick rush of guilt. The fight was my fault. And Jonah's still con-
tending with the fall-out.

"Jonah, I feel for you. I do." Adwoa presses her palms
together, prayer-like, beseeching him. "But if you and your
boyfriend don't get it together and stop fighting before
Nationals . . ."

"No, I understand," he says quickly. "I'll sort this out. I'll
fix it."

"Wonderful. Love to hear it." She turns to me. "Now, Finch:
What's eating you?

I'm wondering how to lie when I realize, suddenly, that I
don't even have to: "Ari said a lot of transphobic stuff during
the debate, and when I started asking her questions, she ran
out crying, so . . ."

Adwoa rolls her eyes skyward, mutters—"Give me
strength"—and sighs. "Okay. I've heard enough. Have a seat,
both of you. We need to talk, but we gotta keep it brief. I
don't want Jas stuck running the whole meeting."

She leans against the wall, then slides to the floor until the
seat of her jeans hits linoleum. With great reluctance, Jonah
and I follow her lead and assume crisscross applesauce. His
knee presses into mine, briefly, before he flinches away.

Why do I feel like he's just left a bruise?

"I know you kids have a lot on your plates right now," says
Adwoa. "Jonah, you've got your boyfriend and his nonsense.
Finch, you've got Ari and her nonsense." She sighs. "And I
was a high school senior myself once. Long, long time ago.
But I remember what the workload was like. Lord, Jesus, do
I remember."

"Right," I say, simply, because I don't want to get into everything else on my plate. My mom losing her job. Me losing my health insurance. Whether I'll go to D.C. for college or stay here, stuck. "I've got a lot going on right now."

"Likewise," says Jonah, just as simply.

I wonder how much stress that one word holds for him.

"But I need you guys to focus on Nationals." She reaches forward—one hand on my knee, another on Jonah's. "Tonight, after practice, the two of you are going to sit in a booth at the Green Bean. You're going to work on your cases, *and* you're going to work through whatever stresses you're dealing with. *Together.* Capisce?"

"I can't prep tonight," Jonah says. "I have to go to Bailey's dress rehearsal. Opening night is this Friday."

"Then see the show on opening night, Jonah." Adwoa, plainly exhausted, rakes a hand through her braids. "You do not have to be present at each and every one of your boyfriend's rehearsals."

I'm not sure I've ever heard Jonah this depleted, this utterly exhausted: "Adwoa, if I don't show up today, he's going to be so, so mad, like—"

Adwoa brings the back of her hand down into her palm, over and over, as she says, "You cannot keep doing this! Carving yourself up into smaller and smaller pieces to make room for your boyfriend!" She puts up her hands when she sees the injured look on Jonah's face. "I'm sorry. I know I'm overstepping. But, honestly, kid, you've got a national championship to worry about. That's your priority. If it makes Bailey mad, well, tough. He can stay mad."

". . . Fine," Jonah huffs, and pulls himself up to his feet. "Can't *wait* to send this text to Bailey."

"The Green Bean. Tonight." Adwoa helps me to my feet. "Fix your case." She points to Jonah. "And fix that attitude."

After debate club lets out, Adwoa frog-marches us to the Green Bean, pushes us into a corner booth, and orders our drinks for us. She is *not* messing around.

"I'm friends with the baristas here." She points to her eyes, then us: *I'm watching you.* "Either of you tries to escape before closing? I'll know."

"You're a dictator," I tell her. "A totalitarian dictator."

"That's why they pay me the big part-time bucks." She laughs, slings her Telfar over her shoulder, and steps away. "Don't let me keep you! Get some work done. Some *good* work."

I wait until she's out the door—until we're really alone, I mean—before I lift my head, meet Jonah's eyes.

"Before we get started," I begin, cautious, "I just want to say, again, how sorry I am for picking that fight with Bailey. Especially if he's still grilling you about the musical, I . . ."

"Oh, no. He's not even mad about the musical anymore. No, he . . . I mean, it's totally ridiculous, but he thinks . . ."

I wait to hear what, exactly, Bailey thinks, but Jonah has stopped talking. He's sighing, stirring his portable straw through his pink drink. I'd say it's a miracle that Adwoa remembered his order, but then, so did I: an iced raspberry white chocolate soy mocha with rose petals; surprisingly indelible.

"What?" I ask, finally; he's been quiet too long. "What does he think?"

"Honestly? He thinks that I . . . that I sided with you, in the *Millie* argument, because I . . ."—he is really struggling here—"because I have, um . . . feelings. For you."

". . . For *me?*" The words come out a pair of startled squeaks that might be—that I *hope* are—inaudible to human ears. It's one thing when Lucy spouts her conspiracy theories on the bus. It's quite another to hear them coming out of Jonah's mouth. "But that's . . . that's bananas."

I don't so much choose the word *bananas* as vomit it out because my cognition's left me. But Jonah—relief of reliefs—thinks it is funny, and he laughs, and the tension that forced him to take three or four tries with his last sentence evaporates.

"Thank you," he says, and slaps the table lightly. "It *is* bananas." His eyes go wide, suddenly, and he seems to backtrack. "Not that I wouldn't . . . I mean, you're not, like . . . like, *anyone* would be very lucky to . . ."

"Oh, no," I interrupt, eager to spare us both some embarrassment. "You don't have to say that." Among the many things I'm not in the mood for: false flattery. "And if you're going to talk to Bailey about this, maybe leave out the 'anyone would be very lucky' business."

"Oh, trust me," Jonah laughs, "I've spent the past two days trying to convince him that I'm not in love with you."

"You know what?" I lean forward; so does he. "I've been trying to convince *Lucy* that I'm not in love with *you*."

He laughs out loud, right up close: "*What?* Why?"

"Because I got so mad at Bailey on Saturday!" I laugh when Jonah laughs, and I take a sip of my drink, relieved that he finds this as ridiculous as I do. "I was texting her about the argument, and she said something like, 'You can't white-knight for Jonah just because you . . .'" I hesitate—should I say it? "'. . . because you have a *boner* for Jonah.'"

"A *boner?*" Jonah exclaims, voice not low in the least. He slaps the table; people stare. "Right. Totally. Because this is a *very* sexy secret affair we're carrying on here. In the corner booth. At the Green Bean."

"Oh, definitely," I concur. "All these torrid nights of . . . of reading the *Financial Times*, and . . . and color-coding cue cards . . ."

"Seriously!" Jonah says. "Bailey is *so* mad that I've been spending all this time with you, and I'm just like, 'Dude, we're literally at the Annable library on a Saturday afternoon. What do you think we're doing, exactly? We're in a *library*.'"

"I was actually reading an article in *Law and Crime* the other day about a porn star who shot—well, a 'film,' I guess, in a library in California." I sip my lemonade. "So it *can* be done, apparently."

"Good to know," Jonah says. He lifts his drink: *Cheers*. "Next time you find yourself alone in a dimly lit library with a certain Miss Ariadne Schechter . . ."

I lunge across the table, throwing a punch that he dodges, giggling. "I do *not* . . ."

"You guys were out there in the hallway for a *long* time, dude," Jonah says. "And you still won't tell me what you talked about."

"I don't want to get into it," I tell him. There's a bit of magical thinking here: If I never tell Jonah what I told Ari, it'll be like I never told her. "But I can tell you it had nothing to do with, uh . . . carnal knowledge."

"Whatever you say," Jonah flicks his wrist, dismissive. "Twenty years down the line, when I'm bringing over a casserole for the Schechter-Kelly Chrismukkah celebration . . ."

"Okay, okay. That's enough. We should probably get some work done." I lower my eyes to my laptop, pausing to wipe a thin layer of silt from the keys. "Just so we've got something to show Adwoa."

"Fine," Jonah says, and opens his own laptop. "But I'm not done razzing you about Ari."

"You'd better be," I say. "Or I'll punch you."

"Well, you'll try," he says. "You don't have a great track record."

I scowl at him, and he scowls right back, and then we crack up, both of us, and settle into a comfortable, companionable silence. We trade links to long-form articles. We highlight typos. We pin suggestions and emoji-encouragements to each other's speeches. It's like a weight's been lifted; there is no proof, none, to Lucy's and Bailey's conspiracy theories. I'm not in love with Jonah. And he's not in love with me. He is sitting across from me, pasting a study from the *Lancet* into our communal doc. Ours is a thoroughly unsexy evening.

And then, suddenly, the silence shatters. Jonah's phone,

facedown on the table, begins to peal: seven messages, almost all at once. That incoming-text tri-tone rings out so many times in such rapid succession that I wonder if the phone is broken. I startle, knocking over my lemonade. The butter-yellow wave heads right for the ringing phone. So I grab it, lift it, save it, as Jonah lunges for a napkin. It should be the other way around, maybe, but here we are: Jonah mopping up my mess, me holding his phone.

"What's it say?" Jonah asks. "My phone, I mean."

"I don't know." I hold the phone out, away from me. "I don't want to read your texts."

"Can you just read them out? Please?" He waves a hand at the spreading puddle of lemonade. "I'm trying to save our laptops here."

"Fine," I say, and flip the phone. "If you say so."

I press *home*; the screen glows.

Seven texts. All from Bailey. I read, out loud, with a shrillness that makes Jonah giggle:

BAILEY LUNDQUIST: really nice of you to skip my dress rehearsal lmao

BAILEY LUNDQUIST: not like i'm having the most stressful week of my fkn life or anything

BAILEY LUNDQUIST: idk why i'm bothering to text you since you're CLEARLY busy

BAILEY LUNDQUIST: but ms elliott just asked if i'm gonna have a plus one for the opening night party

BAILEY LUNDQUIST: so what should i tell her

BAILEY LUNDQUIST: are you going to come

BAILEY LUNDQUIST: or are you going to flake out on me again to go hang out at the green bean with the little red-haired girl

"Oh my God." Jonah's staring at me—mouth open, face ashen. The napkins balled up in his left hand, the color of weak sunlight, drip and drip and drip. "I am so, so sorry."

I couldn't tell you why, but all I can do is laugh. I should feel cratered by Bailey's *girl* dig. And maybe I am, deep down. But right now, at this moment, in this coffee shop, I can't stop thinking about how *funny* it is.

How long have I looked at Bailey and seen the kind of boy I'd love to be? But all that confidence, all that charm—he never had it, not really. I do, though. He knows that. It scares him. It scares him so much that he's septuple-texting Jonah, weaponizing *Peanuts*, worrying that I, Finch Kelly, virgin and a half, am out to steal his man.

"Finch, really, I can't believe he would . . ."

"*Peanuts!*" I'm finally able to form words again, instead of just bellowing laughter.

"Sorry?" Jonah looks at me, mystified. "*Peanuts?*"

"You know? The comic Charlie Brown's from?" I see the recognition on his face; I keep going. "The Little Red-Haired Girl is . . . she's a character. From *Peanuts*."

That "dot dot dot" there? That's how close I come to telling him that Charlie Brown's hopelessly in love with her.

"He's never done anything like this before," Jonah says. "Called you a girl, I mean. I can't think why he would . . . I mean, I never told him you were trans." Jonah picks up his phone—dry, but sticky with lemonade—and pockets it. "He's just under a lot of stress right now and . . . Yeah, no. I got nothing. No excuses. I'm just . . . I'm sorry."

He's barely gotten out this very sincere *sorry* when another text from Bailey pings through. I don't get to see this one, though—just Jonah's reaction, a deep frown at the screen.

I crane my head. "What did he say now?"

"Oh, nothing. Just a string of question marks." Jonah exhales, lifts his head. "I'm trying to figure out how to answer him. Any ideas?"

I'm tempted to help Jonah draft a breakup text so cataclysmic that Bailey never loves again. Just rots in his bedroom like Miss Havisham in a pile of yellowing *Playbills*. I'd be in the wrong, of course. I'd be doing exactly the thing Bailey—and Lucy—have accused me of doing: conspiring to wreck Jonah's relationship.

So I don't offer ideas. Instead, I shrug.

"I can't tell you what to write, Jonah. I'm sorry. He's your boyfriend, not mine."

Jonah doesn't answer me, not at first. He stares at his phone, thumbs moving slowly over the screen. He's at this for a while. I've just drifted back to my laptop when I hear Jonah tapping the table in front of me.

"How's this?" he begins. "'Hi, Bailey: I know that—'"

"Jonah, I *just* told you that I can't tell you what to write."

"'I know that this has been a really stressful week for you,'" he goes on, ignoring me, "'but it's not fair to take your stress out on me. We're both working hard to balance all our commitments right now. I've been patient with you, and I hope you can be patient with me.'"

He takes another breath; I can't find my own. My mind is racing, questions firing. Is Jonah really not going to mention the "little red-haired girl" thing? Do I matter *that* little to him? Or does he think that Bailey is right? That I am, deep down, a little red-haired—

"'And I'm deeply disappointed by what you said about Finch,'" he says—like he can read my mind, like he knows precisely what to say to stop my spiraling. "'Finch is not a girl. It is not okay to call him a girl. He saw the message when it popped up on my screen, and it really hurt his feelings. I want you to apologize to him as soon as possible.'" He stops there, looks up, searches my eyes. "How's that?" he asks me, anxious now, with none of the confident indignation of his reading aloud. "Is that okay?"

. . . Is it *okay?* Yes, it's okay. More than okay. He's standing up to Bailey. Not because he's in love with me; because he loves me.

I can't form words; I nod. That's enough for him. He presses *send;* I listen to the quiet *whoosh* of the paper plane, flying away.

I return my eyes to my laptop and pretend the earth didn't just move.

"Hold up. Bailey called you a girl?"

"No, not just 'a girl.'" I'm honestly not sure whether Bailey knows I'm trans—if he deliberately misgendered me, I mean, or if he just picked a highly unfortunate insult. "'*The Little Red-Haired Girl.*'"

I'd booked some time with Lucy because I knew, after the hurricane of this weekend, that I'd need a quality vent with my best friend. Plus a plate of pad thai from that great hole-in-the-wall around the corner from her place. Good thing I did. Monday wound up being just as much of a shitstorm.

"Unbelievable." Lucy shovels a bright orange forkful into her mouth, ignoring the noodles that fly from the fork to the bedspread. She can be an awfully messy eater when she's angry. "I'm going to beat his ass at school tomorrow."

"No, you're not," I tell her, from my seat at her desk. "You're not beating anybody's ass."

"Why not? You don't think I could take Bailey in a fight?"

"Lucy, you've never even been in a fight."

"Only 'cause my mom *refuses* to let me join Puget Sound Antifa."

"Really?" Most parents would have reservations about their kids hitting the streets and slugging Nazis. Not Lucy's mom. "I would've thought she'd be all over that. Sewing balaclavas for the black bloc, mixing up little bottles of saline solution to ward off the tear gas . . ."

"I wish, man." Lucy sighs, flopping back onto her mattress, arms out wide as a starfish. "I mean, she and I *do* hit protests all the time. We blockaded ICE up in Tacoma just last month. But it's not the same, you know? Sometimes, you just wanna *smash.*"

"Don't beat Bailey up," I tell her, again. "I don't want to strain my relationship with Jonah any more than I already have."

"Sorry—*strain?* I thought you guys were in great shape. Didn't you *just* tell me that he defended you? Like, tapped out a text right there in front of you, demanding at gunpoint-emoji that Bailey apologize to you?"

I'm still working on my portion of pad thai, but Lucy's had two spring rolls and two and a half helpings of the main event. She's horizontal on her mattress now, fully in a food coma, cheek buried in the down of an enormous Porg.

"He did ask for an apology, yeah." Bailey's apology—no surprise—has not been forthcoming. "I was really impressed by that. Especially after how awful I was this weekend."

"Are you kidding?" Lucy lifts her head, rests her cheek upon the Porg's fat belly. "What Jonah did was the bare minimum, Finch. If he were *really* on your team, he would've dumped the motherfucker on the spot."

"I honestly don't think they'll ever break up." I abandon my plate, and then, against both my better judgment and my standards for laundry, I lie down on her bed, and make a pillow of the Porg's wing. "I mean, they're Jonah and Bailey. Homecoming kings. They've been together for ages."

"Teenagers break up all the time, Finch. Nobody ever actually marries their high school sweetheart."

Does she have a point? Jonah still hasn't told Bailey about his plans for college. Bailey still hasn't quit the outrageously racist musical. I'm having a hard time squaring the boys I've seen these past weeks with the matching Halloween costumes, the affectionate phone calls, the kisses on the bus.

"All I'm saying," I continue, though I'm sure Lucy can hear the doubt in my voice, "is that they seem . . . different. Don't you think? It's like they're not built to break up. Not like . . . well, not like us."

"What are you talking about? You and me, we're the best-case scenario." Lucy lifts the Porg's other wing and wraps it around herself, like it's giving her an extraterrestrial hug. "We dated for a while. We broke up. But we're still friends, and you still crawl into my bed and cuddle on bad nights, and you still happily eat the breakfasts my mom makes for you." She reaches out, taps me lightly on the nose. "That's a way better deal than the bullshit Bailey's putting Jonah through, don't you think? I know you've got a pretty pessimistic view of all this love stuff, but . . ."

"Pessimistic?" I sit up, squint at her. "Just because I don't want to waste my time dating?"

"Dating isn't a waste of time, honey."

I roll away from her; my eyes roll, too. "If it's distracting me from studying, and getting into college, and becoming the first trans person in Congress . . ."

"If Alice Brady doesn't get there first, you mean."

"You know what I mean."

Lucy reaches out, presses a finger to my lips: *Stop talking, Finch.* "I think you're just scared."

"Scared of what?"

"Scared of telling girls you're trans," she says. "Remember what happened with Ari? During that party after Senior State?"

I haven't briefed Lucy on my more recent chat with Ari—

that I *did* tell her I'm trans, that it went even worse than I'd feared.

"Well, maybe I'm right to be scared," I say. "What if I were to hook up with a girl, and she stuck her hand in my pants, or—I don't know—up my shirt, and she found out that I wasn't cis, and she . . . she *attacked* . . ."

"Oh, yes," Lucy says, flatly. "Ariadne Schechter of the Annable School transforming into a violent hate criminal the second she smells clam juice. Totally plausible."

"Didn't I ask you to never say 'clam' again?"

"So you admit that you're scared to tell girls you're trans?"

"Uh, I admit that most straight girls don't want to have sex with someone who has a vagina," I fire back. "Just like most gay guys don't want . . ."

"Wait." Lucy puts up a hand. "Gay guys? You're into guys? It's official?"

"*No*, Lucy." I groan into the Porg's wide wing. "Why does everyone keep saying that? Bailey thinking I'm after Jonah, you asking me if I have . . . if I have a *boner* for him . . ."

"Oh, right. I completely forgot I said that." Lucy rolls onto the Porg's belly, laughing. "You know I was just joking, right?"

"No! I assumed it was part of your ongoing campaign to make me question my sexuality!"

"Well, if I didn't know any better," Lucy says, leveling her eyes at me, "I'd say that campaign's working."

"I'm not questioning anything, Lucy. I've been there, done that, signed the papers, popped the puberty blockers, bought the binder, stabbed the syringe into my thigh . . ."

"I said 'questioning your sexuality,'" she says. "Not 'questioning your gender.' Two completely different things."

"Look, Lucy, we have to settle this, once and for all." I reach out, hands on her shoulders. "I'm not gay. I'm just not. And you, of all people? You should know that."

"Should I, though?" She shrugs my hands from her shoulders. "I mean, I know we've never really talked about this, but back when we dated? Before you transitioned? You never really wanted to make out."

"Yeah, because making out isn't fun for me!" I lower my voice, fast. I don't want Lucy's mom to overhear me and think that Lucy and I are back together. "And sex sounds *terrifying*. I don't like being naked. I *really* don't like being naked in front of other people. I don't even like to touch *myself*."

"Okay. I hear you." Lucy nods. "But, still: would you feel the same way about sex with a man?"

I consider it—and then I shudder. "No. No. I'd feel worse." Visions are dancing in my head: men, men, big, hairy, muscular *men*. If I had a boyfriend, would I even look like a man next to him? "Being with a boy would just make me feel like a girl."

"Finch. Honey." There is a devastated look on Lucy's face. She crawls across the mattress to me, taking me up in her arms. "You *know* that's not true. Being with a boy wouldn't make you any less of a boy."

It's easy for her to say that. Harder for me to live it. This fear I feel when it comes to dating? These worries about being with a boy, being with a girl, being with anyone? They are *very* real to me.

Even if I did want to fall in love—and I don't, because I have school to focus on, and then college, and then law school, and then my campaign for Congress—my body will always be a barrier. I'll have to apologize for it every time I meet somebody new.

And Lucy doesn't get that. How could she? If I try to tell her how scary love seems to me, how bleak and lonely my future looks—well, she wouldn't tell me the truth, would she? She'd just paint pictures of a fairy-tale world where love is possible for people like me. Where it's pure. Uncomplicated.

"Oh, Finch," she says, looping her arms around my shoulders. Here it comes, the fairy-tale pabulum: "Love is going to sneak up on you when you least expect it. There's no escaping it."

"That sounds ominous," I say, as best I can with my cheek smushed to her chest.

"No escape," she says, and squeezes me tighter. "None."

chapter nine

The first thing I see when I step into the senior hallway on Friday morning is Jonah, leaning against the last locker on the left. He holds an enormous bouquet of roses—pink, fat, ripe. The occasional petal flutters to the floor as he shifts, side to side.

"Those for Bailey?" I ask.

"Opening night," he says—all smiles, all strained. "Had to show him some love."

"Of course." I should have remembered—lately, this stupid musical has been dominating my life almost as much as debate. "I'm sure he'll love them."

"I hope so." Jonah laughs uneasily. "He and I haven't really talked since . . ."

"The other night?" I ask, more than a little uneasy myself. "When Bailey called me a girl? And never apologized?"

"Wait." Jonah's fist tightens on the flowers. "He didn't . . . ?"

I shake my head.

"Not even a text?" he says. "Nothing?"

"Nothing," I repeat.

The cellophane in Jonah's hands is a symphony. Why's he fidgeting like this? What's he thinking?

Then, suddenly, Bailey turns the corner, flanked on all sides by a cloud of his friends from the drama club. When they see Jonah with roses in his hands, they erupt—cheering, whooping, clapping.

"*Baaaaaaaby*," Bailey sings—actually *sings*. He folds his hands over his heart. "Roses? For me?"

Jonah, smiling only on one side, says, "All for you."

He's just barely pulled the bouquet out of harm's way before Bailey is surging forward, crashing into him. There's a kiss—a long, lingering one, on the lips—that Jonah isn't ready for. His eyes are still open.

Bailey's buddies are *ooh*ing and *aww*ing—phones out, red lights flickering. In minutes, this will be all over Instagram. Another perfect vignette. People will see this perfect kiss and get jealous of Jonah and Bailey. Just like I used to.

"These are stunning, Jojo." Bailey takes the bouquet from Jonah and spins it around and around, a floral kaleidoscope. He's been cold-shouldering Jonah since Saturday, but you'd never know it, not from the way he's cooing. "I love that you couldn't even wait 'til after the show."

Jonah's grin is lopsiding even harder. "Actually," he says, "I wanted to talk to you about that. Talk about tonight's show, I mean."

"Uh-huh?" Bailey extracts his phone from his pocket. "Hold on. I'm just gonna get this for Instagram."

Jonah's eyes flicker to mine. Is this a cue? Should I step back? Whatever's about to go down, I can't be in Bailey's line of sight when it does.

I sink back behind a concrete pillar as Bailey puts his phone in his pocket.

Jonah turns to him. "Bailey, babe," he says. "I can't make it to your show tonight."

"What?" Bailey is staring at Jonah like he's just sunk a knife into the space between his pale ribs. "Why not?"

Jonah's gaze is level, his voice gentle. "You know why, Bailey."

"Really?" Bailey laughs, incredulous. "Fucking *really*?"

Jonah answers with a nod. *Yes, Bailey—fucking really.*

"I can't believe this." There's water welling in Bailey's eyes. I'm not moved. He cried on cue as Valjean, too. "What the fuck? I thought you loved me."

Jonah glances past Bailey, past me, to the drama club. Their phones are still out, the red lights still glowing. Guess they specialize in more than one kind of drama.

"Let's go somewhere private," Jonah says, voice low. "Talk this through alone."

"If you have something to say," Bailey says—a hand flies out, sweeps over the dramatists—"you can say it in front of everyone."

Jonah swallows. He squares his jaw, his shoulders. I *know* that look on his face, know what it means when he holds himself like this.

It means he's about to eviscerate the person at the podium.

It means we're about to win.

"This musical, Bailey? It's racist. You know it, I know it, and that's why I never auditioned." Other people might raise their voices in a fight. Not Jonah. He is calm, level, utterly in command. "I didn't want to play Bun Foo or Ching Chong or whatever. I didn't want to sing in pidgin English." He shakes his head. "And I kept quiet about it, right? Because I knew how happy you were to be playing this role. But you never, ever thought about how *I* might feel."

"Oh my God, Jonah, it's set in the nineteen fucking twenties." Bailey is in full-on tears now, rivers just sprinting down his cheeks. Whatever he pays his acting coach, it's not enough. "It's not gonna be the most woke thing ever!"

"But you could update the script to make Millie a boy, yeah?" Jonah pulls back, says this at a cool remove. "You could make up a completely fictional version of the 1920s where it was totally fine to be gay."

"I literally can't even, like . . ." Bailey holds his roses the way a nightmare-menaced toddler clings his teddy close. "There is, like, *zero* gay rep in musical theater, and . . ."

"Really, Bailey? Gay men are underrepresented? On *Broadway?*"

"Oh, so now you're just . . ." Bailey lifts his sleeve, mops away another wave of tears. "You're just being openly homophobic now. Okay."

"*Openly homophobic?*" Jonah laughs. "Bailey, I'm gay!"

"Really?" Bailey laughs just as joylessly. "Because lately, it seems like you're way more interested in—"

"Don't." Jonah lifts a hand, giving Bailey a wicked warning glare. "Don't even start."

Bailey steps forward, his eyes skating over the audience.

He's scanning every head in the hall—looking, no doubt, for a flicker of red. He doesn't find it.

"Did Finch put you up to this?" Bailey demands, whirling back to Jonah. "Did he tell you to humiliate me in front of everybody?"

"No, he didn't," says Jonah. "I am *your* boyfriend, Bailey."

"Not anymore you're not."

A low, scandalized hum comes over the crowded hallway. Bailey opens his hands; the bouquet dives to the floor. The cameras in the crowd float higher, higher, to capture Bailey's heel crushing the fat pink head of a rose.

"Bailey," Jonah says, voice low. "Listen—"

"Fuck you," Bailey cries, "*and* your flowers."

His foot descends on another rose, and lingers, grinding its fine pink petals into the tiled floor. I'm sure, for a second, that Jonah will turn, leave Bailey to the flowers. Instead, he steps forward. He takes Bailey's arm in his hand.

"Don't fucking touch me!" Bailey says, wrenching his arm away. "We're done, Jonah! It's over!"

"It's not over until you apologize to Finch."

Bailey turns his head, then, to follow Jonah's gaze. I do not pull my head behind the pillar fast enough, and his blue eyes meet mine, just for a second.

"Say sorry," he says, eyes still on me, "for *what?*"

"You *know* for what," Jonah says. "Tell him you're sorry. Right now."

He doesn't. He turns, and he blows right past me, past my pillar, protected by his thick hull of friends. They march with him up the hallway and around the corner. It only takes a few moments for the regular flow of traffic to resume. Kids step over the destroyed bouquet without a second thought. Jonah looks at me. People pass between us. His mouth forms the words *I'm sorry* just as the very same words leave mine.

BAILEY LUNDQUIST—@BaileyOnBroadway

Love Too get brutally dumped the morning of the biggest opening of my entire life lolololololololololol i really might k-word myself

BAILEY LUNDQUIST—@BaileyOnBroadway

apparently it's racist to portray racism in a musical about racism wow wild who knew

BAILEY LUNDQUIST—@BaileyOnBroadway

ykw maybe this is for the best! like! i'm going to juilliard! bitch! i'm like a witch and you can't kill me! bitch! there's nothing holding me back! bitch!

BAILEY LUNDQUIST—@BaileyOnBroadway

YouTube: Shawn Mendes—There's Nothing Holding Me Back (Official Video)

BAILEY LUNDQUIST—@BaileyOnBroadway

honestly when i bring my husband shawn mendes to the tonys to watch me accept best actor in a musical its OVERRRRRRR for you hoes

BAILEY LUNDQUIST—@BaileyOnBroadway

and by you hoes i mean j*n*h c*br*r*

BAILEY LUNDQUIST—@BaileyOnBroadway
anyway come see billie tonight lmao forget about the boy bouta be LIT. UP.

After what may be the worst day of school ever endured by a human being—just hours on hours of speculation flying between desks and lockers about my mysterious role in the catastrophic public break-up of Bailey and Jonah—it is with profound relief that I haul myself back to my house and up to my room. Friday nights, understand, are the only time I give myself to do nothing at all. To recover, in a way, from the week. I've got a bag of peanut butter M&M's, a pint of Rocky Road, and absolutely no commitments but a brand-new feature-length *ContraPoints*.

So why, then, have I shattered my own calm by scrolling through the car crash that is Bailey Lundquist's Twitter profile? I don't follow him—I'm surprised I haven't blocked him—but one of his tweets popped up on my timeline, buttressed by one of those 4 *people you follow liked this tweet* banners. And so, here I am, spelunking through a feed that has become a dedicated shrine to the derogation of Jonah Cabrera. I'm just reaching into my pocket for my phone—whether to text Jonah *Sorry about Twitter* or *Don't look at Twitter*, I'm not sure—when I feel it buzz in my fingers.

JONAH CABRERA: hey i know we were planning to meet up at the green bean tomorrow morning but i'm so sorry i have to cancel

JONAH CABRERA: i know we're getting close to nationals and every minute counts but i need a mental health day

JONAH CABRERA: i'm so sorry

I begin to type:

FINCH KELLY: You have nothing to apologize for. Are you okay?

Wincing, I stay my thumbs on the keys; of course he's not okay. I had a front-row seat—well, front-pillar—to this morning's catastrophe. And I didn't have another chance to check in with him all day. Jonah deserves much better from me than *Are you okay?*

FINCH KELLY: You have nothing to apologize for. I know you're having a hard day. I saw what happened this morning.

FINCH KELLY: And I'm seeing what's happening on Bailey's Twitter right now

JONAH CABRERA: yeah maria warned me to stay off twitter lol

FINCH KELLY: well thank god for tech savvy little siblings

JONAH CABRERA: yeah no kidding lol. she's keeping ren & ben busy in the playroom downstairs so i can have some space to myself rn.

JONAH CABRERA: most of my friends are either in the musical or at the musical so i am just by myself in my room listening to the same jay som song over and over

I stare at the phone. Then I lift my head and stare at my laptop. The never-ending churn of Twitter. The bag of M&M's tilting against the side of the screen. I have no real plans tonight. Nothing, really, to do.

I've only ever been over to Jonah's place to prep for debates. I'm not even sure I've been upstairs—maybe twice, if that, to use the bathroom. I've certainly never seen the interior of the bedroom where Jonah is presently lying on his side and listening to the saddest of sad music.

But I could go over there tonight. I could ride my bike, be with him.

I could help.

FINCH KELLY: Well, listen, I understand if you just want to sit in the dark and cry

FINCH KELLY: But if you need a distraction, I can bike over. No time flat.

I wonder if I'm being too forward. Inappropriate, even. I mean, what am I doing, insinuating that he's shut up in his room, weeping? That was rude, wasn't it? Oh, God. I tap the timestamp of my message. Fear lurches through my gut: It has been *two full minutes* since I got a reply from Jonah. Oh, no. No, no, no. Is he upset? Did I offend him? I'm going to throw my phone into Puget Sound. I'm going to—

JONAH CABRERA: thanks finch but i think i'd be pretty useless for debate prep right now lol

No! That's not what I meant! Not at all! Does he really think I'd crack the whip at a time like this? Force him to pile stress on top of stress? I was trying to make him smile, not stress him out. My thumbs fly across the screen.

FINCH KELLY: No, no, no, sorry, that's not what I meant at all

FINCH KELLY: It's just that I'm sitting here in my room

eating peanut butter M&Ms and watching Youtube and I thought, well, if you wanted a friend, I am available to be a friend

A moment ticks by. I hope I haven't hurt his feelings.

And then, mercifully . . .

JONAH CABRERA: peanut butter m&ms you say?

The knot of fear coiled up in my chest shakes loose.

FINCH KELLY: I'll be over in fifteen.

JONAH CABRERA: Can't wait:)

I did it. I made Jonah smile.

It's a quick bike ride over to Jonah's, where I'm greeted by a warm smile, a barking dog, and a gorgeous smell wafting from the kitchen. Jonah plays a kind of Tetris to hang my coat in a closet already stuffed to the gunwales. By the time he's figured it out, I've unloaded half the bounty from my backpack: the much-anticipated peanut butter M&M's; the aforementioned pint of Rocky Road, and a bottle of lemonade, just so we won't get scurvy eating all these snacks. Jonah peers into my backpack—in search, I assume, of more junk food—and looks up, a little startled.

"Is that a book?" he says. "Did you bring a *book* into my house? When I explicitly told you this would be a zero-work night?"

"Oh, no, no, no. That's not prep. Or work." I reach for the book, fish it out, put it in his hands. "This is a 'sorry Bailey broke your heart' present."

He laughs, but it's a softer, sadder sound than his usual doubling-up.

"*Capital in the Twenty-first Century*," he reads aloud, running a hand across the cover. "Finch, this thing is a brick. It's literally . . ." He flicks it open, fans through the pages, arrives at the final number: ". . . 730 pages long."

"I know. But that's 365 times two. If you read two pages a day, you'll be done in a year. It's perfect."

He looks at me, baffled. "Perfect how?"

"Well, I was doing some research," I begin, "and, apparently, if you're trying to get over a breakup, it usually takes about half the time you were together."

"I've heard that, yeah," he says, one corner of his mouth ticking up. "But keep talking. I wanna see where you're going with this."

"Well, you and Bailey were together for two years," I say. "So, like I said before: Read two pages of this book every day. A year from now, you'll be over Bailey, *and* you'll be an expert on inequality."

He's very quiet as I talk, and when I finish, he's even quieter, looking at me with an expression I can't quite read. I worry for a second that I've stepped in it—that this gift is bananas, insane, the worst possible thing I could have offered him. I mean, for Christ's sake, Finch: You comfort people with chocolate, ice cream, cheesy movies. You do not heal hearts with Thomas Piketty.

But then, before I even know it's happening, he's wrapping his arms around me, pulling me in, close. I don't quite hug him back, I'm so shocked. I simply stand, and let myself be held, my arms at my sides, the thick copy of *Capital* in his hands pressing into my back.

"I love it," he says, quietly, right into my ear. "Thank you. So, so much."

I'm still reeling when he steps back. "Go on and wash your hands," he says. "We're having dinner in a minute."

I hadn't realized our evening would include dinner with the Cabreras. I'd assumed we'd be up in his room, gorging ourselves on junk food, maybe burning Bailey in effigy. I'm friendly with Jonah's family—and with his mom's cooking—but I've never claimed a seat at their table. Still, when I step into the kitchen, his mom lights up at the sight of me, like I'm part of the family.

"Finch! So good to see you again." She flaps her arms, and waves me close to where she stands, stirring a tall pot of peppery stew. "You want a hug?"

As a matter of fact, I do. I sink into the soft warmth of her gingham apron and sigh. She lifts a hand, mid-hug, and signals to Jonah's dad across the kitchen.

"Finch is here," she says. "Come, say hi."

He looks up, over his shoulder, and waves at me with a can opener. "Hello, hello, hello," he says. "Jonah said you were coming by to cheer him up."

I look at my slippers, shy, suddenly, as Jonah's mom returns to her soup. "That's the plan, anyway," I say. "Cheer him up with copious amounts of junk food."

"Well, let's have some real food first," says his mom, sliding on a pair of oven mitts, checked pink like her apron.

Renata, the littler of the little sisters, is laying out mismatched placemats, and Maria—the elder—is rolling a scratched-up swivel chair into the kitchen from Mr. Cabrera's office. How all seven of us will fit around this table is a mystery to me. It seems like a stretch to seat six here, let alone seven.

The answer, I'm surprised to learn, is that we're seated almost shoulder to shoulder. "You say grace at home, Finch?" Jonah's mom asks me, as the kids scurry into the kitchen, taking their seats. "You could say grace tonight."

"Oh, no, thank you." I shake my head; I wouldn't even know how. "We don't pray together all that often."

"That's okay," she says, and smiles brightly. "Jonah's turn, then."

"I'm not really in a grace mood," Jonah says glumly, elbow on the table, chin in his hand. "Maybe Benjie can."

"Hay nako," says Mr. Cabrera—and I don't know what he's saying, but I figure he must be scolding Jonah. "So you had a bad day. Even more reason to say grace."

And so, all around the table, the Cabreras cross themselves, close their eyes, and bow their heads. I'm just about to do the same when I feel a tiny hand brushing mine. Renata, on my left, has claimed my pinky finger.

I look to my right: There it is, Jonah's palm, laying open on the table like an invitation. I slip my fingers through his. When he begins to pray, I can hear the smile in his voice.

"Jesucristo," he begins, "thank you so much for the gift of this day, and for the wonderful food Nanay made for us."

I'm just thinking how calm he looks, how serene in prayer,

when I realize that I'm not supposed to be looking at all. We are, for Christ's sake, *praying*; my eyes really should be closed. As fast as I can, I screw them shut. And then, along with Jonah's prayer, I offer up a tiny, silent one of my own: that nobody noticed me, just now, staring at him.

"Thank you for the gift of family, and the gift of friends . . ." He pauses here. His fingers locked in mine, I feel a little squeeze. I'm his friend; I'm a gift. "Sa pangalan ni Jesucristo na aming tagapagligtas at manunubos na kasama mong naghahari sa iyong kaharian at ang Espiritu Santo, Diyos na walang hanggan. Amen."

The stew that Maria ladles out smells gorgeous, intoxicating. On my first bite, I taste something that might be peanut butter, and then a chunk of spicy meat, slippery with cartilage. Next to me, Renata's having the time of her life, blowing bubbles into her broth. On the other hand—literally—Jonah is savoring every spoonful.

"I made Jonah's favorite for dinner," his mom explains, pouring me a second helping. "He had a bad day, thanks to that rotten boy."

"'*Nay*," Jonah moans. "Can we not talk about Bailey? Please?"

"Fine," she says, and lifts her hands in surrender. "We can stop talking about rotten boys and talk about someone who deserves my anak."

"That boy from Riverdale," says Mr. Cabrera, quite seriously. "What's his name? The one you like so much?"

"'*Tay!*" Jonah cries out—mortified, clearly—but Maria,

across the table, is already snickering. "Cole Sprouse," she says. "Jonah's in *love* with Jughead."

"*Jughead?*" Jonah's dad throws his head back, crowing. "That string bean?"

"He's a good actor!" Jonah insists.

"I've heard that one before," says Maria—a *great* dig at Bailey, though I do Jonah the favor of not erupting into laughter like his parents do.

"Enough good actors," says Jonah's dad, with a dismissive flick of the wrist. "You need to find a good *man*."

I'd known, of course, that Jonah's parents were all right with him being gay. But I hadn't grasped until now that their support for Jonah wasn't the grudging kind you see sometimes in religious families. They're not tearing into Jonah with the fervor of bigots who don't want their son to bring home a boyfriend. They're ribbing him with the sympathetic sarcasm of parents who believe their son deserves a *better* boyfriend.

"Okay, but like, admit it," Maria says, laughing, "you've got to be a *little* relieved that this is finally over."

"*Relieved* isn't the word I'd use." Jonah spins his spoon, slow, in his half-empty bowl. "I mean, I mostly feel like he just yanked my heart out of my chest and stomped on it."

"We should go to Bailey's play tonight," says Mrs. Cabrera, conspiratorial. "Throw rotten tomatoes."

"'Nay!" Jonah crows. "No!"

She absolutely does not heed his refusal. She balls up a cloth napkin and tosses it overhand, across the table. It hits Mr. Cabrera square in the forehead, and he mimes shock only for a moment before crumpling up a napkin of his own and volleying it right back. Renata and Benjie, of course, get in on the fun, right away, hollering "rotten tomato!" and aiming at one another in rough, high arcs. Maria cringes, but I can tell from the small smile she shoots to Jonah that she's loving this.

"Sorry," Jonah says to me, ducking a cloth tomato. "My family's full of dorks."

"No, no." If I shook my head any harder, it would fall off. "I love your family. I wish I were an honorary Cabrera."

I can't even remember the last time I sat down for a meal with Roo and Mom and Dad. Oh, no, wait: I *can* remember. It was the day after Mom lost her job, when she told me I wouldn't be having surgery this summer. *That* was the occasion that brought the four of us to the dinner table. Yikes.

"Leonardo DiCaprio!" Mr. Cabrera calls out, aiming a finger across the table. "How about him?"

Jonah winces. "Ew, 'Tay, he's so *old* now."

Maria chimes in: "I mean, *Titanic*-era Leo? Definitely. Middle-aged Leo who exclusively dates Scandinavian supermodels? No way."

"What about Eddie Gutierrez?" Jonah's mom brings her palm down on the table, insistent. "*That* is a handsome man."

Jonah laughs. "Isn't he, like, eighty years old, 'Nay?"

"He has sons," she says, sipping her soda. "*Handsome* sons."

I notice too late that the seat to my left is empty. When I turn to look, Renata's on her hands and knees, tugging a photo album loose from a cluttered sideboard. Jonah's eyes follow mine, going wide when he sees her.

"Renata, no," he begs. "You can't."

"Oh, yes, she can." Maria leaps up, grinning, and hurries over to help Renata. "Who wants to see all of Jonah's baby pictures?"

I want to say *yes, please, absolutely*, but I can feel the sheer mortification radiating from Jonah's every pore.

"I don't know, guys," I say, with great reluctance. "I think Jonah would be too embarrassed."

All around the table: laughter. Even from Jonah himself. His mom lifts her spoon, aims it at me.

"You," she says, "are a *good* friend."

"You really are," says Maria, propping the photo album open on the table. "But we're gonna embarrass Jonah regardless."

Jonah, I'm pleased to learn, was an extraordinarily chubby baby. In every single one of these photos, his legs and arms are little rolls of crescent dough. The cheeks framing his wide, toothless smiles look as soft and squishy as marshmallows— nothing at all like the high cheekbones on the lanky boy sitting next to me. I don't even attempt to keep the grin off my face as I flip through page after page of Jonah's babyhood. There are several solemn portraits with Santa Claus, a baptism in a filmy white gown, and a few faded snapshots from a Sears photo gallery, his parents decked out in clothes that scream *the '90s may be over, but we're not over the '90s.*

Maria arrives a few pages in, when Jonah's a toddler. There is a truly choice triptych here, depicting Jonah's initiation into big brotherhood. In the first photo, he stands over Maria's crib in the hospital, absolutely glowering. In the second, his mouth is open, his eyes are shut, and he appears to be screaming at the top of his tiny little lungs. In the last photo, Jonah's being carried away—against his will, by the look of his blurry, flailing limbs—in the disembodied arms of a medical professional.

Maria laughs. "Thanks for the warm welcome," she says.

"I was out of line." Jonah slings an arm around his sister. "I didn't know how cool you'd be."

He smiles at her; she smiles back. And then, gently, she elbows him in the ribs.

I keep flipping through the pages. Jonah ties his shoes. Jonah rides a bike. Jonah plays dress-up in a frilly pink gown, glitter smeared all over his face. I look to him to get his reaction; he moans into his hands.

"So," I ask him, "when did you know you were gay?"

"Not early enough, apparently."

"All right, all right," Mrs. Cabrera jumps in, pulling the album away. "I think we've embarrassed Jonah enough for one day."

"Next time you come over, Finch, you'll have to bring *your* photo album," says Mr. Cabrera. "I mean, it's only fair."

"I don't know." I shake my head. "My baby photos are way more embarrassing than Jonah's."

"Really?" says Mrs. Cabrera. "Tell us more."

"Just . . . lots of pictures of me in dresses."

The joke goes over their heads. But when I tilt to Jonah, he's smothering another round of giggles behind his palm. And I like it, how much he's laughing. I don't know if the laughter's just a cover for sadness—I don't think so; it sounds real—but it's nice, all the same, hearing it.

Jonah, owing to his broken heart, is excused from helping with the dishes. So after the stew, and after the fruit salad, we make our way up the stairs to his room.

The Cabreras are a big family, and this isn't an especially big house. Siblings share bedrooms here. Maria and Renata have one room to themselves, and Jonah shares another with Benjie. It's a fascinating split down the middle: One side of the room is strewn with action figures and Happy Meal toys, and the other clearly belongs to a teenager—one with a lot of trophies, and a lot of empty space on the wall where I'll bet Bailey's headshots used to hang. I glance at the trash can on Jonah's side of the room: yep, brimming.

It's while my eyes are thus occupied that I step on a tiny brick of plastic and let out a howl that would shatter the space-time continuum.

"Oh, shit," says Jonah, eyes going wide. "Are you okay?"

"LEGO," I grumble, slumping onto Jonah's bed, "is *such* a safety hazard." I roll my sock down over my left ankle to check the damage. What the hell? I'm *bleeding*. Not badly, but still, Jesus. "Bad for the environment, too. Are you really okay rooming with this much plastic?"

"Oh, those LEGOs are made of corn." Jonah takes a step into the tiny en suite bathroom and emerges with a first-aid kit the size of a shoebox. "They're not compostable, mind you, but if we're choosing between corn ethanol and petro, it's a no-brainer."

He kneels before me and reaches for my foot. I spring back, fast, before he can touch me.

"What are you doing?"

"I've got three little siblings." He opens the kit, pulls out cotton balls, a bottle of disinfectant, a thin accordion of Band-Aids. "I'm used to patching up scrapes."

I don't like to be babied. I truly do not. I've got half a mind to snatch the Band-Aids out of his hands, tell him, *I can put on my own Band-Aid, thank you very much.* But he's already going to work, pressing a cotton ball to my heel, right in the place where the brick cut deepest. I feel a sting—the disinfectant, I guess—and then, something else, some kind of full-body tingle that's harder to identify.

Oh, no, is this a sex thing? Is *this* why people have foot fetishes? I was already pink in the face, but now, I'm sure, I'm crimson. You can't hide *anything* when you're a redhead.

The best course of action—really, the only one—is to bend away from him, and bury my face in a pillow. This way, he can't see me, and I can't see him. Also, if I'm still red in the face when I emerge, I can attribute it to temporary suffocation. Brilliant!

Jonah, laughing under his breath, asks, "What are you doing, dude?"

"It *stings*," I whine into the pillow.

"You're a bigger baby than Benjie." He presses the Band-Aid to my skin, and then I feel his hands leave. "There you go," he says. "Good as new."

He leaps onto his twin-size bed as I lift my head, then roll my sock up and over my ankle. He pulls out his laptop. The light from the screen washes blue all over his face. I assume I'm still red.

"I was thinking we could watch a comfort movie to go with all the comfort food you brought me." He pauses, smiling. "Do you want to come up here? Pick something out?"

He wants me to *come up here*. As in: Sit on his mattress. Next to him. This is, of course, something we've done—oh, I don't know—a million times? In a million hotel rooms, relaxing after a million long days of debating, scrolling through a million mediocre late-night channels. So why, now, am I so nervous?

"You don't need me to help," I mumble, copping out. "You've got better taste in movies than I do."

"Well, that's a given." He pats the mattress. "Still, though— come on, get in here."

I crawl on my knees and hands to the empty place next to him, and I settle in. What I don't do is touch him. Not with my hands or my elbows or any part of my body. I find the pillow in which I buried my face and I grip it tight—make a barrier of it, even: This is where he ends; this is where I begin. When I feel the first pinpricks of panic, I try, with everything I've got, to push it back. I barely register Jonah navigating through Netflix, scrolling past the reams of little posters.

"Is this angle okay?" he asks. "Can you see the screen?"

"Yeah." I've been reduced to monosyllables. "Sure."

This, in my frenzied, anxious state, is the best guess I've

got: We are alone. In his room. On his bed. His family's home—I can hear them all bustling around downstairs, cleaning up in the kitchen—but, still. He's a boy. A boy who *likes* boys. And I—by the more inclusive definitions, anyway—am a boy. A theoretically likeable boy. This fact has never felt as relevant as it does now, in this brave new post-Bailey world.

But it's not like *I* like boys—no matter what Lucy says or Bailey venomously spits. So why am I on the verge of something that feels like a panic attack? Why are my nails digging craters into Jonah's poor pillow?

"Finch?" he says. "Are you okay?"

"Yeah. Totally. Yeah." I'm sure I sound very convincing, gasping for breath after each *yeah.* "It's just . . . I just . . ."

"Deep breaths." He reaches out, places a hand on my shoulder. "One, two, three . . ."

I repeat the numbers, and breathe along with him. I do not tell him that the hand on my shoulder is only making it worse. I already had to contend with the fact of lying next to him, on his bed, and now he's touching me. What is *happening* here? Does he want to . . . *do* something? With *me*? Or is it the opposite—that the very idea of doing something with me would be a joke to him? Maybe it's neither. Maybe I'm being *incredibly* homophobic by interpreting his good-faith effort to calm me down as a sexual advance.

"Come on, Finch," he says, before I can spiral any further. "What's going on? Tell me what's happening."

"I just . . . I . . ." What should I say? In search of something, anything, that sounds like a plausible explanation for this sudden fit of mine, I land, finally, on: "I am *really* mad at Bailey."

"You and me both, kid."

"The way he treated you this morning . . . the way he's *been* treating you . . ."

"Hey, hey. You don't need to bash my ex. My fam's got that covered."

This makes me laugh. I'm grateful for it. I can feel my psychological temperature falling a few notches. He bought my excuse. He's moving away from me. I am, at last, off the ledge. I think so, anyway. I hope so.

"I don't know why they got so heated just now," Jonah says, returning to Netflix, scrolling. "They always really liked Bailey. I mean, I thought they did, anyway."

"My guess," I begin, slowly—forming sentences is always harder after an anxiety attack, even an aborted one, "is that they like you much more than they like Bailey. And they want what's best for you. And he was not that."

"Bailey used to come over all the time," Jonah says, like he didn't even hear me. "He'd help me babysit. He was so good with Renata and Benjie. He'd read aloud to them, do all these little voices for the different characters. They loved it." He laughs glumly. "They were four chapters into *The Lion, The Witch, and The Wardrobe.* Guess we'll have to abandon it now."

"Well, maybe you could do the voices," I suggest.

"I guess so." Jonah shrugs. "But I can't voice the White Witch like Bailey does."

"Your parents," I start, "they're really . . . I don't know, tolerant. Especially with your dad, being a pastor and all."

"Well, those things aren't mutually exclusive," Jonah says, a frown lighting on his face. "Our congregation actually has a lot of gay people. We've had weddings for some couples, baptisms for a few families . . ."

Oh, God. I've offended him. "I'm sorry," I spit out. "I just thought . . . you know, since so many Christians are so . . ." I stop, search for the right word. I don't find it. And so, helplessly, I shrug. "You know what I mean."

"I do," he says. "But my dad's never been like that." He stops, and smiles to himself. "There's a story behind it, actually. It's kind of sad."

"A story?" I pull the pillow closer to my chest. "I'm listening."

"Well, growing up, my dad had this brother, Ferdinand," Jonah begins. "They called him Ferdy for short. My uncle. He and my dad, they were really close, growing up together in Lucena. They had a big family too. I mean, I have a zillion aunts, but he and Ferdy were the only brothers."

"Like you and Benjie," I say.

He grins. "Exactly like that." And then that grin disappears: "So, um . . . when my dad was in college, and Ferdy was in his last year of junior high school—so, like, our tenth grade—Ferdy called him up one day. Crying. Asking if my dad could pick him up and take him to a doctor in another town to, uh . . . to go get tested."

"Jesus," I whisper. "It wasn't . . . ?"

"It was." Jonah nods. "Yeah. Apparently, Ferdy'd been going to these bars in Malate, in Old Manila—like, he'd tell his parents, my grandparents, that he was on the school's basketball team, and he was going out of town for tournaments.

But he was actually driving the three hours to Manila, with friends, and, like . . . Anyway. He'd started noticing these cuts. I forget what they're called. It's, like . . . I want to say . . . Sarkozy's . . . glaucoma?"

"That sounds right," I tell him. I spent a lot of time reading *And the Band Played On* a couple of seasons back, when we debated about HIV at this big tournament up in Vancouver. "Something like that."

"And it was the '90s, so treatment was still pretty, uh . . . well, the disease was still a death sentence, at that point. Even in the United States. And the medical system in the Philippines was—I mean, still is, in some places—pretty underfunded. And so . . . he died. Ferdy died."

"Oh, Jonah." I know I'm risking another bout of panic here, but I have to be—no, *need* to be—closer to him. My hand on his shoulder is tentative at first, but when he leans into the touch, I squeeze. "I'm so, so sorry."

His eyes begin to well with tears. I feel ashamed that my own are so dry.

"And my grandparents," he says, "when they found out Ferdy was sick—I mean, when they found out *what* he was sick *with*—they put him out on the street. Told him he was evil. He deserved it. God was punishing him. And my dad, he knew it wasn't true. He didn't want his brother to die."

"Jesus, Jonah. I had no idea."

"So my dad, he took care of him." Jonah's voice is shaking. "For those couple months before he died, my dad looked after Ferdy, and made him comfortable. And my grandparents didn't visit. Not once. Not even to say goodbye." He stops. He turns to face me. "But you know who did show up?"

"Who?"

"Like, every single one of Ferdy's friends." And even though he's crying now, Jonah's face is cracking into a wide, giddy smile. "They'd come over on the weekends. Bring meals. Read to him. Turn the pillows. And my dad, when he tells this story, he always says Ferdy had been a part of something really special. He'd been, like, really, deeply loved."

"You're loved, too," I tell him. "You know that, right? Your parents—they love you so, so much. I wish that my own . . ." How do I say this? How, without sounding like an ingrate? "I mean, they accept it. Me, being trans. But I don't know if they really *love* it. And your parents—it's so obvious, Jonah— they *love* this part of you. Since you were that little kid, dressing up like a princess, they've loved it."

I am aiming here for comfort, for reassurance. So why is Jonah's face caving in on itself? Why is he crying *harder*?

"They *do*," he says. "They *love* me. You know how rare that is?"

I remember the early talks with my own parents. The fear on my dad's face when I cut my red hair down to the scalp in the bathroom sink. The disappointment on my mom's when I told her that, no, I didn't think I'd ever want to carry a baby.

"I know," I tell him. "I know exactly how rare."

"My parents would come to Pride with me and Bailey. March in the parade right next to us. They were so proud of me for being in love. For being open about it. For doing all these things that Ferdy never got to do. And now . . . now, it's over. Like, I just threw it all away."

It takes me a moment to understand what, exactly, he's saying here. "Wait," I begin, slowly. "You think that they're . . . what, disappointed in you? Because you broke up with your boyfriend?"

He looks to me. His eyes are full of tears, and when he nods, they spill over, fall in beads onto his cheeks. I hook the sleeve of my sweater over the heel of my hand. I lift it up, to his face.

"They are *not* disappointed," I tell him, brushing my sleeve across his skin. "They're so proud of you, Jonah. Anyone could see that."

"Yeah, but here I am, like . . ." He waves his hands: his cheeks, my sleeves. "Having an emotional breakdown, when it's like—they worked so hard to make sure I could be with Bailey, and like, bring him to church, even, without anyone saying anything, and, like . . . you know how many kids would kill for that? For a family like that? And I'm sitting here, and I'm not even happy . . ."

"Well, Jonah, people don't . . . I mean, they don't come out of the closet to be happy. They do it to be honest."

Jonah rests his head on my shoulder. He nods against my collarbone. I have to lift my chin, rest it on the crown of his head. It's a funny feeling; I'm not used to being taller than him.

"I wasn't always honest," he says; the faintest hint of a sniffle. "Like, if I was having problems with Bailey, I'd keep it to myself, you know? I wanted my parents to think I was happy.

And that, like, the support they were giving me, it was all worth it."

"But, Jonah, you don't *have* to be happy all the time. You don't. You really, truly don't." I can hear my own voice climbing, insistent. "You're allowed to fight with your boyfriend, and break up with him, and just . . . be messy. Like anybody else."

Jonah leans away from me, laughing through his tears. "Since when are *you* the one who calms *me* down?"

"Since you're the one who got brutally dumped twelve hours ago, buddy."

"Buddy?"

"Or, I don't know." I look down, away from him, and pick at a loose thread on his yellow bedspread. "Partner."

"Pardner," he says, with a Texan twang.

And for that, broken heart or no, he gets a soft pillow to the side of the head.

At the end of the night, Jonah pulls my raincoat from the closet. I look out the window and wonder: Is it going to rain again? Should I leave my bike here, come back for it? Take the bus instead?

"Well," says Jonah, "thanks for coming over, cheering me up."

"Oh, of course. Nothing like a pillow fight to lift a person's spirits."

He claps me on the back. Or, at least, he means to. But as I'm turning to him, his hand falls, and he brushes me ever so slightly against the side of my body. I'm not sure he meant to do it; I know I wasn't expecting it. And I definitely wasn't expecting my skin to burn where he touched me, like he seared somehow through my coat, my sweater, the rumpled button-down beneath it.

He's pulling away already, with a look on his face like he's done something wrong. I want so badly to tell him that he hasn't. But his mouth is already saying sorry, and I'm already stumbling over my own reply—"It's fine, it's fine"—and clipping my bike helmet beneath my chin. I fuck up; I pinch the skin. "Ow," I say, out loud, and before either of us can say anything else, I'm stepping out into the cool, wet night. There's my bike, still propped against his porch, not locked down. With a final wave, I'm gone.

It isn't 'til the first stoplight, when I'm absolutely certain he can't see me, that I let go of the handlebars and press my fingers into my side. The soft space just below the bracket of my ribs, the place where he touched me—it's still warm.

The light turns green. And even though the intersection is clear, I don't move forward. I leave my hand where it is. I feel the pulse glowing beneath my skin.

chapter ten

I hear the fight on my way up the walk, louder and louder with each step. It sounds worse than usual, pouring through the thin walls. This isn't just Mom and Dad's familiar rumble; Roo's in the mix, too, roaring like a feral animal. I'm tempted on the front steps to click my heels together and wish myself back to Jonah's house. There was all the love in the world in that dining room. There's none here. Why? What's wrong with us?

I tiptoe down the hall, following the noise to Roo's bedroom. They're standing in an uneven triangle in the small space. It takes me a minute to break their voices down, really hear the words buried in each shout, before I understand: They seem to be arguing about . . . video games?

"Are you out of your minds?" This is Roo, at the top of her lungs, which are not large. "You couldn't even get five bucks for this at GameStop!"

"Five bucks? Really?" Mom, arms across her chest, is well on her way to fury. "For an Xbox 360 that cost us hundreds of dollars?"

"Yeah, when you got it used, like, a decade ago," Roo

fires back. "You must be a fucking idiot if you think anyone's gonna—"

Dad comes in, thunderous: "Did you just call your mother—"

And I know Dad would never get physical, but he is so big, and Roo is so small, and she's backed into a corner with her body as her only barricade—I have to do something.

I know I shouldn't. If I were smart, I'd retreat to my room, close the door, leave them all to carry on. But if there's a chance, even a small one, that I could make peace? Get the screaming to stop—or, at least, pull the anger away from Roo? I'll take that chance.

I step forward. "What's going on?"

They swivel to face me, all with veins popping, faces glowing, chests rising and falling fast.

"Finch," Mom says, her voice hoarse, her calm so unconvincing I wonder why she's even bothering. "We're having a garage sale, and we're just deciding—"

Roo breaks in: "They're trying to take all my stuff!"

It's only then that I notice what, exactly, Roo's guarding, with her arms stretched out wide: her old cathode-ray television, and the console as old as she is, and the collection of games she's packed into cases held together with dense geological layers of masking tape.

"Even though this stuff is so ancient," she goes on, "that it's literally worthless!"

"Ruby, unemployment is going to pay me a *fraction* of what I used to make," Mom says—no, shouts. "And your father *still* hasn't found work . . ."

"Oh, right, because this is all my fault," Dad booms. "Doesn't matter I've been pounding the fucking pavement, doesn't matter I haven't had a drink in eight goddamn months . . ."

"I could use this stuff to *make* money," Roo insists. "There's people who make millions of dollars streaming video games. If you guys got me a half-decent webcam . . ."

"Now she's asking for more stuff." Mom throws her hands skyward. "Unbelievable."

"I've actually read a few articles about this"—I'm aiming for calm, rational—"and Roo isn't wrong. A lot of video-game players make money online, and Roo's so passionate, she could easily build a following."

"What, she's gonna pay the mortgage playing video games?" Dad says. "That's where your tuition payments are gonna come from? Your little sister playing video games on the fucking internet?"

"Oh, no, not at all." I put my hands up, and I take a very deliberate step back, through the door. "You know I'm planning to pay for college with scholarships and grants, and . . . I mean, especially if Jonah and I do well at Nationals, I'm sure that I can scrounge up—"

"Oh. Finch. That reminds me." Mom turns to me, a pained look on her face. "I'm so sorry, honey—I know how much you were looking forward to your debate tournament—but we had to refund your plane ticket to D.C."

What? "What?"

"Three hundred and fifty dollars." Dad pronounces every

syllable. "We need that money right now, Finch. We need it bad."

"But . . . but I have to go to Nationals." That panic I felt before, on Jonah's bed: It's back. My vision is going blurry, my pulse sprinting. "This is my last chance to impress George-town, and . . ."

"You might just have to settle for in-state, sweetie," Mom says—and, weirdly, it's the *sweetie* that twists the knife, kills whatever little shreds of hope I had. I don't know how I manage the three steps across the room to Roo's bed. I only know that if I don't lie down, I'll faint, and gravity will force the issue.

"Why didn't you ask me?" I know my parents aren't villains; we're poor. But still: *Why?* "You know how much this meant to me."

"It's just one tournament, kid," Dad says, as I stumble. "What, you don't have enough gold medals already?"

My shoulders are falling heavily to Roo's mattress, my head dizzily to her pillow. She is standing just steps away, saying, quietly, "Finch, I'm sorry."

Her games, my debating: These are the things we've used to escape our gloomy present, to imagine something better.

And now, they're for sale.

"I'm flying to D.C. next weekend," I say, half smothered by the pillow, like saying it will make it real. It's all I've got left: delusion. "*And* I'm going to college in D.C."

"With what money, Finch?" Mom sounds exhausted, more depleted than angry. "We don't have fifty thousand dollars for

D.C. tuition. Hell, we can't even pay for your plane ticket."

I can't look at her, at any of them, in the odd, queasy silence that settles in the room. I can only gaze, eyes unfo-
cused, at the stain on Roo's carpet. It is made of Mountain
Dew and shaped like a kidney. Someone should really clean
that up, I think, and then I think how silly it is, how stupid, to
be staring at a stain on a carpet at the end of the world.

Eventually, I go to my own room, close the door behind me
and lock it. Nobody bothers me as I plant my face into my
pillow and scream, scream, scream 'til my throat is hoarse.

By the time I lift my head, the sky outside has blackened,
swallowing up the shapes of trees and roofs. I must have fallen
asleep. I reach for my laptop to check the time. Logging in
takes an eternity, blue circle spinning endlessly. When the
clock appears, finally, and tells me it's half past one o'clock in
the morning, I feel like I'm being mocked.

I wonder if I should climb out of bed and walk over to
Lucy's. She'd never turn me away, not even at this hour. Thing
is, though, I'm tired. Too tired for a walk in the dark. Besides, if I know anything about Lucy's sleep habits, I know
this: She's still awake right now, up late, reading fanfiction.

So I navigate to iMessage. I'm not ready for the burst of
bright white light. It springs out of the screen into the dark,
searing my eyes, as I click on Lucy's name. I can barely see
the keys to type.

FINCH KELLY: Hey so everythign is awful

FINCH KELLY: Just really really really messed up a nd bad

FINCH KELLY: Please please please message me back when yo see this

I wait. I watch the blank white space where I want the gray bubble of her response to appear. But it never comes, that bubble. Not so much as a read receipt. Why? Where is she? I was banking on her being awake right now. Should I wait until Monday for our ride to school? Can I wait, even? Closing my computer and drifting off to sleep is nowhere near an option, not now. My pulse is still thrumming, my chest still tight. If I don't speak everything I'm feeling—well, type everything, anyway—the grief will bloom up within me and vine around my lungs 'til I choke.

FINCH KELLY: Okay well I guess you're asleep in which case good job you're presently better at life than I am

FINCH KELLY: I'll just leave this all here adn you can read it when you wake up and we can talk about it at school on Monday

FINCH KELLY: Okay. So. Tonight I came home to this massive fight, Mom & Dad trying to sell all of Roo's video game things for extra cash, and when I tried to help my parents dropped the BOMB that they cancelled my flight to nationals

FINCH KELLY: And when I told them nationals was my last chance to impress Georgetown and the other schools in DC my mom was like "well maybe you can just settle for in state" lolololol

FINCH KELLY: So now I guess I am not going to DC for college or debate or anything unless someone gives me $350 for another plane ticket. Or someone else gives me a million billion dollars to pay DC tuition

I'm surprised to find my chest feeling heavy, still, even after spilling all this. What more is worrying me? Before that fight, before the refunded ticket, what was I . . .

Oh. Right.

Jonah.

FINCH KELLY: Oh and then earlier on Jonah invited me over to distract him from the breakup so I biked over and had dinner with him and his family, we looked at his baby photos, that part was nice

FINCH KELLY: But then we went up to his room and we were lying on his bed together watching a movie and this is so ridiculous, I'm sorry, but I thought he might be coming on to me? I mean he didn't do anything, we were just lying there, and I know it's bad of me and probably homophobic but I did start to freak out, that he might try something

FINCH KELLY: And then we talked

I stop here—the story of Ferdy, of Jonah's long, complex familial history, of all his shame and fear; it seems way too private to share, even with Lucy.

And so I skip to the end. The end of the night, I mean. That touch before I left.

FINCH KELLY: And then we talked about really personal things and he sort of well not sort of he really did cry in my arms on his bed and then at the end of the night he, I don't know, touched me? On the side of my body

FINCH KELLY: BEFORE YOU SAY ANYTHING obviously I

am not attracted to boys and I don't even think he likes me that way either, he's definitely just heartbroken over Bailey and maybe he needed a hug tonight, or something, I don't know

FINCH KELLY: I mean this is JONAH and it has NEVER been like this with us and nationals is right around

FINCH KELLY: Oh wait! No it isn't! I'm not even going to nationals because mom and dad refunded my ticket!

FINCH KELLY: So there you go, I'm not goign to Nationals, I'm not going to George town, or any school in DC, I'm not. getting srugery, things are WEIRD with Jonah, and on top of it all, I can't even see hte screen it's so fucking bright

FINCH KELLY: Please message me when you get this or just come over to my house and bonk me on the head with your softball bat

FINCH KELLY: I love you

I can't look at the searing white sun of the screen a second longer. I power it off, and fall back onto my mattress, letting out a long, loud sigh as my head craters the foam.

It's funny, but I *do* feel better having ranted at Lucy. Already, my anxiety is dissolving. In its place, I feel anticipation, the warm kind. Lucy will meet me on the bus to school tomorrow. She'll give me a hug. She'll tell me everything is going to be okay. She'll be lying, but it will, at least, be nice to hear.

On Monday morning, Lucy bounces onto the bus and into the seat next to me, radiant in Pantone polka dots. She looks as full as I feel empty.

"Hey, you," she says, and kisses me on the forehead. "How you doing?"

"I haven't heard from you all weekend." I blink at her, baffled. "You didn't get my messages?"

"Messages?" She shakes her head; twin pink pigtails flutter like wind socks. "I don't think so. When did you send them?"

"Friday night. Just after one o'clock?"

"Would it surprise you to hear that I was asleep?"

"There were, like, fifty of them." I nudge at her, insistent. "Check your phone."

"I mean, I *could* check my phone," she says, not making any movement in the direction of her pockets. "Or you could just tell me what ails thee."

I could, couldn't I? But how would I find that frantic midnight energy now, exhausted, on the bus to school? How would I say, out loud, the ugly things I typed about my parents? Let alone the things I wrote about Jonah, about him touching me—words that weren't ugly so much as unspeakable.

"Actually, I don't think I want to talk about it."

"Aww, come on, Finch." She puts her head on my shoulder. "You *always* want to talk about it. You're literally a competitive talker."

"Not today," I tell her, and my head falls against the cold glass of the window.

"Well, I have some good news," she says cautiously. "If I share my good news, will I make you feel better or worse?"

I look at her—the way she's hesitating, chewing her lip against the words she can't wait to spill. And I soften.

"Better," I say.

She brightens. "So, you know how I've been booking interviews for my channel, right?"

I'm not sure that I did know. She'd mentioned the one woman before, Linsay Ellfis, who'd gotten back to her. But interviews? Plural? I really had no idea she was this far along. Am I a bad friend?

"Well, last night, I finally got an email back from the person I wanted to talk to most." She's speaking fast, each word tripping over the next. "And that person is . . ."

She fans out her fingers: jazz hands, Bob Fosse style. Wait. Why do I know to call them jazz hands? Why do I even know Bob Fosse's name? I regret every moment I've ever spent in the vicinity of Bailey Lundquist.

"Alice Brady," she says. "Future congresswoman."

"Lucy!" I forget, for an instant, everything bad, everything wrong in my life. "That's incredible!" I pull her into a hug. *"You're* incredible."

She tries to shrug, but I'm holding her too close. Those shoulders aren't going anywhere. "I mean," she says, all false modesty, "it's a *start*."

"It's a huge start! You're doing an on-camera interview with a congressional candidate!"

"Well, hoping to do more than that," she says. "If it goes well, maybe she'll want me to do some freelance video work for the campaign." Her eyes are gleaming. "You know, like, a TV spot here, an online town hall there . . ."

I can't help it: My face falls. I'm happy for her—I am, I

am—but it stings, too. The same night I find out I'm not going to Nationals, Lucy gets the go-ahead to interview a congressional candidate. She might even work on this woman's campaign, for God's sake, while I . . . while I . . . what *am* I going to do after I graduate, anyway? Work retail? Scrounge up some money for surgery? Wish my parents could have afforded to send me to D.C.?

"Oh! Almost forget." She's digging into her polka-dotted backpack, pulling out a brown paper bag. "I got you something. A gift for your trip to D.C. this weekend."

Oh, wow. She wasn't kidding. She didn't see a single word of those messages I sent last night. I take the bag, her gift. I upend it: a pen falls into my hand. Just a plain white plastic cylinder. I lift my head, look at her: What is this?

"It writes in seven colors." Plainly thrilled, she picks it up. "See? Just press on these tabs: red, green, blue, pink . . ."

"Can't be without pink ink at Nationals."

"You'll never run out!" She grins, triumphant, and hands it back to me. "See? One less thing to worry about this weekend."

I can't take it, the look on her face. She thinks I'm going to put this pen in my pocket and bring it with me to Washington, D.C., and use it to make magic. The rest of the world seems pretty agnostic when it comes to Finch Kelly. Not her. Never her.

"Lucy, I . . ." My fingers close around the pen. It hurts to touch, almost. "I'm not going to Nationals this weekend."

"What are you talking about?" She sits back, confused. "Why the hell not?"

"We can't afford it." Saying this out loud isn't as awful as I thought it would be. It's worse. "My parents had to return the plane ticket."

"Oh, Finch." Her head falls on my shoulder. Her fingers stroke my hair. "Well, you'll just have to save that pen for college in D.C. in the fall. Those lectures at Georgetown, you know?"

"I'm not going to Georgetown, either." The pen falls back into the bag; the brown paper rolls back into place.

"Well, you never know," she says, and sort of pets my hair. "You might get a scholarship."

I unzip my backpack, press the paper bag into what spare space I've got. "Yeah, like I might find a unicorn grazing in my front yard."

"God, you're cranky today," she says, and starts to reach into her backpack, rummage for our breakfast. "Let me do you a solid. Get some food in you."

Let me do you a solid. Above my head, a lightbulb goes off. There may be one real solid Lucy can do for me.

"Lucy." I reach for her, squeeze her shoulder. "Lucy, Lucy, Lucy."

"Yeah?" she says, not looking at me, still searching for our food. "What's up?"

"You should talk to Alice Brady about me." My turn to talk a mile a minute, trip over my words. "Tell her that I'm looking for a job and I could be a big asset to her campaign, like, whatever she needs, whether it's writing speeches or like, helping her with debate prep, or . . ."

Lucy lifts her head, brow cocked. "You're asking me to get you a job on the campaign?"

"I mean, if you wanted to just talk to her, tell her I'm interested, give her my résumé . . ."

". . . I don't know." She gnaws on her lip. She looks away from me. "I mean, I keep inviting you to go door-knocking with me and you keep saying no."

"I'm not talking about *door-knocking*. I'm talking about helping her with speeches, and . . . and sending out press releases, and . . ."

"She's got people doing that stuff for her already," Lucy says. "She needs boots on the ground. Voices on the phone. And you don't need me to, like, refer you for that."

I can feel that dizziness again, that quickness in my blood. "So you . . . you don't want to talk to her? About me?"

"I just wouldn't want to jeopardize, like . . ." She pauses, scratches at the side of her nose. "I mean, I might get to film some videos for the campaign, yeah? But not if I'm going around with my hands out, like, 'Hey, you should hire my friend . . .'"

"But I would be good for the campaign!" I insist. "I know how to write a speech, I know how to prep her for a debate, I could—"

"Finch, I'm not going to ask her to give you a job," Lucy cuts in, voice rising. "I'm sorry. It's not going to happen."

I don't know what to say to this. I don't know if I'm even capable of saying anything to it. I only know that I can't look at Lucy, can't sit next to her even a second longer. And so I rise, clumsily, and shift my standing body past her seated one.

"Finch! Come on. Don't be so pissy. Sit down. Talk to me, at least? Eat your breakfast?"

I do not turn around. I move out into the aisle, and I stand there, shaky, one hand on the high rail against the motion of the bus.

"You know," she says, "you can be a real fucking baby sometimes."

"I'm not being a baby!" I turn, face her, nearly fall as the bus lurches forward. "You're joining this campaign and you're not bringing me with you!"

"Yeah! Because you didn't give a shit about this campaign 'til five minutes ago!"

She isn't wrong. I didn't care—and definitely didn't have time to knock on doors—because I was so focused on Nationals, on D.C., on Georgetown. But all of that is gone now, and this—can't she see?—is my last chance to break into politics, to do something, to *be* someone.

There's that feeling again, that tight heat behind my eyes. I screw them shut; deep breaths, Finch. There's got to be another way. There has to be. But what is it? And how do I find it?

"Finch! Just the man I've been looking for!"

Adwoa is downright jolly when I walk into debate club after school. It's the very opposite of my dark mood, still lingering after this morning's bus ride. She leaps merrily down from her perch at the desk, braids swinging, as soon as she sees me. Me, I freeze. It's a bad time to freeze, too, even by my own exceptionally awkward standards. I'm standing in the only en-

trance to the classroom. A small line's forming. I don't thaw
'til Adwoa's hand lands on my shoulder, a touch that makes
me flinch, hard.

"Let's take a walk." Her voice softens like she's soothing a
spooked horse. No more exclamation points. "Okay?"

I manage, just barely, to nod. "Okay." Adwoa turns, waving
to get Jonah's attention.

"We might be a while," she says. "You good to run the
meeting with Jasmyne?"

"Sure. Of course." Jonah gives me a glance. A look that
says, *Is everything all right?*

I shake my head at him. I don't know what Adwoa wants
from me right now, but if this unfolds like any of the other
dozen difficult conversations I've had in the past week, it's
bound to be a nightmare.

"Okay!" Jasmyne, behind a worried Jonah, claps her hands.
"Today, we're going to practice delivering a dynamite P.O.I.
Let's start with . . . okay, Ava? And Jesse? You two want to . . ."

As Adwoa leads me out of the classroom, down the hallway, Jasmyne's voice fades away. All I hear for a while are
footfalls as she steers us forward.

"I thought we'd grab some hot chocolate from the cafeteria,"
she says, still in that spooked-horse voice. "Sit and talk, yeah?"

I nod. I would wonder, normally, what this was about, but
I'm so worn down these days. Nothing would surprise me. She
could sit me down in the cafeteria and say, "Finch, I've dis-
covered evidence linking you to the death of Princess Diana,"
and what could I do but roll with it? I have *no way* of proving
my whereabouts on the night of August 31, 1997.

Besides that I wasn't born yet.

Adwoa buys two hot chocolates: one for me, with whip, and one for herself, without. We sip them in the center of the room, all but empty in these after-school hours. A few stragglers are sitting, studying, waiting for parents or for volleyball practice, but we've got a fairly wide berth.

"So," she says, and takes a sip, "I got your messages."

"You . . . you got my . . ." Oh, no. Oh, no, no, *no*.

"Yes." She puts me out of my stammering misery. "I have to assume I wasn't the intended recipient, but . . ."

But she received them. All two dozen or however many puddles of digital word-puke. The fight with my parents, and, oh, Christ, most mortifying of all, the blow-by-blow of my evening at Jonah's.

"I am so, so sorry," I leap in, before she can say another word. "It was the middle of the night, and the screen was so bright I couldn't see, and I was trying to message someone else, and if I clicked on your name, it was definitely an accident, and, just, *please* don't tell Jonah that I . . ."

"Hey. No." She lifts a hand. "I'm glad I got those messages. I'll keep everything between the two of us." I take this as a pledge that she'll refrain from telling Jonah about my . . . crush? Is it a crush? "I wish you'd talked to me sooner," she goes on. "You should never be embarrassed to ask for help."

I'm embarrassed to wake up in the morning most days. I'm definitely embarrassed that Adwoa was the unintended recipient of a middle-of-the-night diatribe that ended with me typing "I love you." This is calling your teacher "Mom" times a hundred, supercharged, on anabolic steroids.

"I just feel bad," I say, "because my parents never talked to me about refunding that ticket, and now Nationals is ruined, and—"

"Stop. Please. You *have* to stop."

Up 'til now, Adwoa's been operating in the gentle mode of a guidance counselor. Now, though, there's a hard edge to her voice, the one I hear whenever she goes on a tear about corporate tax evasion or ICE or the cancellation of her favorite show on Netflix after only one season.

"You are a brilliant kid," she says, in this voice, the *no human is illegal* voice, the #RenewTheGetDown voice. "But as long as I've known you, you've been swimming upstream, and every time the currents get stronger, you blame yourself. And you can't make it in this life on willpower alone, Finch. You've got people around you who love you, who want good things for you. Try asking one of them for help sometime." She leans back, spreads out her palms. "Go on. Ask me for help."

Confused, I ask, "What kind of help?"

"The kind you need," she says. "And right now, that's a new plane ticket. Isn't that right?"

Before I can answer, she reaches into her pocket: a white envelope. She places it on the table, daring me, without words, to open it.

So I do.

AMERICAN AIRLINES, I read. *Thank you for your reservation, Ms. Douna.* And then *Passenger Name,* and then, in confident bold: *Mr. Finch Kelly.*

A near-minute passes in silence, stunned, before Adwoa says, "You're welcome."

"Adwoa, I can't accept this." I press the paper back into its envelope. "This is so much money. And you . . ." You have debt from college, I think, but don't say. And even more debt from law school. And you're interviewing for the job of your dreams, aren't you? The one that will take you to the middle of nowhere, to earn nothing.

"I know what you're thinking," she says. "I didn't take that job in Alabama." She sighs; I hear regret in every syllable. "I'm staying here. Well, near here, anyway. Redmond. Going in-house at Microsoft. I accepted the job last week."

I stare at her, wide-eyed, horrified. "But, Adwoa," I begin, "you . . . you said Alabama was your dream job."

"Yeah, but it's not just about me." She props her chin in her palm. "I've got a mama who's getting older. Who's gonna need home care sooner rather than later. I've got loans to pay off." Her long, glittering fingernails dance across the table and tap on the envelope. "And I've got students who need plane tickets."

"But everything you said about . . . about doing good in the world, and . . ."

"That's not good in the world?" She nods at the envelope. "That plane ticket's not making you feel good?"

I don't know how to answer her. I think this may be the kindest thing anyone's ever done for me. And it's not without blood, this gift. Not without sacrifice.

I lift my eyes to Adwoa's. "I honestly don't know . . . I mean, how do I even begin to thank you for this?"

"Thank me," she says, "by winning Nationals."

———————

We rise from our seats not long after that. I pocket the envelope, and she tosses our empty cocoa cups into the recycling bin. It's a short walk back to debate club, and just when I think we'll spend it in a comfortable, stressless silence, Adwoa turns to me.

"Now, that other thing," she says, as we push through a pair of double doors. "That boy thing."

"No!" I pull on her sleeve, try to bring her back to me. We're nowhere near Jonah—not yet, anyway—but, still, better silent than sorry. "You said you'd keep everything between us!"

"And I will!" she says, and laughs. "But you boys have a big weekend coming up. And I *know* you both got a lot going on right now. So: Extra distractions?" She stops here, puts her hands on my shoulders, and looks hard, insistent, into my eyes: "You don't need 'em."

I'd love to melt into the floor, but her grip won't let me. "You don't have anything to worry about," I tell her. "I'm sure he was just sad the other night, and I was just . . ." I swallow, search for words: "Confused, I guess. I was confused."

"Well, we don't need confused right now," she says. "We need focused. Focused on *winning*. You hear me?"

"I do. I hear you."

She lets go of me. I'm ready to let the issue die. I'm also ready to die of embarrassment. But our next stop, of course, is debate club. And Jonah looks up when I step into the room. He sees my skin, rosy with humiliation, and lifts his brows in silent concern. I settle into the seat next to him, trying to focus on the freshmen arguing against one another. It's something about the British museum, about drawings of Buddha, Burmese diamonds. I watch, but I don't quite listen.

Instead, I worry. I worry about the future, rolling on whether any of us likes it or not. Where will Jasmyne and Tyler be in twenty years? Where will I be? And where, crucially, will I be at the end of this weekend? When all the rounds are through, when all the votes are being tallied up?

This is where my mind is wandering when Jonah lifts his hand. He brings his thumb to my forehead and smooths the frantic ridges. They vanish under his touch.

"There you go," he says, as he runs his thumb over the last worried lines between my brows. "All good?"

"Yeah." I'm having trouble breathing, suddenly—not from anxiety, but from its lack. The way he managed to rake all my worries away with a single touch. "All good."

"Good," he repeats.

He slings an arm around me then, and directs another two freshmen up to the front of the classroom. He gives them a topic. Something about Narendra Modi, Hindu nationalism. I don't completely hear it. My left ear's sort of buried in his side, dampening the sounds. It occurs to me that I'm exactly the right height for him—like this space, right here, under his arm, was designed with me in mind.

I shouldn't think too hard about what that means, should I?

chapter eleven

I wake up groggy and disoriented before our hideously early flight to D.C. on Friday morning. It doesn't help that I was up 'til the wee hours, packing and prepping. Mom passed by my door sometime around half past one and laughed at me, up late, ironing the navy-blue jacket I got at Gap Kids for this august occasion.

"I swear," she said, "you are the only seventeen-year-old boy in the world who knows how to work an iron."

Most of the kids at Nationals hail from top-flight private schools. All of them wear their uniforms to tournaments. There are crisp blazers in navy blue, maroon, and forest green. Starchy dress shirts, too, snow white. You'll see plaid skirts in hundreds of different colors, and wool trousers in just the one. Whatever the uniform looks like, though, and however they wear it—formally, or with a sort of campaign-stop-in-Iowa tilt, sleeves to the elbows and the top button popped loose—they look, in these clothes, like they belong in any room they walk into.

So I can't just stroll into this tournament in slouchy, lint-speckled separates. The judges will take one look at me and assume that I'm stupid. Or, well, that I'm poor. But the two are usually one and the same in their minds.

So I iron my clothes. I stash them in dry-cleaning bags. I carry a lint brush at all times to tidy up any oopsies. And I wonder, as I pack this de-linting device into my suitcase, if I *am* gay, after all.

Just as quickly, though, I put the thought out of my mind. I don't have time for an identity crisis on the morning of Nationals. I don't even have time for . . .

"Breakfast!" Mom calls from the next room.

Breakfast? Really? We sit down for a meal together once, maybe twice a year. After that one spaghetti dinner, we're already well on our way to hitting that quota. And I don't think we've ever actually sat down and consumed breakfast as a group. There's a reason, after all, that Lucy and I partake in those bus-ride breakfasts every morning.

And yet, when I walk into the kitchen, there they are: Mom, Dad, and Roo, a broken circle around a sweet-smelling spread of scrambled eggs and bacon and buttered toast. There's a pitcher of orange juice, even. And I know—I *know*—it's got to be the stuff you buy frozen, in a can, and stir into water with a great big wooden spoon, but still! I'm very impressed.

Dad pulls out a seat for me. "Look, kid, we're sorry," he says. "We know how much this tournament matters to you. We should've at least talked to you about the ticket."

Am I dreaming? I take the seat, and Mom nods, agreeing. "I'm so glad your coach could come through for you."

Roo reaches out, passing me an envelope. I slip my thumb

beneath the flap, tear it open, and find . . . a card. A card? A group breakfast, a genuine apology, and now, to top it all off: a card.

I'm just beginning to suspect body-snatchers when my eyes fall on the front of this card: a field of white and yellow stars on blue-black cardstock. They spell out GOOD LUCK, these stars, in a dazzling, glittery constellation. ALL THE BEST, it says, inside, TO A GUY WHO SHINES LIKE THE STARS IN THE SKY.

A lump forms in my throat as I take in Mom's signature, Dad's. Roo has signed it too, with a postscript: You better kick . . . and a rudimentary drawing, in her perfect fourteen-year-old scrawl, of a pair of hairy buttocks.

Am I ready to forgive them? I lift my head. I take in the softness—the love, even—on the face of my dad, my mom, my little sister. Ever since Dad lost his job, my life at home has been little more, sometimes, than a series of screaming matches to sleep through.

But this morning, Roo rushes forward, and wraps her arms around me, squeezing me hard. And I feel, just for a second, the way I felt at Jonah's. Like we're a family. A real one. There's a card in my hands, and a pitcher of orange juice on the table. We love each other. We're trying our best.

"This morning was nice, wasn't it?" Mom glances at me; I nod. We're on that familiar tree-lined highway now, driving fast to Sea-Tac so I can catch my plane. "I can't remember the last time I fixed a real breakfast. Mixed blessings of unemployment, you know? We may be behind on our bills, but I've got all kinds of free time."

"You know, there are these researchers at Yale who came up with this thing called 'time affluence.'" I scratch at the side of my nose, trying to remember where, exactly, I read about this. "They did this study, and they found out that the happiest people weren't actually the ones with the most money. It's the most free time. That's the ticket."

"Heard that one before," Mom says, snorting.

"No! Really!" I lean over the divide. Mom, being a reporter, is usually the only person who lets me info-dump like this. Who finds it interesting, even. "If you're making tons of money, but you're coming home at the end of your hundred-hour workweek to screaming kids and a messy kitchen and a garden full of weeds . . ."

Mom nods, less skeptical than she was before: ". . . then all the money in the world won't make you happier."

"Exactly! Unless you use your money to *buy* time—like, ordering takeout instead of cooking, or hiring maids instead of cleaning."

"Christ, but that makes sense. Rich people have more time, and poor people have less." Mom looks sideways at me, smiling. "You're so smart, you know that? You're going to do great things. Someone in our family should."

"Mom. Come on." Why'd she have to give me a compliment that *hurts*? "It's not your fault, what happened to the paper."

"Oh, I know. I just can't help feeling a little stupid. These past few years, a paper goes kaput every five seconds. It's constant. Another newsroom, cleaned out. Another friend of mine walking past me with that goddamned cardboard box. And the whole time, I kept telling myself it'd never happen to me, but . . ."

She sighs, then goes silent, staring through the broad windshield at the tall rows of trees.

"You know, Lucy's starting a YouTube channel." I start speaking before I remember that we're fighting, me and Lucy. I wince. "She says she's going to use it to reinvent journalism."

Mom lets out a laugh—a less than kind one. "Anyone told Lucy that journalism's a dying industry?"

"Yeah, but she's got this whole plan to crowdfund it," I say. How weird, to be speaking in spirited defense of someone who isn't even speaking to me. "She launched a Patreon for it. Racked up something like two hundred dollars of monthly pledges in the first hour."

"I don't know, Finch. I've spent decades watching these V.C. vultures pick this industry down to the bones." She shakes her head. "And I just can't help feeling your friend's bringing a knife to a gunfight."

"She really believes she can do it. And she's already making it happen. Booking interviews. Making videos."

"Maybe that's my problem," Mom says. "Maybe we just got to a point where none of us believed this thing could actually be saved."

She stares again through the rain-spattered windshield, lost in thought. We're at the curb now, right outside the bustling departure gate. I should get out, grab my suitcase, say my goodbyes. But something keeps me in my seat.

"Mom? Can I ask you a question?"

She waves a hand at the signs dotting the curb. "This is a five-minute parking zone. A kiss-'n'-fly."

"A quick question. It won't take five whole minutes. I promise."

"Fine," she says. "Shoot."

"Do you think you'll ever be a reporter again?"

"No," she says, much quicker than I was expecting. "No, I don't think so. I mean, I hope so. But hoping and thinking—very different things." She puts a hand on my shoulder, and squeezes. "I'm glad you told me what Lucy's up to. Glad someone's keeping the dream alive, I mean. It makes me think I can still win. All of us could, maybe."

She lets me go, then, with a rare smile.

"You most of all, honey," she says. "Go, fight, win."

I step out of the car. "I will," I tell her. "I'll bring home a trophy."

I'm just boarding the plane, shoveling my plain black suitcase into the cramped overhead bins next to Adwoa's (leopard print, bulging hugely) and Jonah's (sleek, economical, doubles as a backpack if the urge to hike hits) when I realize: I've got precious little time before I'll be forced to switch to airplane mode. And so I open Twitter. I scroll through my timeline the way a runner throws back water before the final stretch of a marathon: sloppy, quick, and already exhausted.

God, is *this* why I get anxiety? This constant exposure to the worst people in the world doling out the worst takes imaginable? Just for a second, I wonder what it would be like to delete the app. No, delete my account. *No*, unfollow everyone but that one account that posts pictures of possums every hour on the hour.

I'm just contemplating this glorious possibility when I hit a tweet from Bailey Lundquist like a speed bump on a superhighway.

BAILEY LUNDQUIST—@BaileyOnBroadway
i want @tchalamet to lick apricot lacroix off my body

I don't follow Bailey, of course, but three people from school have deemed this likeable, so Twitter's forcing it down my craw. When will this website learn that I don't want to see anything he posts? Ever? *Especially* if he's being horny on main?

I tap on Bailey's name out of morbid curiosity. And that's when I see it:

BAILEY LUNDQUIST—@BaileyOnBroadway
well it's official i just got the email guess who's not going to juilliard next year lololololololololololololololol

No. Fucking. Way.

Bailey Lundquist didn't get into Juilliard? Bailey Lundquist, who built his entire personality around aspiring to Juilliard, *didn't get into Juilliard?*

All the disappointment I felt in December, reading my Georgetown deferral—it transforms, in an instant, into the most delicious kind of schadenfreude.

Adwoa takes in the vivid shock on my face. "What's happening on Twitter?" she asks. "Someone die? Resign from the White House? Say something super racist? All three?"

I can't speak. I can't even shake my head. She's in the center and I'm in the aisle, so I tilt the screen of my phone to her, point to the key words: *guess who's not going to Juilliard.* She gasps.

Jonah, in the window seat, preoccupied with SkyMall, cranes his head. "Wait, what's happening on Twitter?"

I exchange a worried look with Adwoa. Is Jonah ready for this news? Should we break it to him? She gives me a solemn nod: It's better if he knows.

I pass my phone to the window seat and watch Jonah's face—watch as his eyes widen, his lips fall open, his hand fly to his mouth in silent shock.

And then, before I can even blink, he explodes into laughter. I mean, really *explodes*; I've never seen him—never seen *anybody*—laugh so hard, so physically. His hand is shaking so hard that I worry he's going to drop my phone. I pry the device out of his fingers—I do *not* want it to fall and shatter on the floor of the plane—and when I settle back into my seat, he's still laughing.

"He didn't . . . didn't even . . ." Jonah can't get the words out, each one swallowed up by fresh rounds of laughter, a sandcastle caving to a wave. "After all that, he . . . they . . . they didn't want . . ."

It's not long before I'm laughing, too. Even Adwoa, between us, is beginning to break down, giggling furiously behind her hand.

Folks are staring at us, bug-eyed. I know very well why. I also know that we can't stop. Not now.

"Wait. Wait." I'm giggling like an insane person. "Why did Bailey cross the road?"

"Why?" Jonah giggles.

I'm laughing so hard that I can barely get the words out: "To get rejected from Juilliard."

Jonah fully bends over at the waist, wheezing. "*Jesus.*"

"Okay, boys," says Adwoa, dabbing at her eyes, trying to catch her breath. "Let's behave."

I don't really feel like behaving, though. Neither, judging from the giddy look on his face, does Jonah. He reaches across Adwoa, tugging insistently at my arm.

"Hey, Finch," he says. "How many Baileys does it take to get rejected from Juilliard?"

I know we're being mean. I know. But this is the balm my soul needs after the past few long, hard weeks. I smother a laugh. "How many?" I ask him, and he crows, "One!" and then we're both falling all over Adwoa, shrieking with laughter.

"Okay. Fine." Adwoa lifts an imaginary champagne flute high. "A toast to the exquisite discernment of Juilliard's admissions committee."

Jonah clinks his Hydro Flask against her imaginary glass. As the plane tears through the open sky to our final destination, all, for a moment, feels right in the world.

chapter twelve

After the flight, there's a shuttle bus, and after the bus, an arduous walk through the terminal to the Metro, which takes us on a dank and clattering ride into the heart of Washington, D.C. I should be exhausted, running on little food and even less sleep, but I'm not. Every part of my being is thrumming, pressing up against the windows of the train. There are no spectacular across-the-Potomac views of the monuments, but even underground, seeing the names of the stations is a thrill: Smithsonian! Dupont Circle! Pentagon!

Well. Not that last stop so much. The Pentagon's maybe the only place from which I'd *prefer* to be banned.

Our host this year is the Gray School, a dour castle in a chi-chi corner of the Palisades—not like there are any un-chi-chi corners of the Palisades, I mean. Before we do anything else, and before we *go* anywhere else, we need to sign in at the school's front office. We'll all be billeting in the dorms here. This is how it works whenever boarding schools hold tournaments. No hotels. If we're lucky, we'll sleep on common-room sofas. If not, we'll get a sleeping bag on a floor. It's probably the least luxurious element of this weekend. Everything else about this place screams inherited wealth.

Adwoa heads into the office for registration while we perch on our suitcases in the Gray School's cavernous Gothic lobby. I'm chewing a hangnail and falling asleep upright when, suddenly, Nasir blows by us.

"Fuck is up, Olympians?" he calls out—and then, mysteriously, he slaps his own ass. "How you liking Foggy *Bottom?*"

I heard a rumor that Nasir's going to Oxford next year. I hope it's true. I can't wait 'til there's an ocean separating me from this guy.

"So far, so good," says Jonah, cordially. "How was your flight?"

"Oh, man, the *worst*, even in biz class," Nasir groans. "Food was shit, too. Broken crackers. Camembert cold as a witch's tit." I look at him, confused, and he clarifies: "Camembert's cheese. You serve it hot."

I nod, nervous. If Nasir's here, Ari can't be far behind. I haven't spoken to her since that day at Annable, outside the library. I'm still terrified of what she might do with the truth I told her.

"All right, Nas." Speak of the devil: Ari's walking out of the Gray School's office, juggling a thick packet of maps and schedules and tournament regulations. We're all wearing the clothes we traveled in; she's wearing her Annable uniform. Does she *ever* take it off? "We're up against West Virginia Red, and then—"

"*Nice*," Nasir interrupts, and pumps his fist. "Country bumpkins! Gon' be a breeze. Thank fuck we're not up against Massachusetts first thing, am I right?"

"Nasir, no. Do not underestimate the competition. Ever."

She pauses, gives me and Jonah a curt nod, and then looks back to her partner. "Speaking of which, let's go strategize somewhere quieter."

"Hold up a second, Rodham. I'm socializing." He pulls out his phone, glances up at us. "You guys coming to this party tonight? Up at Georgetown?"

"Nasir, we've got *four* competitive rounds tomorrow." Ari is not amused. "What part of 'the North American Debate Association National Championships' do you not understand?"

"Uh, I understand that I need to cruise for chicas tonight," he says, and again flicks his eyes at us. "And these guys are gonna come cruise with me. Ain't that right, fellas?"

I should tell him no, shouldn't I? I should refuse his offer of chica-cruising and get a solid night of shut-eye before tomorrow's rounds.

But something holds me back, stalls the *no* in my mouth. A party up at *Georgetown*, he said. If Nasir's party can take me there, well . . .

"Sure," I leap in. "Sounds fun."

"Wait." Jonah turns to me, disbelieving. "You actually want to go to this party?"

I nod. *Georgetown*, I mouth; mercifully, he gets it.

He turns to Nasir. He nods. "We're in," he says. "We're cruising."

"Wait. Don't you have a boyfriend, Jonah?" Ari looks up from the schedule she's busily highlighting. "I thought I saw him on your Instagram. Blond guy? Looks like an elf?"

"Oh. No." Jonah's clearly startled by Ari's recon. "I mean,

yes, he does look like an elf. But we're not together anymore. We just broke up."

"Oh, Jonah, my *man*." Nasir plants a sympathetic punch on Jonah's shoulder. "On *God* we gon' get you laid tonight."

Jonah winces. "I'm not really sure if . . ."

"No, no, no—we're making this happen." Nasir speaks like he's doing some kind of gracious public service. "Lemme ask my friend at Georgetown if she knows any guys who'd be good for you."

"Really, Nasir, I'm not—"

"And you're, like, fully gay, right?" Nasir asks, tapping away on his phone's keyboard. "Not even a little bi? A hundred percent into dick?"

"Correct," Jonah says, unsmiling. "Guys only."

I step away from them, shrinking into myself. *A hundred percent into dick; guys only*—that absolutely doesn't include me, does it? Not that I want it to. Not that it's relevant in the least. There's nothing between Jonah and me. He just touched me. Once. That's all. I'm getting worked up over nothing. Jonah didn't even say the part about "dick."

But he didn't call Nasir on saying it, either.

"What about you, ginge?" Nasir asks, and nudges me in the ribs. "What you into? Girls? Boys? Gender liquid?"

I stare at him, bewildered: "Gender . . . *liquid?*"

"Leave my boys alone, Nasir," says Adwoa, emerging from the front office, welcome packets in hand.

"'S'all good!" Nasir puts his hands up, defensive. "Gotta bounce anyway."

He flits away to bother another pack of debaters. Ari doesn't follow him, though. She wanders away from us, leaning by herself against a patch of stone wall. Her hands are full, and her eyes are busily scanning the tournament schedule. But she seems to be sneaking glances, every few seconds, at me. Even after we leave the lobby, hoisting our bags and heading to the dorm where we'll sleep, I can feel her eyes on me.

Whatever she's up to, though, I don't have much time to theorize about it. A bell is ringing through the Gray School's gray halls. A voice is speaking through an intercom: *First round, thirty minutes.* Half an hour to wash our faces, get changed, and run through our speeches one last time.

We're on the starting line. No turning back now.

When I saw *Texas Red* on our schedule, I wondered what we were in for: rich white liberals from Austin, the spoiled sons and daughters of South by Southwest? Or rich white conservatives from Dallas, descendants of decades of oil barons? As soon as I walk into the classroom, I have my answer: two boys, six feet tall each, in mustard-yellow blazers that make their blotched pink skin look downright rosaceous. One wears a signet ring; the other, a tie clip. They look like they could buy our present environs—Chemistry Lab 3; regular rounds always take place in normal classrooms, with desks as podiums—and turn it into their own personal country club.

We take our seats in front of a frankly colossal plasma-screen television. What it's doing in a chemistry lab, I haven't the foggiest. I'm on one side of a microscope, and Jonah's on the other, and it's welded to the table so neither of us can run off with it. Back home, at Johnson Tech, a class of thirty shares a single microscope.

It's clearer to me, suddenly, why my chemistry grades are so bottom-of-barrel.

The moderator for our first round is a freshman from the Gray School with a cloud of curly black hair, tiny, in knee socks and a sweater-vest. She does not look like she'll be able to intervene if a brawl breaks out between us and Texas Red. "Good evening," she reads, from a sheet of crisp white paper, "to all debaters, judges, and honored guests."

The only "honored guests" in the room are Adwoa and another woman who must be the Texas guys' coach. She's wearing a pink suit, black piping at the hems. All that's missing is a pillbox hat. Why is a woman from Dallas going for Jackie's motorcade look?

"Debating for the proposition today," the moderator goes on, "from Washington State Blue, we have Jonah Cabrera and Finch Kelly."

We nod, and we smile; the woman in the back can't disguise her disdain. Is it our lack of uniforms? Our shaggy haircuts? The fact that Jonah is Asian and I'm trans? I mean, not that she's capable of clocking me. I'd be shocked if she's ever met a trans person.

"And debating against the opposition, from Texas Red, we have Grantley Fairview and Remington Beveridge."

I only just swallow a loud, rude laugh. My hands scramble

for a pen; they close around the one that Lucy gave to me. I feel a pang of guilt, missing her, as I scribble a note to Jonah: *Those cannot be their real names.* He glances at the notepad, then sucks in his cheeks, inhales deeply. I can tell he's straining not to laugh, putting every bit of his drama club breath control to good use.

The Texan coach, though—she's onto us. She's glaring daggers, like we're in a Bath & Body Works, and Jonah and I are polyester-vested employees, and her debaters are a couple of three-wick candles she's desperately trying to purchase with an expired coupon. On his way up to the teacher's podium, Jonah tries to calm her with a friendly smile.

"Evening, everyone," Jonah begins. "Today, we'll be discussing the rights of transgender and non-binary students who—"

"On that point, sir," says Grantley—or Remington, I can't remember—leaping to his feet, flinging out his arm.

Now, any debater worth their salt knows to reserve their questions. Lie in wait 'til the middle of the speech, then pounce. You want to time your questions carefully, chop up the other person's flow. You absolutely do *not* want to leap up in the first five seconds to spit out a fervid "On that point, sir!" Not if you want to win, anyway.

"Yes, sir?" says Jonah, still smiling. It's a smart move on his part: If the question's coming this early, it can't be a good one. "You had a question?"

"Sir, do you not agree that if we are to have a productive conversation today, then we must be in agreement that"—God, Brantington, get on with it—"this whole notion of 'non-binary' is facially unsupportable? From a biological standpoint?"

Jonah exhales. "Madam Speaker, my colleague from Texas is mistaken," he says, in the most polite voice he's got, his purest, cleanest, Grandma-is-listening diction. "Many biologists have proven conclusively that humanity is not a perfectly sexually dimorphic species. Hundreds of thousands of intersex babies are born each year with both 'male' and 'female' sexual characteristics, and—"

"On that point, sir!"

The other one—Rentleyton, or whoever—is on his feet. Jonah stops talking and nods like, *yes, please, dig yourself a deeper hole.*

"We concede that a tiny fraction of babies really are born that way," says the Texan. "But what about the people who *are* born boys, and *are* born girls, and just claim they're not, just because they feel like' it?" He pauses, laughing in a theatrical way. "I mean, do you know of any *real* biologists who support these so-called 'special snowflakes'?"

On "snowflakes," Jonah turns to me, very slightly, and grins like a shark.

Oh, yeah. We've won this round.

After we leave the room, we wait a polite minute 'til Ridgeview and Fremley are well out of earshot. And then we turn to each other, our faces breaking into wide, giddy smiles. I lift my hand for a high five, but Jonah has other plans. He reaches out, arms around my shoulders, and hugs me tight, trapping my arm between his chest and mine. When I pull away, I can feel my face going pink, warm.

"So," I say, and hope I'm not *too* flushed, "that was . . ."

"The easiest round we'll have all weekend," he finishes for me.

"But you can't get complacent!" Adwoa says, pushing us gently down the hall. "You have to bring it! Every! Single! Time! Even against the dodo birds!"

"Right on," says Jonah. "Doesn't matter how many rounds we win. If our scores aren't high enough, we're not highest-seeded."

"Definitely." I'm about to give him a quick critique of his speech—almost perfect, except when he said Foster-Sterling instead of Fausto-Sterling—but I can feel my phone buzzing in my pocket.

My first thought? It's got to be Lucy, reaching out with a digital olive branch. I've been waiting for it—feeling guilty, and wanting to apologize, but not wanting to make the first move, lest she refuse to talk to me at all. I reach into my pocket and scan the screen for her name.

Instead, I see a white banner. Two lines:

Georgetown University—Edmund A. Walsh School of Foreign Service

Subject: Your Admission Status

Oh. My. God.

This is it. The moment I've been anticipating for months. Years. My whole life, even. I will open this email and the long, wintry purgatory of my deferral will be over. I will know where I stand. *Finally.*

"Everything okay?" Jonah glances at me, a worried brow going up. "You're, like, vibrating."

"Yeah, yeah, yeah. Everything's great." I'm falling behind him and Adwoa, so I slip out of the stream of the hallway. "Hold on. I just got . . . I really need to check this . . ."

Jonah was right: I *am* shaking, my phone rattling in my hands as I punch in my passcode. One, two, three nanoseconds go by.

And then the letter loads.

Georgetown University

Edmund A. Walsh School of Foreign Service

Office of Admissions

Finch Kelly

9230 Dibble Ave NW

Olympia, WA, USA

98508

Dear Ms. Kelly,

The Committee on Admissions has completed its review of applicants to the incoming class. Following a very careful consideration of your application, I am sorry to inform you that it will not be possible to offer you a place in the

This can't be real. It's a mistake. I'm sure of it. The letter is addressed to *Ms.* Kelly—and didn't I note, specifically, in the very first line of my essay, that no matter what my gender marker might say, I *am* a boy? So, there we have it: a mistake. I'll get an acceptance letter any minute now, addressed to *Mr.* Kelly.

And even if it's not a mistake, this letter—even if I *have* been rejected—well, that's not so bad, is it? I'm competing at Nationals, right now, this very minute! If all goes well, I'll be a national debating champion by Sunday! How could George- town say no to that? I'll appeal their decision; they'll reverse it. They'll have to. I may be hanging by a thread here; so be it. I'll cling until every last fiber's frayed.

"Finch?" Jonah's hand. My shoulder. His hands seem to be finding my shoulders a lot these days. "Are you sure every- thing's okay?"

I shove my phone back into my pocket, and I half nod, half shrug. "I'm fine," I tell him, even though I can hardly breathe to get the words out.

"We did a fantastic job in that first round, okay?" His voice is low, gentle, soothing; he clearly didn't buy my whimpered *I'm fine*. "And now we're up for our second round, and we're going to do a great job on that one, too."

I manage another nod, a more deliberate one. And then I follow him into the Gray School's dining hall to get our sec- ond-round pairing. He's doing his best, I know, to keep me calm. I have to reach down inside myself and do my best, too. This is absolutely no time for panicking. In fifteen minutes, we'll be arguing *against* trans rights, not for them.

This is how it always works. If you argued *yes* in the first round, you'll be arguing *no* in the second. Tomorrow, we'll run through four rounds: two yes, two no. On Sunday morn- ing, the highest-scoring teams from these first six rounds will advance to the final round. Who will triumph? Will it be Min- nesota Red? Nevada Blue? Any of the other randomly red-

dened or blued teams who qualified from their state tournaments? The final is less than 48 hours from now. It feels like
an eternity.

And *I* feel like I'm swimming through thick, dark mud for
our entire second round. We wind up debating Florida Blue,
a couple of Cuban American kids from a Catholic school in
Miami. They're better—*leagues* better—than the Texas team.
And they've got an edge: They don't have to stand behind a
podium and argue against their own right to use a bathroom.

For maximum winnability, we built our opposition case
on a soft concession: Transgender students shouldn't use the
bathroom that corresponds to their gender, but rather, a single-stall, unisex bathroom. To protect trans kids from bullies,
see? To keep them safe.

The only place I've ever really felt safe, though, is behind
the podium. This is where I first learned to defend myself, to
hold my head high, to declare that I was worth listening to.

So why am I using these skills to tear myself down?

We crush Florida Blue in the end, but it's a joyless victory. A wave of guilt rolls over me as we walk to the dorm
where we'll sleep. Maybe it's cosmic punishment, that rejection letter. For betraying trans people.

For betraying *myself*.

"Okay, Finch, what's up with you?" Jonah reaches for me,
rubbing my shoulder. "Ever since we won that first round,
you've been dragging your feet."

"I'm just tired," I mumble. "I didn't get a lot of sleep last
night. And it's been a long, long day."

"You're sure there's not anything else?" he asks. "You're not feeling bad about how that round went?"

"It went great," I tell him bluntly. "You were great. Now, let's get back to the dorm and go to sleep."

I pace forward, through the courtyard. Jonah sort of half jogs, hustling to keep up with me.

"But you wanted to hit that party!" He ups his pace, steps in front of me—those long, long legs. "You were so excited to see Georgetown!"

The word is a knife to the gut.

I push past Jonah, grumbling. "I don't want to go anymore. I'm too tired."

"Look, Finch. I know you. And this?" He sweeps his hand from my yawning head to my shuffling feet. "This isn't 'I'm tired.' This is 'I'm stressed.' Getting some fresh air and catching a glimpse of your dream school will help you decompress. A lot more than curling up in your sleeping bag and hate-reading *InfoWars*, anyway."

He's right. That's exactly what I'd planned to do: wash my face, brush my teeth, and "unwind" by reading whatever nonsense that one gun nut who pooped her pants posted on Twitter today.

But somewhere, deep inside me, a voice is crying out: *Fuck it! I just got rejected from Georgetown! I'm spending this whole weekend parroting terf talking points! Nothing means anything anymore! Let's go to a party! Let's be bad for once in our lives! Let's finally find out what alcohol tastes like!*

I can already feel the rational side of my brain sprinting to catch up to this outlaw. He's repeating Alateen slogans.

He's droning on about sleep, nutrition, personal responsibility. He's telling me I can still persuade Georgetown that I'm worthy, but only if I win Nationals. And if I want to do that, I'd better get some sleep tonight.

But the outlaw dodges the sheriff, and against all my better judgment, in this hail of internal gunfire, I open my mouth. I say, "Sure." I say, "Why not?"

Nasir is a liar. The party is not "at Georgetown." Not in any way, shape, or form. It's in a house rented by Georgetown *students*. Google Maps tells me the campus is a brisk half-hour walk away. There will be no breathless, consolatory stroll across the quad. Not tonight.

Instead, I get to spend my evening in a row house whose occupants are treating it like a public toilet—beer-sticky floors, pungent smoke, tartan uniforms askew. Half of Louisiana Red is riding half of Michigan Blue's lap on a low-lying bench in the mudroom. I pull my eyes—up, away—to Jonah.

"What," I ask him, "are we *doing* here?"

He doesn't give me an answer. He just pulls me, gently, by the wrist, into the kitchen. We pass dozens of sweaty bodies, but the only one I care about is the one that belongs to him. He steers me to a counter strewn with beer and wine and a single measly six-pack of Coke. There may be time, later, for hard liquor. Right now, though, I think I'll settle for softness. I pry a can out of the dolphin-choking six-ring packaging and hope Jonah will forgive me.

A few more steps, and we're in the living room, where

people I don't know are dancing to a pop song I don't know. I take a swig of room-temp Coke. It is not delicious.

"This tastes disgusting," I tell Jonah. By way of reply, he passes me his beer, and—oh, what the hell? I take a drink. I grimace. "*This* tastes disgusting."

There's some relief in this revelation, actually. I can't imagine *ever* becoming addicted to this stuff. It tastes like raw sewage. With one sip, I may have just broken an intergenerational curse. Go, Finch!

"We'll get you started on the fun alcohol," says Jonah, as I hand back the half-empty bottle. "The alcohol that doesn't taste like alcohol at all."

"No way," I say, newly committed to the temperance movement. "Alcohol is a class-one carcinogen."

"Says who?"

"Says WHO."

"Really?"

"Yes. As cancerous as cigarettes." I lift my hands: this crowded room, these kids all swilling liquid cancer. "And nobody cares because the beverage industry fights tooth and nail to keep the public in the dark. It is a scandal. It is a national scandal."

Jonah doesn't respond to my excellent points. He looks at me like you look at a feverish child, brows bent in concern. "Are you okay?" he asks. "You seem really anxious tonight. More than usual."

"I'm always anxious." Another swig of lukewarm soda. "I don't need a *because* to be anxious."

"Is it the tournament?" he asks. "Is that the *because*?"

"No, it's just that I got a letter from . . ." I catch myself *just* before I can say "Georgetown." ". . . No. Sorry. I'm anxious because this was a bad idea. We've got four rounds tomorrow, and we're out here carousing."

"'Carousing,'" he repeats, and laughs. "Oh, Finch." He slings a hand around my shoulder, tucking me under his warm, sweaty wing. "Don't worry so much. We'll be fine. We worked our asses off. And we've only ever lost one round in our whole lives."

"Just the one," I mumble, my words getting lost in the soft fabric of his sweatshirt. "Just the state final."

"And we *still* made it to Nationals," he says. "We're in Washington, D.C., baby!"

He lifts his hands, and he sweeps them around the squalid room. Beer puddles. Weed smells. People fornicating on the formicating furniture. This is *not* how I wanted to see D.C. Oh my *God*, why did I come to this party? What did I think it would do for me? Why, why, *why* did I listen to the outlaw in my head?

"I have to go." I leap to my feet. "Right now."

Jonah takes a very calm sip of beer. "How are you getting home?"

"On the Metro," I answer.

"In the middle of the night?"

"When else?"

"By yourself?"

"I just need to not be here, okay?" I abandon my Coke,

search for a door. "If I don't go back and get some sleep, I'll screw up tomorrow's rounds the same way I've been screwing up everything else lately."

"Hey. No." Jonah's hand presses into my side, just for a second—that same place he found before, the other night, at his house. I stop moving. "Don't go anywhere. We're going to turn this night around."

And then he steps away, and I'm alone in the center of the room. The party flows around me. I'm not a part of it—more like an obstacle in its way, a rock in a river, parting the current.

Jonah strides up to the DJ—well, the guy with the laptop and the headphones, anyway. They put their heads together and talk for a few seconds.

Then a beat begins to boom through the speakers. It comes through low, but loud, a pulsing drum. Jonah dances back to me, singing along with the silky voice pouring out of the speakers. "What song is this?" I ask him, and he sings, *"Don't worry 'bout it."*

Then he takes my hand. Takes it, holds it, laces fingers through fingers. And there's his other hand, again, at that place on my waist, and . . . what is he doing? Is he . . . *leading* me? Like we're in a ballroom, and not something less than a frat house? Like that's Beethoven on the speakers, and not whoever's voice keeps chanting *don't worry 'bout it*?

I'm not ready for the beat to explode, for the room to erupt in light and color, for Jonah to send me spinning out across the floor, and then spinning back to him, his hand tight in mine all the while.

Then he lets go.

And I let go.

I don't want the song to end, but that's what songs do.

After a stop in the kitchen for cool water, we step out onto an empty balcony and take our first breath of fresh air in forever. It's hot on the balcony—too hot for March, but I'm judging by the standards of the Pacific Northwest, and this is a whole new kind of Washington.

It occurs to me about five seconds too late that falling onto the lounger is a very dumb idea. Reaching for the first rumpled blanket I see—doubly dumb. How many bodily fluids have these objects absorbed in their long careers as furniture? How many communicable diseases am I contracting just by sitting here? I'd like to leap up and douse myself in Purell, but I can't move without disturbing Jonah. He's seated on the balcony's concrete floor, resting his head on the top of my thigh. The blanket is a kind of pillow for him.

His head is in my lap, I think, and shiver.

For the first time ever, I'm grateful I don't possess a penis.

"Are you feeling any better?" he asks me.

He doesn't lift his head, or turn, or look at me. He doesn't really have to. We're alone out here, in the quiet dark. He's so close he can probably hear my pulse racing under my skin.

"I feel like I was carrying a suitcase." I feel my shoulders fall. A knot inside, coming loose. "A really heavy suitcase. And I got to put it down for a minute."

"That's good," he says. He reaches up, finds my hand in the tangle of the blanket, and squeezes. "I'm glad."

"But I'll have to pick it up again," I tell him, pressing my fingers into his palm. "Keep hauling it along."

"I know what you mean," he says, and sighs. "I keep waiting for Bailey to get the hell out of my head. And I think he must be on his way, because I'm thinking about him less and less."

"That's good," I say. "I'm glad."

He saw what I did, echoing him: *That's good; I'm glad.* He tilts his head, smiles widely. "It helps that I'm here with you," he says. "You're a good distraction."

I reach down to pull the blanket closer, but my hand brushes his head. It's an accident, this touch. A week ago, I would have apologized for it. Now, though, something holds me back. Maybe it's that single sip of beer in my system. Maybe it's the newfound outlaw in my head. Something compels me to leave my hand where it is. To stroke his soft, blue-black hair. If he asks me why I'm doing it, I'll tell him I'm drunk, and he'll believe me.

"It might take a long time." My fingers brush up against the tip of one ear. "You loved him a lot."

"I don't know, actually. I don't know if I really loved him."

My hand, in his hair, goes still. All I can manage, in the smallest voice I've got, is a single word: "What?"

"I thought I did. At one point. But these last few weeks, all this fighting over the musical, the way I was too afraid to tell him about UDub because I knew he wanted me to follow him to New York . . ." He exhales; it sounds like a weight coming loose, falling from his chest. "Maybe I was just calling it love. Maybe it was something else."

I try to keep my voice calm, neutral. "That makes sense."

"It's less like I lost someone I loved than, like, I lost a part of myself." He lifts his eyes to me. "I didn't have a ton of friends before I got with Bailey, you know? I was the awkward, closeted Asian kid who never shut up about saving the whales." He pauses; a sad laugh. "If people at school like me, it's probably because they liked me with Bailey."

"I liked you before Bailey," I tell him. Instantly. Honestly. "In freshman year, when you still had braces, so you talked with a lisp. You saw me writing with a mechanical pencil before our first round at that invitational in Walla Walla, and you gave me a lecture about ocean plastic. Then you handed me a pencil made out of recycled newspapers, and you said, '*Uthe thith inthtead.*'"

"My lisp was *never* that bad."

"Oh, no, it was. But it was nice, your lisp. I liked it."

"Well, thanks," he says, "for being a Day One friend."

I'm awake, suddenly. Deeply, profoundly awake. I bend in half to rest my cheek on the crown of his head. I need to be closer to him. It shouldn't be a shock to learn that Jonah didn't really love Bailey. But it sets something in motion within me, sends me hurtling to some point of no return, some ledge. I want to fall over it, drop like a falcon. I can't stop.

"I know what you mean," I tell him. "About losing an important part of you. And thinking everyone will look at you different."

"What do you mean?"

"I mean, uh . . ." It is so hard to say this. Even here. Even to him. I let out an utterly joyless laugh: "How many Finches does it take to get rejected from Georgetown?"

"Oh, Finch." He turns his head, knocks my hands out of place. "*No.*"

I can't cry, haven't cried in ages. But I can feel my face growing hot, feel the pressure building behind my eyes. Jonah must sense it, too, because he's reaching up, his hands aiming for my temples, like he's trying to wipe away any tears that might come falling.

It's not until his fingers are brushing the round curves of my cheeks, not until his face is very close, too close, that I realize this might not be comfort at all.

It might be a kiss.

"Finch?"

The screen door hits the plastic siding. Jonah springs up, away from me, rolling across the deck. It's so sleek it looks choreographed. I lurch back, pulling the blanket up to my chin. There's a stain: someone else's vomit, vividly green. I fling the fabric away.

Ari is swaying in the doorway, still in that goddamn uniform, red plastic cup in her hand. For a long, terrifying moment, I worry she's going to mock us. But then she yawns—loud, wide, and undignified. I realize, with relief, that she's way too drunk to have noticed our almost-kiss.

"Finch, hey," she calls out. "Need to talk to you."

My voice comes out a raw, anxious chirp: "Talk about what?"

She groans effortfully. "That thing we talked about. When you came to my school."

That thing. Me, being trans. I do *not* want my secret to come tumbling out of her drunken mouth. Not now. Not in the middle of this crowded party, where it'd spread like wildfire.

"Ari," I say—my voice serious, warning her—"let's get you home, okay? Before you do anything that you—"

She stumbles toward me and crashes into my lap—the very same place where, just a second ago, Jonah was laying his head. Across the deck, half hidden by a potted plant, Jonah blinks, as bewildered as I am.

"When did you, like . . ." She pauses, hiccups. "When did you *know* that you were, like . . ."

"Come on, Ari." I try to lift her up and out of my lap; I don't succeed. Did I mention she's twice my size? "You're way too drunk right now. Let's go back to the dorms, okay? We can go together."

"'Cause I've been thinking about it," she says, not moving from her perch on my thighs. "I've been thinking, since we talked, and I think that maybe I . . . you know, I might be a . . . a *you.*"

Am I hearing her right? How drunk is she? She wobbles, threatens to fall; I hold her steady. "What do you mean?" I ask, leaning in, repeating slowly: "You might be *like* me?"

In the low light, I see her eyes glimmer: excitement, maybe; terror, more likely. "Yeah," she says, and rises to her feet, wobbling. "I might . . . I might be like . . ."

And then she turns, opens her mouth, and aims for the potted plant.

She misses. Drowns Jonah in a toxic soup of Grey Goose and Red Bull—all those colors, all those animals.

He handles it like a perfect gentleman, tells her that we'll get her home, and asks me, over her shoulder, to call us all a cab. We ride back to the Gray School together, in silence: me on the left, Ari snoring on my shoulder, and Jonah, still drenched in puke, being cussed out by the woman in the driver's seat.

That's the last thing I remember thinking before my head falls against the dusty pane of the cab's rear window—not, *Did Jonah really mean to kiss me?* and not, *What did Ari mean, "I might be a you?"* No, my very last thought was: *How weird, a female cabbie.*

chapter thirteen

At breakfast the next morning, Ari is nowhere to be seen—
and I am *relieved*. I've never been so grateful to be stuck at the
far end of a long table in the dining hall. I nod and mumble
and *uh huh* my way through the conversation, happy to be
mistaken for a participant in it.

I'm grateful, too, for the bland food on offer. My stomach's
still upset about last night's thimbleful of beer. I smear tepid
cream cheese onto an unseasoned, untoasted bagel. Across
the table, Jonah forges through a plate of French toast and
bacon and eggs. He eats his feelings; I starve mine.

The kids at our table veer into gossip about this year's
frontrunners. The girls of Connecticut Blue are, apparently, a
force to be reckoned with. So are the boys in Massachusetts
Red—who hail, weirdly, from a tennis academy. I'm craning
my neck to hear more when Jonah, suddenly, reaches forward
and touches my wrist.

"So," he says, in a low voice, just for us, "should we, uh . . .
talk about what happened? Last night?"

I leave my bagel on my plate. I wasn't hungry before; now
I'm on the verge of retching. What is Jonah *doing*? Not just

mentioning "last night," but saying it at the breakfast table, surrounded on all sides. The Alaskans can hear us, for God's sake. The Alaskans!

I swallow air and shake my head. "It's okay," I tell him. "There's nothing to talk about."

"All right." He lets out a breath: disappointment, or relief? I don't know. "And you're not feeling too hungover this morning?"

Relief, then; he's feeling relief. What happened last night was a fluke: Jonah, broken-hearted, reaching for the nearest warm body; me, desperate for acceptance after Georgetown's rejection.

"I had, like, *one* sip of beer." I swirl my orange juice in my cup, praying it'll restore my blood sugar. "But, still, when I woke up this morning, all I could think was, 'Now I know how Trotsky felt when Mercader showed up with that ice-axe.'"

Nasir, a few seats down, barks with laughter. "Damn, you guys are *obsessed* with this Soviet shit."

"Don't worry," Jonah says. "Our communist role-playing days are over."

"You sure about that?" Nasir says. "'Cause I got some Stolichnaya if you need a little hair of the dog that bit yo' ass." He reaches into a backpack freckled with little G's and retrieves, from these designer depths, an eco-friendly aluminum water bottle, just like Jonah's. Its silver is dotted with green leaves, blue waves. "Love these things," he says, tapping on the metal. "Genius. Can't see into it. Teachers don't know if you're drinking water or white wine."

"No, thanks," Jonah says, and tosses his napkin onto a now-empty plate. "I'm trying to cure this hangover the good old-fashioned way."

I'd give Nasir and Jonah another lecture about alcohol being cancerous, but I don't have it in me this morning. No, I've got carcinogens in me. A full sip's worth. And I swear I can feel this microdose blooming, deep in my stomach, spreading through my bloodstream, making me sick.

Or maybe it's just nerves.

As I'm contemplating all this—anxiety, or beer-induced cancer?—there's a minor commotion at the front of the dining hall. Ari Schechter is striding through the double doors of the dining hall, looking like she woke up five minutes ago. Her short hair's stuck in a wicked cowlick. She missed a button or two when she was doing up her shirt. And there's no makeup, not even a stitch of concealer, covering the grisly pallor of her hangdog, hungover expression.

"Looking good, Rodham." Nasir claps her on the back. "Ready to hit the marketplace of ideas?"

"Oh, yeah," Ari grumbles, settling heavily into place at Nasir's side. "Really reveling in the life of the fucking mind this weekend."

"Not my fault you can't handle a hangover," says Nasir.

Ari scowls, snatches the bottle out of Nasir's hand. She takes a long, slow *glug, glug, glug*, wipes her mouth with the sleeve of her blazer, and levels her eyes at Jonah.

"I am very sorry about what happened last night," she says to him. "I will pay for any and all dry-cleaning bills." And then, without missing a beat, she shifts her eyes to me. "I was not in control of my faculties. I definitely did not mean the things I said."

The flicker of fear in her eyes tells me what her words don't: that she *did* mean it, last night. But she's determined— for now, at least—to ignore it. To stay in her fragile eggshell as long as possible, even though the cracks are showing.

I remember what that was like. I know exactly how much it hurts. And as I watch her pour vodka down her throat, a lump swells in my own.

"You missed a button," says Nasir. "I can see your bra."

"One of these days, Nasir, I'm going to light this bra on fire. And then I'm going to throw it into a trash can, and then I'm going to throw you into that very same trash can."

"What the hell?" Nasir yelps. "Did you really just threaten to murder me?"

"Sure did," she says, and drains the bottle.

We're facing Massachusetts Red first thing—the boys from that tennis academy in the suburbs of Boston. It's unclear to me why they're here, debating, instead of playing tennis. But what do I know about sports? Maybe debating helps them strategize out on the court. Or something.

The first speaker's called James, and he's about as threatening as one of Renata's My Little Pony figurines. He's slight, and only slightly tall, and he's fidgeting something fierce, clearly nervous. The other guy, Matthew, is more how I imagine a tennis pro, sturdy and stoic. I can see muscles bulging beneath his rumpled blazer, an enormous, mustard-yellow stain visible above its only button. Eyes on this smear, I elbow Jonah.

"Watch out," I whisper to him. "The prep schoolers brave enough to walk up looking like shit?"

"They're killers," Jonah finishes for me. "Always. I know."

We're on opposition—arguing, again, that trans kids should be kept out of bathrooms for their own safety. Jonah gives a solid opening speech, peppered with enough statistics and studies to keep us from coming off as ideologues. But James, the skinny, shivering one, hits back *hard*. He knows every study Jonah cited, and he knows them *better*: this one had a too-small sample size; *that* one was authored by a professor fired for fudging numbers. He's relentless. No stone left unturned, no statistic left unquestioned. "Photographic memory" doesn't do it justice. This kid's a walking, talking JSTOR. His speech is a *massacre*.

When the moderator calls my name, I can't move. How am I supposed to follow that? It takes a forceful nudge from Jonah—and a frantic "Come *on*, Finch," whispered under his breath—to propel me up to the podium.

"The proposition would . . . would have you believe . . ." I begin, shakily, then stop.

I don't want to do this. I don't want to give a speech full of terf talking points. Especially if we've already lost the round. I turn my head and look miserably to Jonah. He meets my eyes, his mouth a grim line. "Come on," he repeats, mouthing the words: *When have I ever steered you wrong?*

I laugh under my breath, and I turn away from him, fix my eyes on the judges. They wait, expectant. I open my mouth. No statistics this time. I'll speak from the heart. The deeply conflicted heart.

I can do this. Of *course* I can.

"The proposition claims that transgender students are safe in bathrooms with cisgender students. But they're mistaken." I sound steadier now, I think. More sure of myself. What I'm about to say, after all, is, *technically,* true: "Allowing trans students to carry out these intimate functions in close proximity to their cis peers, Mr. Speaker—it only exposes them to *more* abuse."

I'm in this vein for a while before the boy with the burnt nose stands. "On that point, suh?" he asks, in a Boston brogue that he *must* be putting on, because there's no way anyone actually talks like that. Outside of the Damon-Affleck Cinematic Universe, I mean.

I pause, nod at him. "What's your question, sir?"

"You say we should separate the transgenduh students from the othuhs, to protect them from bullies," he says, and *God*, that accent's thick. "But aren't you just trading one kind of violence for anothuh? Bullying for loneliness? Loneliness that could lead to suicide?"

I want to say yes. Of course. He's right. Herding trans kids off to our own bathroom might make us safer. But it won't solve the problem of bullying, and it *will* make us feel other, and less than, and bad, wrong, dirty.

But I can't say yes. I don't. I put my hands around the throat of my conscience and I press down.

"No, sir; single-stall bathrooms are not a slippery slope to suicide." I say it smug, cocky; I earn a laugh from the last judge on the left. "The real danger is to the trans children *you* would force into close quarters with bullies."

Matthew stands again. "Point of—" he begins, but I wave him down.

"My opponents talk about 'inclusivity,'" I say, my fingers curling into quotation marks. "But their definition prioritizes assimilation over the well-being of vulnerable kids."

Matthew rises; I flick my hand at him, forceful. I can't stop now. The judges are leaning forward, listening to me, hanging on my every word.

"Our friends from Massachusetts would ask a transgender boy of fourteen, a freshman, to share a locker room with upperclassmen. Nearly full-grown men, Mr. Speaker, who might be harboring hate in their hearts. Is that the 'inclusivity' we should strive for? Forcing a child into a space where he'll be hurt? And then cooing about how we're protecting him? Welcoming him? Saving him from suicide?"

It's only when I pause that I notice the judges aren't even writing notes anymore. They're staring at me, wide-eyed—*wet*-eyed, in the case of the guy on the left, reaching up to dab away tears with his thumb and forefinger. To my left, James covers his face with his hands. Matthew glares at me, beneath dark brows, like he wants to stab me.

And to my right, Jonah's mouth hangs open, his face a mask of plain and total awe.

I may be going against everything I stand for, but goddamn if I'm not doing a great job.

"Thank you," I finish. "The opposition rests."

The tennis players don't look us in the eye when we shake hands. That's how bad it was, this round: a slaughter. When we make our way to the judges' table to thank them for their time, that man on the left gets teary-eyed all over again, his eyes welling as he takes my hand in both of his.

"That was excellent," he says in a low voice. "Truly spectacular."

"I'm pretty sure judges aren't allowed to say stuff like that," I mumble to Jonah as we pack up our things.

He laughs. "Pretty sure the rules don't apply when you're listening to Finch Kelly, the G.O.A.T."

Before I can ask him why he's calling me a goat—I mean, is it a term of endearment? Why?—Adwoa swoops up behind us. She shepherds us, not unlike goats, into the hallway.

"Finch!" she whisper-shouts, because James and Matthew are still well within earshot. "You made the judges *cry!* Over *bathrooms!* That might be the best I've ever seen you. Actually, no—that might be the best round I've ever seen, period. You didn't come to play with those little tennis boys, Jonah. Your P.O.I. in Matthew's speech? *Flawless.*"

"Yeah, yeah," Jonah says, smiling, all modest, "but this is Finch's moment."

Before I can stop him, he's wrapping an arm around me,

and then Adwoa, bringing us together for a tight group hug. His chin rests, light, on the crown of my head. I feel scared and cozy, all at once. I want to wriggle out of this hug; I want to never, ever leave it.

The celebratory mood continues when we reach the dining hall. Adwoa finds the other coaches and regales them all with the tale of our monumental victory just now. The proverbial fourteen-year-old trans boy of my speech, menaced by Neanderthal upperclassmen in an all-male changing room. I'm nodding along—and, truthfully, feeling antsy about all the attention—when something catches my eye across the room.

Massachusetts Red.

They're slumping in a couple of wooden chairs in a far, dark corner. James, the one with the photographic memory, is rubbing at his watery eyes. He might even be crying. It's hard to tell. His partner, Matthew, is stroking his fine, dark hair, and nodding. Total compassion is written all over his face. He leans in, close, and whispers something in James's ear. James laughs. He lowers his hands. His eyes are shining now.

When he turns and kisses Matthew on the forehead, I'm sure I'm seeing it wrong. I blink: There it is again! Another kiss, quick, on the mouth. And then they're pulling apart, bowing their heads to the notepads in their laps, like nothing just happened, nothing at all.

It's the smallest thing—you really could blink and miss it—but it tears through me. I jerk my head away, but I can still see them, even when I screw my eyes shut. Those boys, that kiss, seared in the pink dark on the back of my lids.

They have everything. Don't they? Everything I want, and everything I'll never have. They have more money than they'll ever be able to spend. They have athletic ability on top of academics, enough to kick down the doors of any selective college in the country.

And they have each other. In this sad, quiet moment, they have someone to hold. To kiss. I've never wanted that before. But now, watching them, their closeness, I realize: I do. I want someone.

And I'm afraid of what I want.

chapter fourteen

"So, Finch, tell us how it went."

I'm in a concrete stairwell off the Gray School dormitory, laptop on my knees. It's eleven o'clock my time, eight theirs. Mom and Dad are leaning into the camera, eager to hear all about my arduous day. Roo, in the back, occupied by a video game, looks much less eager.

"It went well, I think." It's hard to muster much enthusiasm after the excruciating twenty-four hours I've had—the bad news from Georgetown, the wildly confusing almost-kiss with Jonah, the long speeches that go against everything I stand for. "Really well, actually."

"*Really* well?" Dad repeats. As he leans close, the pixels of his face blur. "Today was . . . how many rounds?"

"Four," I answer around a yawn.

"So you've done six rounds total," Mom says. "Two last night, four today. Is that right?"

"Right. And tomorrow are the"—I yawn again, a great big world-eating one, this time—"finals."

God, but it's been a long day. Jet lag has done me no favors. I'm practically sleepwalking through this call, actually *nodding* every few minutes. I might not be able to keep my eyes open much longer.

"And you think you won all your rounds?" Mom sounds more optimistic than I feel.

"Well, we're a little worried about the last round of the day, against these two girls from Connecticut. But I think we won, still. And even if we didn't, our overall scores might be good enough to make finals."

"Right on," Dad says. "And you'd better believe we'll be watching the finals tomorrow. Do us proud, kid."

"Wait." I'm confused: We couldn't even afford *one* plane ticket. "What do you mean? How are you going to watch the finals?"

"They're filming the final round," Roo says, glancing up from her game. "You didn't know that?"

"Really?" I yawn, scratch at the stubble forming along my jaw. "A livestream or something?"

"No, no," Mom says. "It's going to be on CSPAN, they said."

". . . *Oh.*" I'm wide awake, suddenly, wired with fear. "Are you sure? Where'd you hear that?"

"On the website," Mom says. "In big capital letters, right along the top."

"CSPAN. Huh." I run a hand through my hair—greasy, gross. I'll have to shower before I go to bed tonight. If we advance to the finals and I appear on national television with an oil slick on my head . . . "CPSAN is . . . big."

"Damn right it's big!" Dad says, bringing his palm down on the desk. "You're gonna be on TV!"

I'm about to tell my dad that appearing on TV is among the top five most terrifying things I can imagine when a notification pops into the upper-right of my screen: a call request from Lucy Newsome.

We haven't spoken since that disastrous day on the bus. Why now? Did something happen? Something terrible? Rushing through my goodbyes to my folks, I press *accept* as fast as I can. There she is, my best friend, sitting crisscross on her bed in her favorite pink terrycloth pajamas. A bread clip rakes her hair haphazardly out of her eyes.

I half expect to feel upset when I see her. Guilty. Instead, I feel relief. Complete and utter relief.

"Hey," I say, "I'm sorry." I know there's nothing else to say until I get *that* out of the way. "I was a total dick to you on the bus that day. I never should have pressured you like that. The past couple days have been . . ."

". . . hell," she finishes for me, giggling. "I know. I was *really* mad at you."

"Are we good?" I ask her. "Can we be good?"

"I don't know if we're all-the-way good," she says, with a sigh that comes across as an explosion of static. "But I think we can get there."

"You know what? I can work with that. I want to make it right, Lulu. Whatever I have to do. I'll even come canvassing with you sometime. If you don't mind teaching me the ropes, I mean."

"I would love that," she says. "It's just good to talk to you, man. I want to hear all about your—Oh!" She lets out a gasp, leans forward, and firmly seizes the steering wheel of our con-versation. "Dude! How's Jonah doing? I've been *dying* to talk to you about Jonah, oh my God. Did you hear that Bailey didn't get into Juilliard? Has Jonah heard? Karma's a bitch!"

Normally, I'd join her in gloating, but I'm still smarting from my own rejection letter.

"Jonah's doing fine," I say, side-stepping the Juilliard thing. "We went to a party last night."

"No way!" Lucy gasps. "A real one? With drinking and ass-grabbing and everything?"

"Oh, absolutely not," I tell her—and then backtrack: "Well, I did have *one* sip of Jonah's beer . . ."

"Finch!" Lucy crows. "You're a bad boy now! I love it!"

"And me and Jonah, we went out onto this balcony, and we were talking about Bailey and . . ." I trail off; I don't want to tell her about Georgetown, not yet. And, besides, I could still get in. *If* I win the final tomorrow. "And I was sort of, uh, petting him on the head, I guess. I had my hand in his hair. And then . . ."

"I *knew* it!" Lucy drives her fist into a pillow. "I knew you liked him!"

"I don't . . ." I pause, glance around, make sure no one's in the stairwell. "I do *not* like him."

"But you made a move," she says. "Stroking his hair and stuff."

"That was not a *move*," I whisper-hiss. "It was a friendly, supportive . . ."

"Whatever." She waves a hand, dismissive. "So you were

sitting there, platonically stroking his hair for friendship reasons. And then what?"

"You're insufferable," I tell her. "You know that, right?"

"But you love me for it."

"I do," I say. "A lot, I do."

"And while we're on the subject of people you love . . ." She brings her brows up, high and mischievous. "Let's talk about you and Jo . . ."

The door to the stairwell swings open. I look up: Jonah.

"Bye, Lucy!" It comes out a yelp. "Adios! Arrivederci! Nice talking to you!"

She starts complaining, pissed that I'm hanging up without an explanation. I'll have to apologize later. I mash my thumb against *end call*—just in time, too. Jonah's already standing over me, looking very amused.

"Didn't mean to startle you," he says.

"You know me. I'm easy to startle."

He leans against the concrete wall, giving me that easy smile he's got. His hair is slick, still, from the shower, and he's wearing what might be pajamas: soft gray sweatpants, a hoodie somewhere between purple and pink. His fingers play with the dangling drawstrings; I watch, rapt.

"You're out here all alone?" he asks.

"All by my lonesome," I answer.

"I thought you wanted to get to bed early," he teases, "after all our carousing last night."

I open my mouth to protest, but Jonah's already bending, pulling my laptop gently from the lap that housed it.

"Hey!" I leap to my feet, try to snatch back my battered computer. "Give it back! Right now!"

"No," he says, and folds the machine in half. "No more internet tonight. We're going on a walk."

"Shouldn't we be sleeping?"

"Nope." Jonah shakes his head. "You need to relax, dude. We're going out for a midnight snack."

"A midnight snack?" I lift a brow.

"I know just the thing."

Fifteen minutes later, we're perched on a park bench overlooking the Potomac. The dark water rushes past, glowing with the distant light of the National Mall. We can see almost all of it: the glittering dome of the Capitol, the forbidding obelisk of the Washington Monument, and even Lincoln's columns—although not, from here, the man himself.

In the midst of all this majesty, Jonah lifts the lid of the box in his lap and retrieves a Boston Cream for me.

"A dozen doughnuts." I take the first, perfect bite. "You don't think this is overkill?"

"Not a chance." Jonah shakes his head, swallowing a bite of double-chocolate glaze. "We can always save some for the morning."

A bit of cream spills onto my chin, but I can't find it in me to care. "Part of a healthy, balanced breakfast," I say, and earn a gentle laugh from Jonah.

"So," he says shyly, "we didn't really get a chance to continue our talk last night."

"Oh. Right. Last night."

I'm very conscious, suddenly, of how dark it is. And how late it is. And how alone we are, here, overlooking the grandest monuments in the country. Does he want to . . . kiss? I scoot away from him, feeling my body stiffen.

"I just meant about Georgetown," Jonah says, flushing a little, embarrassed. "I know how much it meant to you."

Oh. *Oh.* Never mind. No romance here. None.

"Well, the final is tomorrow," I tell him, "and we went up against those top-tier Connecticut girls tonight, so we could still be in the running."

He lifts a brow. "What does that have to do with Georgetown?"

"Well, if we make it to the finals, and we *win*, I can go back to the admissions committee, right? I can say, 'Hey, look, I'm a national debating champion—don't I deserve to get in?'"

"Finch," Jonah says, his voice small, solemn. "I don't think it works like that."

"They're not going to turn down a national champion, Jonah."

He gives me a look so pained that I can't help but wince, too.

"Before Bailey dumped me, you and I talked a lot about him." Jonah speaks slowly, carefully. "You and Adwoa kept telling me that I deserved better. But it never sunk in, because I just . . . I couldn't even *imagine* better than Bailey."

". . . Right." Where is he going with this?

"I think that's why the breakup hit me so hard," he says. I note the past tense here; *hit me*, not *is presently hitting me.*

"I really thought Bailey was The One—capital *T*, capital O. If he dumped me, I'd never have another shot. Not with anyone."

"So you're saying Bailey is Georgetown." I catch his drift. "And I should give up on . . . him? . . . It?"

"I'm saying the thing you want isn't always the thing that's best."

"But Georgetown *is* the best!" I take a frustrated bite of my Boston Cream. "It's the best college in D.C.," I say, crumbs spilling from my mouth, then swallow. "Am I a bad person for wanting the best?"

"Georgetown isn't the best. *You're* the best. You're going up against all these prep school kids with zillionaire parents, and you're talking circles around them. You're kicking their asses."

"But it doesn't matter how good I am, or how much I study. Those kids are always going to have things I don't. And the only way I can level the playing field is if I—"

"Oh my God, Finch, *stop*," he almost shouts. It shocks me. I reel back, away from him, but he's still going: "You deserve to be here, dude! No matter where you go to school! No matter how much money you've got!"

"I live in the real world, Jonah." I rise from the bench and brush my hands, sticky with sugar, against the seat of my pants. "And I have *one* thing going for me: I'm good at this. At debating."

He looks up at me, sighs. "You're breaking my heart, man."

"*I'm* breaking *your* heart?"

"You have *so much* going for you." Jonah rises from the

bench, his hands closed in loose fists. I can tell that he wants to reach out with them, grab me by the shoulders, shake me 'til I understand. "And there are so many people who look up to you. Want to be like you."

"Like who?"

"Like me."

I roll my eyes. "No, you don't."

"I do! I've said it before!" In the space between us, he shakes those twin fists, insistent. "You're smart, yeah. But we meet a ton of smart people at these tournaments, and you're not like them. You don't lord over anyone. You want to *share* what you know. I've never seen you happier than when you're, like, breaking down the wealth tax thing, or whatever, making someone really get it. You want people to care the way that *you* care." He takes a breath; the fists come loose. "And you care so much, dude. About everything. I swear, before you do *anything*—whether it's the state final or, like, ordering lunch—you weigh all your options. You really think about it. Like, 'What's the best possible thing I could do, right now, with what I've got?'"

I laugh, disbelieving. "It's called having an anxiety disorder, Jonah."

"It's called giving a fuck."

A long silence grows as I look down into my lap. The box of doughnuts we've been demolishing. Jonah bought these for me. He wanted me to relax. To sit on a park bench with him, eat something sweet, and look at something beautiful. This city is spread out before us—this place where good people work hard to make the world better, and bad people work even harder to make it worse. I want to join the fight. He knows that. And he believes I'm good enough to do it.

Do I believe it, too? Could I?

"You'll get here someday." Jonah spreads his arms: *here*, the National Mall, the heart of the free world. "And you don't need Georgetown to do it. There are a thousand ways to get here. Alexandria Ocasio-Cortez was a bartender. Lucy McBath was a flight attendant. Bernie Sanders was a folk singer."

"Was he? Actually?" I giggle, dropping my voice a couple octaves: *"We shall ovah-come, we shall ovah-come . . ."*

He laughs and lifts a hand, strokes my hair. "You'll figure it out," he says fondly. "One day."

I reach down for another doughnut. "Maybe, but I'm at a disadvantage as a tiny trans guy who—"

"I don't think you're tiny," he says. "I think you're thirty feet tall." He pauses, flattens a palm against my cheek. "I'm . . . I'm in . . . I'm in awe. Of you."

I look at Jonah, at the steady movement of his chest—up, down, faster, I think, than usual. His pulse sprints where his wrist meets my skin. Something about those quick breaths, the breaks in his speech, the nervous cast to the look he's giving me—if I didn't know better, I'd swear he meant to say, *I'm in love with you.*

"Jonah," I say, his name coming out so soft, so low, I'm not even sure he can hear me. "Jonah, I . . ."

"Hey!" A voice—an adult's, angry, loud. "This is private property!"

I leap to my feet, hands in the air. The doughnuts tumble into the dirt. I barely have time to mourn the apple cruller rolling untouched in the mud before Jonah takes me by the wrist and swings me to the left, out of the glare of a flashlight. He's running, and I'm running right alongside him, lungs heaving below my binder. We don't stop until we're safe, a block and a half away, far enough that the whole thing's funny instead of fear-inducing. I've got a hot stitch searing my side open, and Jonah's chest is heaving again—with heavy breaths, but laughter, too.

I gasp. "What time is it?" and he pulls his phone out of his pocket, squints at its sunny glare. "It's about . . ." he says, then stops. "Holy shit. Half past two."

"And the final round begins at . . ."

"Nine."

"Okay." I nod, barely able to breathe. "We can totally get, like, six hours, right?"

He crosses his fingers. "Let's hope."

"This is not a disaster."

"No," he says. "Not a disaster at all."

Yeah, no, it's a disaster. By the time we return to our dorm, crawl into our sleeping bags, and close our eyes, sleep is impossible. Everything Jonah said—especially, *I'm . . . I'm in . . . I'm in awe*—is ringing loud between my ears. He's on the other side of the room, wrapped tight in his own nylon cocoon, but I can hear him breathing gently all night.

The alarm on my phone begins to blare at eight o'clock. I just lie on the floor for a long moment, listening to it, miserable, acutely aware that I have not slept even one single wink. Six hours of tossing and turning in terror: That's what I'll be running on today.

I'm still full after last night's jaunt in the park—all those doughnuts, all that sugar, not a lick of it settling well in my stomach. This, plus exhaustion, means my breakfast consists solely of coffee, pumped from the dining-hall samovar into the tallest paper cup I can find. At least I'm not alone in my fatigue. Every debater in this dining hall looks like a gray-eyed zombie.

"Damn, dude," says Nasir—no exception—yawning hugely when I take my seat at the breakfast table. "That is a shit-ton of coffee."

"Leave him alone, Nas," Ari chides, picking at a plate of eggs. "We all slept like shit. No shame in caffeine."

"You'll be fine, Finch." Jonah reaches out, rests a hand on my wrist. "Whatever happens today, you got this."

He means to be reassuring. To help. So why do I feel irritated? It's my lack of sleep, maybe. Or what he said to me last night, still rolling around in my head. I reach out. I push his hand away. When I see the look on his face—not a frown; a wound—I regret it.

"Ladies and gentlemen!" The voice of the headmistress echoes loud from a podium at the front of the hall. "It's been a wonderful weekend, but I'm afraid our time together is coming to an end."

We all sit up a little straighter. This is it. We're about to learn if we made the finals—and, if we did, who we're up against.

"It is with great pride that I announce the finalists for this year's N.A.D.A. National Championships," she says. "The two teams I name will have fifteen minutes to prepare before we assemble in the Gray Auditorium for this weekend's final debate."

Her manicured nails slip into an envelope and retrieve a piece of pink cardstock. She holds it delicately between thumb and forefinger, squinting down her nose, through her glasses.

"The first team that will compete in this final round," she says, "is Washington . . ."

I hold my breath.

". . . Red," she finishes. "Ariadne Schechter and Nasir Shah!"

The room erupts in applause. I'm not among the cheerleaders. I'm looking at Ari and Nasir, and I'm wondering: Can two teams from the same state even advance to the final?

"And the second team competing in this round," says the headmistress, "is Washington Blue! Jonah Cabrera and Finch Kelly!"

I wait for it to come: the perfect, flawless happiness. It doesn't. Instead, it's like every stress, every petty anxiety I've ever felt, grows wings and swarms. Will I have to argue against trans rights? In front of thousands of people? On national television? Jonah hauls me up and out of my seat, lifting me into the air and spinning me, and I want to tell him *no, stop*—I think I might throw up. But I don't want to complain. He looks like he's feeling everything I wished I'd feel.

"West Coast represent!" Nasir crows, when I clamber up onto the stage on shaky legs. He claps Jonah exuberantly on the back. "Showed all these East Coast boarding school mother . . ."

A glare from the headmistress cuts him short. He goes quiet, chagrined, putting his hands behind his back. And then, as the headmistress turns back to the podium, I feel a tap on my shoulder: Ari.

"Hey," she says, in a whisper, "if you have to argue no, will you . . . will you be okay?"

I level my gaze, soften my voice: "Will you?"

The headmistress turns, flinty fury in her eyes. We go quiet. Ari pulls away, worrying one thumb against the other.

"As is customary, we'll flip a coin to determine which team will argue for the proposition," says the headmistress.

It's simple enough: Heads, we argue against trans rights; tails, we argue for them.

I watch the smooth, high arc of the coin as it sails forth from the headmistress's thumb. *Tails*, I think. *Please. I can't argue against trans rights. Not again. Not on TV.*

Tails. Tails. Tails.

She lifts her head, puts her lips to the microphone.

"Heads."

chapter fifteen

I will be sick to my stomach. I know this. I know it as I shake hands with Nasir and Ari and the headmistress. I know it as I stand shakily on that little stage in the dining hall for another minute of polite preamble. It may, in fact, be the only thing I know right now. My mind is a wasteland. A mess. We have fifteen minutes to prep for the final, and all I can think about is painting the floor with my breakfast.

Jonah's hand finds the small of my back. He steers me gently to the side of the stage, down the stairs. When he speaks, his voice is quiet, sober: "I think we're supposed to prep in the classroom in the east—"

"Bathroom," I interrupt.

Jonah, mercifully, gets the message. There's his hand on my back again, leading me forward—ten, twenty, thirty agonizing steps. A door opens. He guides me through it. I see the white gleam of a urinal. It's the signal my stomach needed. Something animal takes over. I lurch out of Jonah's arms, swing through the door of the first vacant stall, and fall to my knees.

I am vividly, horribly, defiantly sick.

It's a strange, scary feeling, throwing up. It's like my body doesn't really belong to me. I float out of my skin and lean coolly against the clean white tiles of the wall. Down on the floor, a redheaded kid kneels pathetic before the bowl and opens his mouth and heaves. All the soft bile of last night's doughnuts, this morning's coffee—it pours out in sick, half-digested shades of yellow and black.

I fall to the floor, back in my body. "Fuck."

Jonah's at my side in an instant, on his knees, water bottle in hand. "Here," he says, and I take a drink. "No, no," he says, gently. "Don't drink it. You're not supposed to eat or drink anything for a few hours after you throw up. Just swish it around. Rinse. Spit."

He's the son of a nurse. I trust his medical advice. The next sip is dutifully swished and spat. Another one; another. Finally, Jonah reaches up to flush the mess in the bowl.

"Are you okay?" he asks.

"I'm sorry." There's a throbbing in my head, a sick, raw feeling in my throat. "It's my fault. Ate too many doughnuts last night. Drank too much coffee this morning." I should have known better; caffeine is poisonous, an accelerant. I was practically inviting a panic attack. "Give me a minute."

"I'll tell them you're sick," Jonah says. "They can postpone the round."

"*No.*" My answer comes out sharp, severe. "I'm not holding up the national final just because I ate too much."

But I know why I'm *really* sick. It's panic, pure and simple, that brought me here, pushed me to my knees, and forced me to throw up in—in the *men's room*, I realize, and laugh.

"First point." I hold up a finger. "Trans students shouldn't be allowed to use the bathroom because they might throw up and make everything smell like rancid Boston Creams."

Jonah doesn't laugh. "Finch, we don't have to do this."

"What do you mean?" I blink at him, baffled. "It doesn't matter what we want. This is the resolution. Period. You don't get to change the topic at Nationals because it's personally offensive to you."

"But, Finch . . ."

"We have fifteen minutes." I reach for the backpack I dropped before I vomited. The notepad inside, thankfully, was spared most of the splatter. "Come on. Help me think of new arguments. Ari and Nasir know all our old ones. Why shouldn't I be allowed to use a toilet?"

"Finch," Jonah says, "*stop*."

"If we want the most persuasive case," I mumble, scribbling on my notepad, "these people in England have gone a long way with this whole 'trans people are destroying women's rights' thing. Like, way more than the American evangelicals being like, 'trans people are an abomination of the Lord.' So if we go with the British angle—"

"Stop," Jonah says. "Stop. Please. You have to stop."

"It's just a debate!" I say—and I realize, with hot, sudden shock, that there is real water springing from my eyes, and falling from them, and staining my cheeks. For the first time in years, I'm crying. Really, truly crying. "All I have to do is go out there and pretend to believe some bullshit arguments for an hour. If I do it well, I win Nationals, and Georgetown might give me a second chance. There is no way—no *fucking* way—I'm giving up now."

"I'm not debating this round," says Jonah.

I look up at him, bewildered. "But it's the final. The national final."

Jonah looks at me like he pities me, and that's it, that does it; I'm over the edge, vocally sobbing. All the water I've been holding in, all these months on testosterone: The dam is broken. It rains from my eyes to the collar of my shirt and it mingles with the green-gold flecks of puke there.

Jonah, inches away, is watching me. Has been watching me the whole time. Watching me throw up, watching me melt down. He can see me right now. Really *see* me, see right into the ugliest, shabbiest parts of me. I cover my face with my hands and I close my eyes. This way, at least, I can't see *him*.

But his hands are moving my hands. And light is coming in pink through my lids. Something soft, and a bit scratchy—oh; toilet paper—is brushing beneath my eyes, and around my mouth, mopping up tears and vomit both. When I look up, Jonah is right there, working carefully, gentle presses of the paper to my skin.

"I will not go out there," he says, "and argue that you're less than human."

"Jonah . . ."

"I am not going to stand on that stage on national television and say that you shouldn't be allowed to exist in public." His jaw is square. "I'm not going to do that to you, Finch."

"You've been doing it this whole weekend!" I feel furious—

on top of all the other feelings surging through me, threatening to make me heave up even more bile. "Why now? Why do you want to throw the final when we're this fucking close?"

It happens so fast: hands on my waist, pulling me forward, into his lap. His forehead on mine. His nose brushing mine. His mouth touching mine.

He's kissing me.

He's kissing me on my puke-stained mouth, on the floor of the men's bathroom, the rim of the toilet pressing hard into my shoulders.

And I'm kissing him back.

All I can think to say is, "Why?"

He pulls away, looking like he's just stuck his fingers in a light socket. "Because I love you. And I don't want us to win. Not if it means having to go up there and . . . and humiliate you, and . . ."

"You love me?" I ask. "Really?"

"I'm sorry," he says, and moves away from me, just an inch. "I know that you're going through a lot right now, and I shouldn't have—"

No, no; none of that. I pull him back to me, into my arms. I want to kiss him again. So I do. And the second time is better—not surprising, but familiar. This is a mouth I've kissed before. A mouth I'll kiss again.

"I love you, too," I tell him. Because I do, don't I? Because I've been lying to myself. Because the thing I feel when I touch him and talk to him and take in his easy, perfect smile— it's love. "I can't believe you're boycotting this round for me."

"I can't believe you thought I wouldn't," he says.

And then he helps me stand, on shaky legs. I cling to him as we cross the tiled floor. He flips on the faucet and I lean forward, splashing cool water on my swollen face.

"What about you?" he says. "What are you going to do?"

He no longer sounds hopeless. He says it like I'm the one in charge. Like no matter what I do, no one will ever be able to hurt me in any way that really matters.

"I'm going to wash my face. And then my hands. And then I'm going to do this round."

He sighs. "If you really want to do this, I can't stop you. I just wish that you'd—"

I cut him off: "Come up with me. But let me take your place. The first speech."

He searches my face, confused. And then—there it is, that smile again. The one I love. *Love*.

"Oh, Finch," he says. "*Fuck* yes."

CSPAN, turns out, isn't the only news crew at the final. The aisles are cluttered with cameras, and people with pads, pens, phones out. *Reporters*, I realize, peering from the wings. My stomach churns, still queasy; I'm glad it's empty.

We walk out of the wings and take our seats to thunderous applause. The headmistress gives a speech that I don't, *can't*, hear. Jonah's hand is under the table, holding mine, reminding me that he's here, reminding me of what I have to do.

"And now, from the Annable School in Seattle, Washington"—this is the headmistress, lifting her beringed hand—"Ariadne Schechter!"

Ari strides to the podium with her head held high, not a stitch out of place in her pristine, girlish uniform. The half-asleep Ari who slumped into the dining hall yesterday, the fully wasted Ari who vomited all over Jonah the night before that—she's gone. This is Ari in fighting form, the best sparring partner I've ever had.

"At stake today," she says, "is nothing less than the right of transgender Americans to exist in public." Her every word is sharp, precise. It's like she's running for president and this is the speech that decides everything. "Take away a trans person's right to use the bathroom and you take away their right to attend school. To hold a job. To receive social services. This policy is nothing less than the slow and calculated removal of an oppressed minority from public space. One might even call it genocidal."

I realize, listening to her, how easy it would be to refute her arguments. So simple. I'd just hold my nose, repeat the words of the people who hate me, and walk away with a trophy. I've done it before. I've repeated so many bad arguments for so many bad ideas. And why? What good has it ever done me? Sure, it's helped me know my enemies—but when have my enemies ever tried to know *me*?

A loud swell of applause pulls me out of my daze, back into the moment, the theater. The headmistress is saying my name. The reporters in the front rows are lifting their cameras.

Jonah's hand curls into mine. He presses, hard, into my

palm. And even as I let go of his hand, the world shrinks to us. Only us. Us, alone. Jonah loves me. He's willing to throw this round for me *because* he loves me.

I only need to find the courage to do the same.

There it is: the podium, the microphone. I take my first deep breath. I open my mouth.

"It would be easy to argue against the right of trans people to use the bathroom of their choice." I lift my head. No less than a dozen cameras are trained on me—broadcasting me live, across the country. I force myself to look down the black barrel of the closest one. "Many lawmakers in this country have made this case. They've done it successfully. They've done it so well, in fact, that many trans people *have* been banned from bathrooms. Nothing we discuss on this stage today is hypothetical. It's real. It's happening."

I'm shocked to find myself short of breath, already, only a few sentences into my speech. And so, here I go: my second deep breath.

"In many countries, trans people are murdered merely for existing." I pause; both hands on the podium, holding myself steady. "The United States is one of those countries."

A wave of long, low gasps from the audience.

"We know that the arguments for bathroom bans—the arguments *against* trans people in public spaces—do what they're supposed to do," I say. "They force trans people into closets. They make trans people out to be monsters. They work, and they work effectively. If I repeated those arguments well enough, there's no question that I would persuade many of you."

There's confusion in the crowd now: He's supposed to be arguing *for* the bathroom ban, right? What the hell is this kid doing?

I turn my head, find Jonah. He meets my eyes; he nods. And that's all I need to swivel back to the mystified crowd, all I need to pull in my third, my final, deep breath.

"So I'm not going to make those arguments," I say. "I won't participate in this debate, and neither will my partner."

Wild commotion in the crowd now. Oh, God. Okay. I wasn't planning to do this, but now?

Now, I don't think I have a choice.

"I am transgender."

The headmistress, who'd been stomping toward the stage on tall heels, stops where she stands. I see her mouth, *What?*

"I am a transgender man," I repeat. My head is beating like a heart. "I will not argue against my own humanity. There are many, many people doing that. They're enjoying great success doing it. I will not—I *cannot*—be one of them."

I wonder if I'll burst into tears again. I hope to God I don't.

"You can call me a coward if you want. You can accuse me of suppressing free speech."

A woman with a camera has moved in, close, to the very lip of the stage, pointing her long lens right at my face, zooming. There are people watching this, watching *me*, all over the country, at this very moment. I want nothing more than to stop. To shut up. To race off the stage and vomit, again, blank bile. But I can't. I won't.

"But this isn't the first time I've had this debate," I go on. "I've been having this debate all weekend. I have this debate every time I get dressed in the morning. Every time I leave my home. Every time I get thirsty and wonder if I should have a sip of water, because I don't know when I'll be able to use a bathroom safely, and I don't want to risk it."

It's only as I say all this that I realize how true it is. How tired I am. I'm aware, now, that I'm about to cry. And I really, *really* wish the dam hadn't burst when it did.

"I've debated this issue enough," I say, and sniff; it's hard, harder than I remembered, holding the tears back. "And I'm done. We're done. My partner and I forfeit this round." I turn my head, nod at Nasir and a plainly horrified Ari. "Congratulations, Annable. You're national champions now."

I step back, away from the podium, and in the overwhelming flurry of noise around me, one thing comes through, very clear: Ari's voice, calling out, as she leaps to her feet.

"Finch!" she yells. "Stop! Don't! You shouldn't . . . you don't have to . . ."

But I can't stay, can't hear whatever she's going to say. I need to be *off this stage*. Right now. I pace into the wings, moving so quick Jonah has to jog to catch up. I am—how *mortifying*—gasping back sobs. The microphone rings out behind me as the headmistress grabs it, urging everyone to stay calm. There are footsteps coming after us, gaining.

I turn to Jonah. I take his hand. He nods at me. He knows what we have to do.

Run.

That's how we leave: running. We run and run 'til we burst through the doors of the Gray School, into the warm spring air, and we keep running, across the courtyard, as the sun beats down on our backs.

I stop in the center of the quad, in the shadow of the fountain. Jonah does, too. He lifts me off the ground. He kisses me.

I don't feel like I've lost a thing.

"You guys sure you don't wanna go to this award ceremony?"

"Yeah, Adwoa," I tell her. "We're sure."

This was Adwoa's brilliant notion: to track us down after the final and spirit us away to her tiny hotel room, out of the Gray School's crowded dormitories and, crucially, away from the prying eyes of reporters.

"We just want to lie low," says Jonah. "Like, take a nap. Order some takeout. After, you know . . ."

"After all that," Adwoa says, and exhales. "Yeah. Can't say I blame you. This debate's the number two trending topic in the country right now."

"Only number two?" Jonah looks disappointed. "Who beat us?"

"A new Kardashian baby." Adwoa leans against the open door of the hotel room, scrolling briskly through her phone. "But Caitlyn Jenner tweeted out how brave you are, Finch, so don't say the Kardashians never did nothing for you."

"Did she really?" I push myself forward, to the edge of the mattress. "I had to turn off my phone. I was getting, like, sixty messages a minute."

"Well, stay here and read those texts, then. I'll go to the banquet alone. Collect awards in your stead."

"You honestly think they'll be giving us awards?" I ask her. "After that stunt we pulled?"

"You do realize that you could still—no, sorry, *will* still win awards as individuals, right? Even if you forfeited the team title?"

"Let's not jinx it," Jonah says.

"Finch, truly," says Adwoa, ignoring him, "if you don't win first individual, I'm gonna throw hands."

I lift my hands, shrug: Who knows? "We'll see."

Adwoa rolls her eyes, but I can see her smiling. "Okay, I'm ducking out now. You two be good, now," she says, and winks suggestively.

Jonah and I both, at once: *"Adwoa!"*

She's out the door with a quicksilver grin, a kiss blown over her shoulder. Great. Now I'm too embarrassed to look Jonah in the eye.

"So," I hear him say, behind me, reclining on Adwoa's mattress. "Do you want to, like . . ."

He lets the words hang there in the air, tentative.

Well? Do I want to? Like? I could do what I've always done. Deny him. Deny myself. Want as little as possible on purpose.

But after today, after that speech, I think it might be easier to just say what I mean. Say what I want.

And so I turn to him. "I want to make out," I tell him, with way more confidence than I was expecting. I lift my head, and I look him straight—well, not *straight*, I guess—in the eye. The very enthusiastic eye, suddenly. "But I need to take a shower first. Or a bath. And brush my teeth. Because I'm reasonably confident that I still smell like puke."

"You smell like roses," he says, and I roll my eyes.

"Okay, loverboy," I tell him as I vanish into the bathroom. "Whatever you say."

As I fill the tub, I peel off my jacket, and then my shirt—which, *wow*, will need a round of dry-cleaning when we get back to Olympia. Did I really go up onstage in this shirt? I can only hope the cameras didn't capture the puke-spatter.

My belt is next, and then my pants, pooling around my ankles. That leaves me staring at myself in the foggy mirror, clad only in binder and boxers. I look at myself and listen to the running of the water in the tub, the rushing of blood in my ears.

I look like a boy. I know I do. After all this time on testosterone, on Lupron, I'm almost never mistaken for a girl anymore. But still, whenever I see myself in the mirror like this, all the layers peeled away, the hard facts of my body appear. Sometimes, it's more than I can bear.

Not today, though. Today, when I remove this last fabric, I look into the mirror and see a boy staring back. A boy who was brave enough to walk away from a national title, a second shot at his dream school, to stand up for himself. To defend the belief—no, the *fact*—that he is a boy. That he deserves to be a boy. That he doesn't have to apologize for it.

I lift my hand to the mirror and look at the body in it. It's a boy's body. It belongs to a boy who kissed another boy today. A boy who's held, treasured, loved by that boy.

It's a boy's body, and it's all mine.

I emerge from the bathroom warm and sleepy and pruned by hot water. Well, not *emerge*, not all the way; I stand in the doorway for a second, clad in an enormously fluffy bathrobe culled from the hotel's closet. In the shower, just now, I'd fantasized about launching myself across the room at Jonah. Just throwing myself at him, tearing off my robe: *Take me, I'm yours.*

Now, though, I hesitate. I'm not binding my chest right now. And I have to wonder: Will it be weird for Jonah? A deal-breaker? Is it silly of me, worrying like this, when he's already made it clear how he feels? He's already kissed me, yes, but not like this. Not without my binder. What if that changes things? What if . . .

"Hey," says a voice I absolutely didn't expect to hear. "We need to talk."

I lift my head, and turn it, and there she is: none other than Ari, standing in the center of the room, wearing, as always, her uniform, shifting anxiously from Mary Jane to Mary Jane.

"Wh . . . why . . ." I am wearing a bathrobe. And no binder. I do *not* want Ariadne Schechter to see me like this. "What are you doing here? Shouldn't you be at the banquet?"

"She said she needed to talk to you," Jonah says, in a voice like a hostage, from the armchair by the window. "And it was really important. And it couldn't wait."

"And you couldn't let me get dressed first? Really?"

"I'm sorry," says Ari. "It's, like, life and death. I wouldn't have come by if it wasn't."

"Fine," I say, but only because I'm still thinking about that party the other night. Her aborted confession. "Five minutes."

We step out into an empty corridor where everything is beige but the plants, which are rubber. Ari laces her fingers together.

"The other night, out on the balcony," she begins, "I heard you tell Jonah that you didn't get into Georgetown."

"Oh, God, *that's* what this is about?" And here I was prepared to soothe Ari, to welcome her into the trans community with open arms. "Well, you *did* get in, and now you have the national title, too. Did you just come here to rub it in?"

"No! I'm asking if you still want to go to Georgetown!"

I blink at her, mystified. "How . . . What do you . . ."

"I only got in because my dad bought a building," she says. "And everybody knows it. Do you know how stupid that makes me feel? How shitty? Like, he honestly didn't believe I could do it by myself. He just *had* to drop a couple dozen mil on a big, fat—"

"Ari, I'll be honest. I am *not* feeling a lot of sympathy for you right now."

"Sorry. Fuck. Look." She takes a step back, tries again. "What I'm trying to say is that my dad has a lot of pull at Georgetown. And if you want him to make a call and put in a good word for you, I can make it happen."

"Holy shit." I need to sit down. I stagger back, all but collapse under one of the rubber plants. It's hard to move in this bathrobe. I have to pull the long ends of the garment down for modesty's sake. "Did you just say . . ."

"I can't, like, promise you admission," she says. "But I can promise you a phone call."

I peer up at her, suspicious. "Why are you doing this?"

"Because you threw that round and handed me a national title. And because you helped me realize things about myself that I'd kind of been, um . . ." She looks down, bites her lip. "Ignoring, I guess? Because I was afraid of what people would think?"

"Oh, Ari." I swallow. There it is: the cracking of the eggshell. "I know what you mean. I've been there."

"I mean, I'm not ready to, like, pick a label or anything." She lifts her hand, swipes a stray tear from beneath her eye. "But you made me understand there are things I can do. Like, I don't have to feel this way for the rest of my life. I have choices. I get to decide for myself."

"You do. You get to choose." I swallow. "And if there's ever anything I can do for you—"

"You can let me do *this* for you," she cuts in. "Why are you arguing with me? Isn't this exactly what you've always wanted?"

She's right. I've wanted Georgetown for years. More than I've ever wanted anything. But I'm remembering now what Jonah said last night: *The thing you want isn't always the thing that's best.* Is Georgetown really the best thing for me?

I've wondered for a long time what it's like to live in Ari's tax bracket. A world where wishing for something is as simple as buying it. She's inviting me into that world. Right now.

But I've always hated the people in her world, haven't I? Not for what they have, but how they get it: by cheating, stealing, cutting in line. If I do this—say yes, and sail past all the other desperate kids on the waiting list—how will I sleep at night?

Would Thomas Piketty ever forgive me?

I take a step back. I shake my head.

"I'm sorry, Ari," I tell her. "But the answer is no."

It's a funny feeling—a sad one—to have your wildest dream handed to you on a silver platter, and to say no. My head's spinning as I return to the hotel room and close the door behind me. Jonah, splayed across the bed, lifts his head, curious.

"What did Ari want?"

"She wanted her dad to call Georgetown," I say, hovering at the edge of the mattress. "On my behalf. To get me in."

"And you said yes?" Jonah rises up on one hand. "Please tell me you said yes."

I shake my head. "No."

"God." Jonah throws his head back, laughing. "That is so *you* of you."

"Don't laugh at me!" I protest. "How would you feel if you were on the waiting list and some kid's dad made a phone call for some other kid, and that kid got in, and you didn't?"

"You are such a good person." He tosses his phone onto the nightstand. "Get over here."

I cross my arms over my chest—I've got no small amount of anxiety, still, about going binderless—and take a seat on the bed.

"You know," he says, with a suggestive wiggling of the brow, "I was hoping you would *lie* down, not sit."

"Lie down?" My heart lurches. "In order to . . ."

"So I can kiss you," he says—and then his eyes go wide, apologetic. "But only if you want."

"Oh, I definitely want," I say, and fall back, horizontal. "I just don't know if I'm ready to do . . . you know, more than that?"

"Of course," he says. "We've got so much time, Finch. So much time."

And then we settle into place: his arms around me, his forehead to mine. His lips on mine. I hesitate, just for a second, before pressing the soft peaks of my chest to the flat plane of his.

He doesn't flinch. He only pulls me closer, kisses me longer. I relax, let myself feel everything, all of it. I still can't believe that he's here, next to me, in this bed, touching my body. I'm recovering from new shock every second.

"Whatcha thinking about?" he says, his mouth never leaving mine. "How you feeling?"

"I don't know," I mumble, between kisses. "I just never thought this would happen."

"What do you mean?" He pulls away from me, propping himself up on an elbow. "Why?"

"I just never thought that you would . . . that you *could* . . . like me," I tell him. "Because you had Bailey, for one."

He lifts his hand, runs a thumb along the curve of my cheek. "But that wasn't all, was it?"

I almost don't want to have this talk with him. It would be so easy to go on without saying any of this, to just pretend it doesn't matter. But I know we can't ignore this, the fact of my being who I am. And I'm lucky: I feel safe enough right now, in this bed, with him, to talk about it.

"I mean, you're . . . gay," I begin. "And it wasn't clear to me if you'd ever—if you'd even be able to—be attracted to me."

"I'm into guys," he says slowly. "And you're a guy."

"It isn't that simple."

"It really, truly is."

"No, but, like . . . listen." I pull away from him. He is saying all the right things, but I don't know yet if he's really hearing me. I need him to know, in his marrow, how scared I've been. "Most people think that being gay means being into . . . well, a certain type of body, right? A body that I don't have."

His hand finds mine, squeezes. "Did I ever do anything to make you feel that way?"

I like him putting it this way: not getting defensive, not saying *I would never* . . . but asking me, instead, if he's ever done anything that hurts.

"When Nasir asked you if you were a hundred percent into dick," I say, "you said yes."

"Oh, Finch." He sits up, shakes his head sadly. "I'm so, so sorry. I wasn't thinking."

"Thank you. It's just . . . it's really, really important to me that you get this. When I was growing up, meeting with all the doctors, they kept quizzing me, trying to make sure I was *really* a boy. Because they don't just hand out hormones like Skittles. Especially not to kids. You have to be really, really sure."

"Right," says Jonah. "I can see that."

"And the biggest question was: Well, are you attracted to girls? It was like you *had* to say yes if you wanted to transition."

Jonah lets out a low whistle. "Jesus. I had no idea." He reaches for me, running a hand along the length of my arm.

"Can I be completely honest with you?" he says.

"I don't know." I'm nervous again. "I'm not sure I can handle complete honesty right now."

He laughs. "Okay, well, I told you things with Bailey had been going south for a minute, right?"

"You didn't have to tell me. I saw."

"And the worse he got . . . well, the better *you* got." He turns red, pushing his face into his shoulder to smother a nervous laugh. Something thrills in my chest at the sound. "And I started to wonder if I'd made the right choice. If you were the one. Not Bailey."

My stomach flutters. Not the way it did this morning. Joyfully.

"You and me, we just *fit*," Jonah goes on. "We work so well together. We're a wrecking crew in debates. We help each other solve all our problems. And I just kept thinking, deep down: Finch is it. He's the right choice. Not Bailey."

If he'd told me a month ago that I was as desirable as Bailey, as deserving of love, I would've laughed in his face. And yet, here he is, saying it. And here I am, believing it.

"I had some similar worries to yours, I guess?" he says. "Like, if I liked you, would it make me less gay?"

I recoil, and he reaches for me, squeezing my arm gently. "I know. I know. I know. It wasn't about you. I promise. It was just this stupid insecurity." He laughs. "I would literally tell myself, 'Of *course* you're still gay if you like Finch. He's a boy. You're a boy. That's the literal definition of gay.'" He pauses; in spite of myself, I laugh, too. "And then I'd go hang out with Bailey, and his friends in the drama club, and he'd make some stupid crack about being allergic to pussy, and everybody would laugh, and I just . . ."

I speak softly: "And you didn't call him on it?"

"No. Because things were already so shaky between me and him. I was already feeling so guilty about UDub." He sighs, lifts a hand, brushes his thumb along my temple. "And I'm embarrassed, Finch. I'm so ashamed." He sighs, falls onto his back. "I was so afraid of what people would say. And it was so stupid! 'Cause, like, if I'd gotten my shit together and dumped him? You and I could've been doing this ages ago."

I look at him for a long moment, taking in everything he's just said, all the guilt and the shame and the fear.

And then I laugh and collapse onto his chest.

"This," I say, "is the worst pillow talk *ever*."

He laughs, and looks relieved, and pulls me close to him.

"Look," he says, our noses brushing, "I love you. I mean it."

"Even though I'm—"

"*Because* you are."

"And you don't think it makes you less gay?"

"Finch," he says, "I am so, so, *so* gay for you."

And then he kisses me with all the tenderness in the world.

We do this for a long time, and it's glorious: aimless kissing, nothing to do, nowhere to be. It's not until there's a buzzing on the nightstand—Jonah's phone—that we stop. Jonah reaches for it, swipes the screen with the hand that's not stroking my hair.

"Hey, check it out," he says. "Text from Adwoa."

He turns the phone's screen to me: a pair of silver medals. One for him, one for me.

"Yes!" I chirp. "We lost!"

"Way to go, loser," he says.

I lean up to kiss him in the space between his brows, the way I saw that boy from the tennis school do it.

"Second place never felt so good," I tell him.

The phone buzzes once more: Adwoa, this time, is dangling a gold medal. And then, seconds later, another text comes in. It's a photo, a close-up, of a certificate printed on thick, costly parchment.

BEST SPEAKER, it says. *FINCH KELLY, JOHNSON TECHNICAL SCHOOL.*

"Holy fuck," I breathe.

"Best in the damn country," Jonah says, and kisses my temple. "Not too shabby, baby."

I look at him, lift a brow. "Baby?"

"What, you don't like it?" He looks genuinely concerned. "It doesn't have to be baby. I could call you, let me think . . . sweetie, or honey, or pumpkin . . . oh, or *mahal*, that's a Pinoy one . . ."

A phone buzzes—mine, this time. I groan as I grab for it. "Hold on," I grumble. I'm really getting tired of these interruptions. "Let me tell Adwoa we need some alone time."

But the name on the screen isn't Adwoa's. It's Lucy's. She's calling me.

I tap on the green icon. "Hey, Lucy, now's not a good—"

"Oh, fuck off with that," she says, and laughs. "I've got someone here. Someone who *really* wants to talk to you."

"Lucy?" I sit up straight, listening to the phone trade hands. "Lucy, what are you—"

"Hey," says a voice—a woman's, deep, and wholly unfamiliar to me. "This is Alice Brady calling."

I rack my brain: "Sorry—who?"

She laughs. "I'm running for Congress here in Olympia," she says. "Your friend Lucy's been canvassing for me."

"Oh!" My heart, for the dozenth time today, is sprinting. "Well, it's nice to . . . to hear from you!"

"It's nice to hear from *you*," she says. "That was a hell of a speech, kid. Brought tears to my eyes."

"Thank you," I tell her, and swallow. "Tears to mine, too."

"God, you're funny," she says, and I can hear her smile in the words. "We could use someone like you on the campaign."

"Wait." My heart's no longer racing; it's at a halt. "Do you mean, like . . . like a volunteer, or . . ."

"Well, we've got a job opening," she says. "I need a comms associate. Pretty junior, but if you put in the work . . . well, sky's the limit, kid."

"Oh my God." I try to take a breath; I don't completely succeed. "You . . . you want me to work for you?"

"Lucy tells me you've got your heart set on some college in D.C.," she says. "But if you'd rather stay here in Olympia—take a gap year, maybe—we'd love to have you."

I stand up, start pacing. "You really want me?" I squeak. "You want my help?"

"Finch, I would *love* your help," she says. "And, of course, if we win the race, there's always the possibility that you could come with us to D.C."

I stop where I stand. Here it is. Everything, *everything*, I've ever wanted. No shortcuts; no jumping the line. Just plain, hard work. Blood, sweat, and tears at the podium, falling onto a puke-stained shirt.

"Representative Brady," I say, "it would be an honor."

"Not a representative yet," she laughs. "But I love that energy. I'll have my campaign manager send you some paperwork."

"Okay." I have to sit down again; I feel wrung out, but not anxious. Satisfied. Ready for a nice, long nap in Jonah's arms. "I'll . . . I'll look out for that."

"Great. And celebrate tonight. You deserve it."

"I will," I say. "Absolutely. Thank you, Ms. Brady."

She laughs again. "Just call me Alice, honey."

"Okay," I say. "I'll do that, Alice."

She's the first to hang up. I turn to Jonah. He takes me up in his arms.

"Did I hear that right?" he says. "Did you just land your first-ever job on a congressional campaign?"

"Yeah," I manage, just barely, tears welling up.

He moves in close, kisses them away. "Congratulations, baby."

I laugh, disbelieving. "We landed on *baby*? Not *sweetie,* or *honey,* or *pumpkin,* or . . ."

"Well," he says, "if you've got any better suggestions."

". . . *Comrade*?"

His eyes go wide. And then, in an instant, we're both reeling with laughter, falling all over each other, nearly rolling right off the bed. Finally, when we've tired ourselves out, Jonah reaches for the lamp on the bedside table. His hand is on the switch. I curl against him; he squeezes me tight.

"I love you, comrade. Let's get some shut-eye."

acknowledgments

At Dial Books: Ellen Cormier for focusing the narrative, trimming the fat, and making Finch and Jonah's love story shine as bright as Paris and Rory's; Felicity Vallence, Carolyn Foley, Lauri Hornik, Jennifer Dee, Regina Castillo, Jennifer Kelly, Kristie Radwilowicz, and the whole team.

At Penguin Canada: Lynne Missen, Peter Phillips, and the whole team.

At Janklow & Nesbit: my former agent Brooks Sherman for seeing something special in me, nurturing it, and steering me through the sale of this book with expert skill; Roma Panganiban, Claire Conrad, Emma Winter, Erin Mathis, Aaron Rich, Murad Mirzoyev, PJ Mark, Kira Watson, and Emma Parry.

At Hill Nadell: my current agent, Bonnie Nadell, for climbing aboard during a difficult and delicate time, reassuring me, and restoring my belief in myself and this book.

At UTA: Mary Pender-Coplan.

At Lambda Literary: Benjamin Alire Sáenz, William Johnson, Tony Valenzuela, Sue Landers, and the entire 2016 Young Adult Cohort.

At the University of Toronto: André Alexis, Anne Michaels, Bex McKnight, Dennis Bock, Brenda Cossman, Michael Cobb, and Rinaldo Walcott, along with the entire faculties of the Political Science and Sexual Diversity Studies departments.

At CHS: Ms. Willis, Mr. McKenzie, Ms. Breeze, Ms. Gloster, Ms. Kennedy-Carter, and Ms. Namini, for nurturing my early love of writing; Ms. Clement, for keeping me safe when I had to leave home at seventeen; Wyll M., Emily C., and Danielle P. for coaching me to Nationals and helping me to see both sides; Ms. McCrae for sponsoring the debate team, and for bearing with me even though I was a TOTAL BRAT back then, I still think about that one time I mouthed off at you and feel ASHAMED, here is my apology in writing; Alisha A. for being a world-class partner and inspiring the incident that opens this book; Noreen W. for being my very first partner and for returning to my life this year to lend invaluable insight into Jonah's life, salamat; Alice C. for being a wonderful co-captain; Samantha L., Verity A., Catherine W., and Beth C. for their extraordinary friendship and mentorship; everyone I ever debated with or against, especially Juliette L., Frank H., Sophie B., Ashley B., Jonny and Iqbal (legends), and the Peters.

At Pitchfork: Jeremy Larson, Anna Gaca, Jayson Greene, Philip Sherbourne, Cat Zhang, Mankaprr Conteh, Sasha Geffen, and Jill Mapes, for helping me to grow exponentially as a writer and critic.

In the family: Dad, for his unflagging love and support when I need it most, and for his willingness to learn and grow; Sandi, the mother I wish I'd had and am lucky to have now; Peter, who I love more than anyone, most of all; Robbie, who continues to give me hope that I can thrive and grow in spite of everything; and Grandma, who has always nurtured my love of reading. Of course, also, my ten beautiful biological children: Kit Kittredge, Rebecca Rubin, Ruthie Smithens, Melody Ellison, Samantha Parkington, Kira Bailey, Hal Incandenza, Cécile Rey, Felicity Merriman, and Courtney Moore.

The Toronto Public Library, for providing the desktop computers on which I wrote much of this book, but not for that dumb stunt with what's-her-name the terf.

Langley School District #35, for facilitating the Write From The Heart workshops that helped me and so many other kids, and to the Vancouver Public Library's Writing & Book Camp for giving me the chance to meet real authors and then read my work aloud on a stage like I was one. I am a proud alum.

For reading early drafts of this book and providing heartfelt, thorough feedback: Lena, Daniel Lavery, Frankie Thomas, Hal Schrieve, Seph M., Shreya M., and Ezra Mattes.

For being my dear friends: Lena, to whom this book is dedicated, without whom I would be nothing; Grace, who materially supported and loved me at my lowest, helping me to blossom; Alex G. from New York; Alex G. from San Francisco; Alex G. the musician, who is not my friend, but *Rocket* and *House of Sugar* are both wall-to-wall masterpieces and I listened to them a lot while writing this book; Alexis Henderson; Alice B.; Allegra Rosenberg; Allison H.; Amal Haddad, whose insight helped to shape the mention of Rachel Corrie in this book; Andrea W.; Ave G.; Bec U.; Bethany Hindmarsh, who inspired much of the substance of Adwoa's speech; Ben Harrison; Blythe P., for getting me and Ezra together, you legend; the Canoe; Celeste Pille; Claire Dederer; Claudia M.; Daniel G.; Daniel Lavery; David B.; Eli S.; Elise G.; Emily E.; Emily I.; Frankie Thomas; Hanna B.; Hannah S.; Harry Y.; Heidi; Ian R.; Jaime Z.; Jackson D.; James S.; James from Australia; Jason Lipshutz; Joe Shapiro; Jules Holewinski; Kaelynn Stewart; Kai Cheng Thom, a shelter in a storm; Kaya B.; Kevin F.; Lindsey G.; Lou B.; Mad J.; Mia G.; Mike Scrafford; Morgan Bimm; Morgan Jerkins; Ness Perruzza; Nick K.; Phillip Crandall; Sophie Shelton; Sam O.; Seyward Darby; Seph M.; Shreya M.; Stephanie Redekop, and her whole family, who saved my life when I was seventeen; Suzanne Greenfield; Taylor-Ruth Baldwin; Thea; Tom Phelan; Waverly SM; Zainab Javed. If I forgot you, I will never forgive myself.

For inspiring me: Andrea Long Chu; Andrew Garfield; Bill Hader; Cardi B; Chris Colfer; Craig's Cookies; Donna Tartt; Fresco Tours; fruitsoftheape100; Hanya Yanagihara; the LGBT Youthline; Jeremy O. Harris; John Elway; John Mulaney; Joni Mitchell; Lemony Snicket; Matt Stone and Trey Parker; Meg Cabot, who won't remember this, but one time when I was twelve I went to see her at Kidsbooks in Vancouver after I'd just been rejected from this writing contest, and during the Q&A I asked her very seriously, "How do you deal with rejection?" and she gave me an answer so compassionate and full of love that I remember it over a decade later; Megan Thee Stallion; Mitski; Natalie Wynn; Richard Siken; Paddington Bear; Phoebe Bridgers; Pleasant Rowland; Sufjan Stevens; Telfar Clemens;

Thomas Piketty; Valerie Tripp; and, of course, wolfpupy. In his immortal words, "[kicks a furby through the goals to score the winning points of the super bowl] Fuck everyone who has ever hurt me."

To Marina, Ned, and Trish: You made me the writer I am. I love you. I miss you. I wish you were here.

To Will Barnes: I pitched this book that week in New York. I'd say that it wouldn't exist without you, but somehow, it does.

To Ezra Mattes: I'm typing this while you sit across the room from me, working on your own book. I wrote this novel at a time when I truly didn't believe that love would ever find me, or that I'd ever be able to live as a queer trans man. I was writing toward you, and I didn't even know it. Your support made this book what it is. You are the love of my life. Uh, um, okay.